DATE			

PRESUMPTION
OF GUILT

ALSO BY ARCHER MAYOR

The Company She Kept

Proof Positive

Three Can Keep a Secret

Paradise City

Tag Man

Red Herring

The Price of Malice

The Catch

Chat

The Second Mouse

St. Albans Fire

The Surrogate Thief

Gatekeeper

The Sniper's Wife

Tucker Peak

The Marble Mask

Occam's Razor

The Disposable Man

Bellows Falls

The Ragman's Memory

The Dark Root

Fruits of the Poisonous Tree

The Skeleton's Knee

Scent of Evil

Borderlines

Open Season

PRESUMPTION OF GUILT

A Joe Gunther Novel

ARCHER MAYOR

Minotaur Books
New York

PRESUMPTION OF GUILT. Copyright © 2016 by Archer Mayor. All rights reserved. Printed in the United States of America. For information, address St. Martin's Press, 175 Fifth Avenue, New York, N.Y. 10010.

www.minotaurbooks.com

The Library of Congress Cataloging-in-Publication Data is available upon request.

ISBN 978-1-250-06468-4 (hardcover)
ISBN 978-1-4668-7091-8 (e-book)

Our books may be purchased in bulk for promotional, educational, or business use. Please contact your local bookseller or the Macmillan Corporate and Premium Sales Department at 1-800-221-7945, extension 5442, or by e-mail at Macmillan SpecialMarkets@macmillan.com.

First Edition: September 2016

10   9   8   7   6   5   4   3   2   1

1859 2074
9/26/16
KHP

ACKNOWLEDGMENTS

I am asked on occasion why I write. The answers are many and varied, but among the most compelling is that I get to interview and collaborate with generous, intelligent, and knowledgeable people—who no doubt later read these books and shake their heads about how little of what they imparted ended up in the following pages. Nevertheless, I thank them all—and all who've come before—while taking full responsibility for any errors or omissions that might strike your eye as you read on.

Corky Elwell

Stephen Skibniowsky

Dawson Lyon

Margot Zalkind Mayor

Castle Freeman, Jr.

Eric Buel

Marci Sorg

Mike Mayor

Arlo Kline

Keith Clark

Jacqueline Calder

Dan Marx

Wally Mangel

Martin Cohn

John Martin

Julie Lavorgna

Steve Shapiro

Entergy Vermont Yankee

Office of the Chief Medical
    Examiner

Vermont Historical Society

Ray Walker

PART ONE

PART ONE

CHAPTER ONE

1970

Tony Farnum waited until he saw Barry's face in the driver's-side mirror before motioning him to back up, looking over his shoulder to make sure the concrete mixer's rear wheels didn't hit the staked wooden form bordering the pour site. Satisfied, he held up both hands to a chorus of squealing brakes and a whoosh of compressed air. Barry swung out of the cab, strolled back, extracting a pack of cigarettes, and threw a wheel chock under one of the back tires with practiced ease.

He offered the pack to Farnum, who shook his head. "Too hot," he said. "And I wanna get this load going. Told my old lady I'd take her out tonight."

"Friday night on the town," Barry intoned. "'Summer in the City.'"

Farnum shook his head. "Brattleboro? That's a bar town, not a city. They should call it Dodge and have done with it. We're going to Keene."

Barry raised his eyebrows. "Works for me. You're the flatlander. Bright lights're like oxygen to you."

"Spare me," Farnum said, removing his hard hat, sweeping his hair back, and refitting the rubber band he used to keep his ponytail in place. He jerked his head toward the gigantic construction site across the driveway from their small warehouse project. "We probably got fifteen hundred people working this job. How many you guess are local woodchucks like you?"

Barry shrugged, not willing to argue. He didn't know it for a fact, but he figured this nuclear plant project was maybe the biggest construction job the state had ever seen. One thing was guaranteed: Brattleboro had lost the majority of its available workforce to it. Every carpenter, electrician, contractor, plumber, ditchdigger, and shit shoveler within a hundred miles had found a way to dip into the till down here.

Sign of the times, the way he saw it, and like the song said, the times were a-changin'. Barry left Farnum to his grousing and his dreams of a heavy date, to return to the truck's cab and enjoy his smoke. From Vietnam and the riots to landing on the moon a year ago, the 1960s were going to be a decade people would remember for a long time.

And that meant not just "away," as many Vermonters called the world beyond their borders. The Green Mountain State had changed radically, switching from a hundred-year-old, rock-ribbed Republican bastion in 1962 to the thing in flux it was now, just eight years later. This plant they were working on was just another example, as far as Barry was concerned.

Farnum adjusted the truck's offload chute to hover above the rebar latticework inside the wooden skirting. The warehouse slab was 150 feet by 40, which they'd opted to pour in sections. The main construction site wasn't messing with ten-yard wheeled mixers for its needs, of course. By the time this project was done, they'd have a zillion tons of reinforced concrete in place. But this was a side project—a two-man job with little to no supervision. Custom made for a single truck.

He reached up, switched the drum's auger from charge to discharge, and began slinging a river of gray slurry off the end of the chute, back and forth over his target area.

Until Barry half fell out of the cab, yelling, *"Fire."*

Farnum threw the flow arrester and stepped back to see what Barry was pointing at. Rising beyond the front of the cab, a thick black vertical cloud of smoke was mushrooming toward the blue sky.

"Far out," he said, and jogged after Barry to see what was up. The Vermont Yankee plant wasn't near being operational yet—much less producing radiation—but that didn't mean that the word "nuclear" wasn't thick in the air. Vernon, the plant's tiny host town, was undergoing a bipolar crisis, reveling in the millions of dollars being spent in its midst, while downplaying the predictions of the nuclear disaster being forecast by the raggedy protesters who gathered weekly by the front gate.

It wasn't a reach for Barry and Tony to imagine something dire in the sight of a dark column of smoke stabbing the construction site's heart like an accusing black finger from above. They were children of World War II, brought up in the dawning light of the Atomic Age, complete with spy trials, missile gaps, bomb shelters, and monster movies like *Godzilla*. Vermont Yankee's anticipated use of nuclear fission ran hand in hand with the latter's ominous reputation.

"What d'ya see?" Farnum asked, catching up.

Barry looked back at him, surprised. "I thought you were pouring."

"I shut it off. It'll keep a few minutes."

"It looks like it's in the parking lot," Barry reported, rounding the corner of the metal-clad turbine building.

"Oh, man. Say it ain't a red Chevy truck."

They stopped side by side at the edge of the dirt parking lot. "Nope," Barry announced unnecessarily.

Before them, surrounded by a small tribe of men, most of them empty-handed, was a tired-looking van spewing fire from under its hood. One person was trying to pour water on the blaze with a garden hose.

"That's not gonna do much good," Farnum judged.

A bullhorn announcement from behind them urged everyone to stay back and return to work, and advised that the fire department was on its way. As if on cue, an anemic wailing could be heard far in the distance, growing louder.

"I better get back," Farnum said, his interest waning.

Barry kept him company, lighting up another cigarette. As they cleared the front of the mixer, he said, "I thought you said you turned it off."

"Fuck," Tony swore, and ran to the chute controls. "I did." The discharge wasn't fully open, but Barry was right—a thin trickle of concrete had deposited a significant lavalike mound within the form. Fortunately, it hadn't spread above grade. Farnum only had to even it out, and all would be well—especially after the subsequent screeding and floating took place.

No one would be the wiser.

PRESENT DAY

Nelson Smith laid down his jackhammer, shifted his ear protectors to the top of his helmet, and settled down beside the now quiet compressor, propping his back against one of its tires. He adjusted the earbuds he wore virtually all the time, and then rethought the gesture—removing them instead—and reached into his shirt pocket to kill his iPod.

The silence almost startled him. Usually, the outside world was kept at bay in preference to music or phone usage or podcasts, virtually all of it piped into him via the earbuds.

But sometimes, rarely, he yielded to his rural heritage and the early influence of his grandfather and father, both of whom used to take him into the woods to tap trees, gather cordwood, or hunt. Those moments of stillness remained fond memories, especially now that he no longer lived at home—the quiet conversations, the creaking of heavy branches overhead, the sound of distant wildlife, most of which the older men could identify from long experience.

Nelson looked around as he opened his lunch box and extracted his thermos and sandwich. He was hardly in the woods now, although at the moment, it was almost as quiet. Even more so.

He was sitting on the edge of a large, flat, exposed building slab, opposite the largest concrete cube he'd ever seen. He'd worked at the Vermont Yankee nuclear plant for four years now, doing whatever grunt work needed to be done, from digging ditches to shoveling snow, gravel, dirt, and rubble—like today—to anything else the foreman asked of him. It paid okay, filled the day, kept him outside, and mostly allowed him to work alone.

Especially lately. The plant, after forty years, had been decommissioned. From a high of maybe six hundred employees, they were functioning with a skeleton crew. It made him think of an aircraft carrier that he'd once visited in New York, as a kid. Now a museum, the ship was moored by the dock, still floating as designed, but almost totally empty near closing time. Nelson had wandered its length and depths, less impressed by the function of its varied nooks and crannies and more overwhelmed by the enormity of its stillness.

Like this place, right now. Once humming with activity, and a monument to pure energy, it had become a huge receptacle for a slowly dying radioactive heart—a comatose patient with no expiration date.

He shifted slightly against the tire. It was officially spring, after what his old man had termed an "old-fashioned winter"—cold, snowy, and hard on the bones. It wasn't quite T-shirt weather, but getting close. The Connecticut River, a few hundred yards away, hidden by the embankment bordering the plant, was fat and swirling with melted ice from the north. The near monochromatic world of a frozen New England was by now lightly tinted with the coming green of renewed vegetation. Nelson had heard that the Inuits used a hundred names for snow. Too bad we had only the one word, "green," for vegetation, he thought, given the varieties of green he could see from where he was sitting—in the trees and grass and hills beyond the razor-wired borders of the plant's periphery.

There was one exception, however, which he noticed only as the sun drifted out from behind a cloud. His gaze was attracted to the contrasting field of gray wreckage that he'd created in his multiday assignment to crumble the concrete slab of a recently dismantled warehouse. In the sun's sudden glare, Nelson saw a flash of something white and thin amid the lumpish shards.

Frowning, he rolled over onto his hands and knees, preserving his line of sight, and crawled to the lip where the old concrete met the edge of his latest efforts with the jackhammer, a few feet away.

"Damn," he said, the word carried away by the gentle breeze.

What had beckoned him appeared to be part of a human hand— a curved finger, bleached white and encircled by a thin gold ring.

CHAPTER TWO

Sammie Martens put down the phone. "Huh."

Joe Gunther looked up from his paperwork. "New case?"

She answered indirectly. "Over the years, how many times did you think tensions at Vermont Yankee might get hot enough to trigger a homicide?"

"You're kidding me." He pushed away from his desk, preparing to rise.

Sam, usually first to head out the door, checked him with an upheld hand. "Not that kind of call. This time, I don't think we're gonna find the doer standing over the body."

They were the only two in the small office, on the second floor of Brattleboro's timeworn municipal center.

"Okay," Joe said slowly, letting Sam have her moment.

"Some guy with a jackhammer was taking apart one of the old warehouse slabs and found a skeletonized hand."

"Only a hand?"

She shrugged. "So far. Unlike some of the bozos we've dealt with, sounds like this one knew when to stop. From what I was just told, right now all we got is a finger with a ring on it. I was being generous, calling it a hand."

"The warehouse inside the inner fence?"

"Right beside the reactor building."

"How'd we get the call?" he asked.

"Through the state police. Guess they figured we'd get it eventually. Plus, I bet the last thing they want is another pain-in-the-ass cold case."

Joe nodded. "Okay. Given how that plant's been a publicity shit-magnet since before it was plugged in, you better call the state's attorney while I let our esteemed director know at HQ."

Two minutes later, after they'd both hung up, Joe looked questioningly at his colleague. "I take it you got the same 'mother of God' reaction I did?"

"Along with a prayer that this can be kept quiet for as long as possible," she reported.

He rose and walked to the coatrack by the office's front door. "People's continual belief in miracles never ceases to amaze me." He handed Sam her jacket. "Good news is that at least we'll have a secure scene. That might help delay things."

She laughed. "And we won't need to rig any lights after hours, according to all those glow-in-the-dark rumors."

Vermont Yankee is located in Vernon, Vermont, about five miles south of Brattleboro. It occupies 130-plus acres, more or less, of sacrificed farmland that sticks out into the Connecticut River like a fat man's belly overhanging his belt.

It's an unusual-looking plant—at least to Joe's eye. Informed as he was by icons such as the four Three Mile Island hourglass cooling towers, he found Vernon's monument brutish and massively squat—a series of huge, utilitarian, blank-faced cubes and boxes, offset only by a single tall, thin, slightly ominous smokestack located on the facility's edge.

He'd been here multiple times over the decades, especially when he'd led the Brattleboro Police's detective unit before becoming head of VBI—the Vermont Bureau of Investigation. Back then, the plant's management was forever inviting local emergency personnel to participate in tabletop terrorist countermeasure exercises, or briefings on catastrophe protocols, or sometimes merely to share security concerns. The latter had become especially topical as relations between the plant's owners and the state's political leaders soured—spurred on by steady protests from area antinuclear activists. Indeed, this broiling antipathy and its attending legal wrangles were touted by observers as having played as big a role in finally shuttering the plant as its advancing years and the advent of cheap natural gas. Certainly Joe was among those who believed Vermont Yankee's management eventually just tired of the squabbling.

One advantage of all this past cooperation was that Joe and his colleagues had come to know the well-armed and highly trained defense force that protected the campus, specifically Jim Matthews, its current leader.

It was Matthews, in fact, who met them at the newly unmanned front gate, on Governor Hunt Road, and directed them to pull over.

He did not look happy.

"Hey," he greeted them, leaning over to look into the car Sam was driving.

"Hey, yourself," Joe answered. "You know anything more than when you called us?"

"Only that we'll be knee-deep in bad press again. I never would've seen this one coming, though. Not in a million." He straightened and pointed them to the right of the entrance road. "Drive down there. One of my guys'll wave you through, right up to the scene. We've had everything cordoned off. You'll see."

As Sam pulled away, Joe saw Matthews reach for his radio to warn others of their approach. For all the talk of decommissioning and downsizing, the power plant remained a nuclear site and, as such, a high-security concern to a lot of people and agencies—a fact highlighted by the number of armed people they saw positioned along their way, not to mention a scattering of watchtowers, camera stations, heavy fences, and even the occasional odd-looking, one-man concrete pillbox, complete with firing ports.

As if echoing his private ruminating, Sammie observed, "Always gives me the creeps coming here. It's like a prison for the undead."

They rolled to a stop beyond the last open gate and got out of the car near the remnants of a flat, half-crushed concrete slab ringed by men with guns, some of whom were further isolating the area with yellow tape and metal barricades.

They were met by a serious young man with a clipboard. "Could I see your identification and get your names, please?"

They complied, although Joe could see Sam suppressing a smile at the formality. But he and she were both ex-military, if a generation apart, and he found value in the ritual nature of the exchange. And as he'd said at the office, he sensed they'd be having few problems maintaining the scene's integrity—often a hassle in the real world.

Free to proceed, they advanced to a couple of dark-clad officers standing next to a twentysomething man in a hard hat—a pair of earbuds dangling over his collar—not far from a jackhammer's compressor.

As they drew near, Joe announced conversationally, "Special Agents Joe Gunther and Samantha Martens, VBI."

One of the security men indicated the man in the hard hat. "This is Nelson Smith. He was breaking up the slab for removal when he found . . ." He paused, groping for a description, and finished lamely with, "what he found."

"I stopped for lunch," Smith volunteered, "and saw the sun reflecting off the white bone. I couldn't figure it out, first. Gave me a real shock."

"So you saw nothing while you were working the jackhammer?" Sam asked as Joe drifted off toward the tool itself, which was lying still and quiet at the edge of the broken field.

"No. It was just dumb luck that I stopped when I did." Smith paused before adding, "I woulda stabbed right through it if I'd kept going."

Joe crouched low, bringing his eyes to within a few inches of everyone's topic of interest.

Sam joined him from the other side. "Damn," she said quietly. "What d'you think?"

Wearing a latex glove, Joe reached out and shifted a small chunk of material that was leaning against the ring finger, revealing a bony mate still half encased in untouched concrete. It vaguely looked like a dollhouse-sized version of a dinosaur dig.

"If I were a betting man," he said, "I'd say these two are attached to an impressively well-preserved skeleton."

They both looked up as Jim Matthews joined them, squatting down to their level. "So?"

Joe tapped gently on the one fully revealed finger. "I was just telling Sam that this is probably the tip of the iceberg. That's a guess, of course— could be these two fingers're all there is. Don't know why, though. If I'd wanted to get rid of a body when all this was going up, this place would've seemed like a gift from heaven."

Matthews shook his head. "Christ. So you know, both the state's attorney and our vice president in charge of operations are here, looking to be briefed."

"I'll get to them in a second," Joe said, unhappy to be facing such conversations so early on.

"When was the slab put in?" Sam asked.

Jim looked at her, his expression showing a preference for facts over politics. "Nineteen seventy. I have the exact date in my office. I looked it up. They documented everything as it went in, almost brick by brick—not that they used bricks, come to think of it."

"Any changes since?" Joe asked. "Additions, repairs to the floor, anything?"

"It was a metal warehouse," Matthews said. "It went up, served its purpose, and they decided to take it down. As far as the records go, this floor's been untouched for over forty years." He paused before reflecting, "Wonder who this is."

Joe smiled grimly. "Unless we get lucky, I'd say somebody who's going to keep us busy for a while." He rose and said to Jim resignedly, "Better take me to the grand pooh-bahs."

They were waiting for him in a small security building built into the inner fence system. The interior consisted of a row of now silent, alarm-equipped, passkey-operated turnstiles, once designed to handle shift changes of hundreds of people in short order.

The Windham County state's attorney was a tall, slim, serious-faced woman with a thatch of close-cropped white hair and a fondness for low-heeled shoes and practical pantsuits. Her name was Janet Macklin, and Joe had heard her referred to variously as Jammin' Janet, Manglin' Macklin, or inevitably, Mack the Knife—presumably, all from people who'd come up short against her. While Joe dealt mostly with the AG's office in his VBI capacity, he knew Janet Macklin and knew her to be sharp, tough, good in court, and supportive of law enforcement.

The Vermont Yankee VP—Roger Goodhugh—he'd never met and didn't know. VY had been sold some fifteen years earlier by its local birth parents to a Louisiana-based monolith named Entergy—to instantaneous scorn by activist opponents. Joe had always avoided the emotional turmoil around the plant's virtues or flaws, but could see that in the person of Roger Goodhugh, the "anti's" had an easy target to parody. Through no fault of his own, he was double-chinned, narrow-shouldered, and wide in the hips. And as Goodhugh extended a predictably flaccid, damp hand and spoke his greeting, Joe also picked up a discernibly thick southern accent. It almost seemed unfair, which immediately made Joe think kindly of him—and made him wonder if some corporate Machiavelli hadn't worked hard to put Goodhugh precisely where he was for precisely the effect he unconsciously made.

Joe nodded to both of them as part of the formalities. "Janet. Mr. Goodhugh. My colleague, Special Agent Samantha Martens. As you can imagine, we don't have much to tell you yet."

"Nevertheless," Macklin said quickly, "thanks for calling so fast," cutting off Goodhugh's soft-spoken, "Call me Roger."

"No problem," Joe told her. "Given how the place attracts attention, I figured you'd want an early heads-up."

He looked at Goodhugh. "And thanks for all the help we've been given. Appreciate your adapting the security routine for our convenience."

"Of course," Goodhugh said with an anemic smile. "Do you have any idea how quickly you'll be done?"

"We've barely arrived. It'll be an excavation, like for an archeological dig. Those are not fast-moving, Mr. Goodhugh—Roger. I do have a related question for you, though."

"Of course."

"Actually, it applies to all of us. How do you want to handle the press? Word gets out about a dead body at Vermont Yankee, all sorts of fireworks could blow up if we don't plan ahead."

"You have to throw them something," Macklin said bluntly, pointing out a window. "Right now, people are phoning and texting whatever they can make up."

Goodhugh surprised them with his response, suggesting that he might have been made vice president for some unexpected prowess. "From the little we know, it's ancient history and unrelated to anything radiological." He reached into his jacket pocket and presented them with copies of a single sheet of paper. "I had our PR people write this up. It refers to y'all as just 'authorities,' since I hadn't had the pleasure of meeting you, but I hope it'll do the trick for the time being."

Joe, Sam, and Macklin quickly read the release and exchanged glances.

"That's fine with me," Janet announced.

Joe folded it up. "Vague, almost boring, and throwing it onto us, as promised. Nice, Roger. You've clearly had practice."

Goodhugh glanced at his feet. "More than you could imagine."

In a large urban area, with a police department of thousands, the process thereafter would have taken a few hours. But there weren't many cops across Vermont, from the lowest town constable to the commissioner of public safety. As a result—and as Joe had implied to Roger Goodhugh—what was immediately set in motion took much longer to occur. By nightfall, although a tent had been rigged over their crime scene and the perimeter sealed to Jim Matthews's standards, they were still reduced to waiting for other investigators and/or technicians to appear, including a forensic anthropologist and scientists from the state's only official crime lab, in far-off Waterbury.

Things were done professionally and effectively in this nation's second least populated state, but their tempo was scaled to the locale's reality. As people were too fond of saying, there was "real time," and "Vermont time."

By the next day, however, everyone necessary was in place, and the wheels put into motion to free Nelson Smith's discovery from its tomb.

Also, Joe and Sammie had been joined by the two previously absent members of the local VBI squad—Lester Spinney and Willy Kunkle—both of whom had been out running other cases when this one came in.

Spinney—absurdly tall and gangly—was a native-born transplant from the Vermont State Police, drawn to the VBI because of its small size and major crimes focus. Kunkle was equally striking, but for radically different reasons. Hailing from New York and NYPD-trained, he stood out because of his demeanor. Sammie's romantic partner and the father of their young daughter, Emma, he was saddled with PTSD, a history of alcohol abuse, and a crippled left arm, which he kept—for the most part—pinned to his side by shoving his hand into his trouser pocket. Kunkle was irascible, opinionated, brusque, and intolerant; he was also one of the best cops Joe Gunther had ever worked with, which played well for Willy, who owed his continued employment to Joe's steadily running interference against everyone from the governor on down—all of whom Willy had alienated at one time or another.

"Can't we rule it a suicide?" Willy asked now, looking down at the calcified finger with the ring, still trapped in place.

Predictably, Lester laughed, Sam rolled her eyes, and Joe answered evenly, "Probably not, but I like the creative thinking."

Given that the next stage here would involve crime scene techs, the consultant anthropologist, and the precisely applied use of more jackhammers, chisels, and finally hand brushes and spatulas, Joe opted to lead his team out of the inner security fence, across the main entry road, to an administrative building housing the company's media relations department. There they'd been told to expect documents and photographs detailing the construction of the same warehouse that was currently being dismantled.

These were delivered by an efficient, pleasant, and professional young woman who met them at the door, escorted them down a hallway, and set them up in a conference room whose table was neatly stacked with file folders and a laptop computer.

She waved a hand at the array as if making introductions. "I put out the computer because I thought you might want to see the old photographs on-screen. You can blow them up that way to see any details, and arrange them into separate folders as you go. Oh," she added as an afterthought, pointing to a machine in the corner. "You can also print them out, if you want, or put them on a thumb drive if you have one. You know how to do that?"

Joe spoke for them all. "I think we'll figure it out. If not, we'll send up a flare."

It took a while to find their footing. The plant had taken years to construct, and the archives covered the progression from farmland to when the switch was thrown in 1972. Every aspect had been documented, from weld and pour inspections to a thousand general site photographs. Nevertheless, they reached their goal eventually: photos and documents detailing the pouring of their warehouse slab. In the end, they not only knew which firm had done the work, but the names of the mixer's driver and the chute operator, as well. Disappointingly, none of the pictures portrayed the actual work in progress.

"They could've taken a shot of the body being dumped, for Chrissake," Willy grumbled. "The one interesting thing that happened, and they missed it."

"Probably because of this," Lester said, holding up a single sheet of paper. "It's an 'unusual event' report," he explained. "A fire in the parking lot at the same time the slab was going in. There's a reference to how all work was momentarily halted by the distraction."

"You think the pouring crew was pulled away so the body could be dumped?" Sam wondered.

"By who?" Willy asked. "A third party or one of the pouring crew? Either one of them could've rigged the car fire to distract the other."

Joe indicated another report. "This is the investigation behind the vehicle fire. Not much to it. Just says, 'engine fire,' without explanation."

"It identify the owner?" Lester asked.

"Yeah." Joe paused to read, "William Neathawk. High iron guy, maybe. I remember when all this was happening. They used a bunch of Native Americans to put up the steel framing. That was common back in the day."

"I heard about that," Willy added. "Totally fearless, to hear the stories."

"Well, whatever Neathawk was, or still is," Sam said, "we'll have to rule him out."

"Good luck with that," Willy said under his breath.

"Good luck with any of them," Joe agreed. "Most folks working here were nomads, moving from job to job. It's going to be a challenge, not just finding them, but even some of the companies that employed them. Vermont Yankee itself was sold in 2000 or so. Rounding up employee lists is going to be fun. We'll have to see if they even bothered keeping tabs during construction. My guess is that lots of people just wandered off. Assuming our skeleton was even missed, he was probably lumped in among them."

He noticed Willy switching from one screen image of the slab pouring to another and back again—repeatedly—comparing the two. "You got something?"

"Something moving." Willy allowed them to see. "That lump there—the tarp. You can see what looks like some leftover rebar sticking out the end of it." He tapped his finger on the screen for emphasis. "When I flip from one to the other, it flattens slightly—like something was moved from underneath."

"And the flap changes position," Sam added. "Like it's been shifted."

"It's right beside where the body was found," Lester pointed out. "Against the skirting."

Joe shrugged. "There wasn't time during the car-fire distraction to do much more than flip the body onto the crisscrossed rebar and cover it with concrete."

Willy sounded peeved. "It means more than that. This whole thing had to've been done in two steps. Whoever did it moved the body under the tarp the night before. Nice catch."

Joe straightened and took them in. "So we go back in time and check what records they have for then."

"Did they have night watchmen?" Sammie asked.

"Guess we're about to find out."

Back at the site, signs of progress were unmistakable. A shallow, semi-circular dry moat, reaching down to the rebar, had appeared around the body, and the debris from within it painstakingly removed and sifted for anything such as a weapon, a bullet or casing, credit cards from a long-rotted-away wallet, or any other piece of evidence. So far, nothing had surfaced. As Joe had suspected, it seemed as if the body had been quickly tipped into the foundation site—as it might have been over the gunwale of a rowboat.

"You get lucky searching the records?" Jim Matthews wanted to know.

"Sort of," Joe conceded. "The body may've been moved in two stages—onto the site the night before, hidden, and then here, presumably forever. Problem is, we just searched the watchman logs of the night before the pour, and nothing was noted."

"Meaning what?"

"Meaning absolutely nothing," Willy said from beside them.

Joe answered the question. "Security was a Band-Aid, mostly to prevent theft or sabotage. You had a guy with a time clock, wandering around like a bicyclist in the Pentagon. Took him all night to make two turns—pretty much hopeless."

Of course, Willy had to add, "Or he was in on it, and moved the body himself. Rent-a-cops weren't held to the high standards they are now."

Joe sighed inwardly as he sensed Matthews stiffen moments before walking away.

"Nice," Joe said in an undertone. "Very diplomatic."

"I thought so," Willy responded.

Joe followed Matthews to where he was pretending to be checking a subordinate's clipboard entries.

"Any media response so far?"

The man's reaction was professional, any response to Willy's comment kept private. "Better than we'd hoped." He pointed toward the entrance gate. "One truck and a couple of cars out there, but nothing like the old days. Probably helped that the press release stressed this happened before the plant even went live. Things'll heat up, for sure, but so far, so good."

Slowly, the crime scene techs broadened the moat until, at last, they were on their hands and knees, their Tyvek suits filthy, chipping away at the emerging corpse like oversized vultures trying to share a meal.

The process was all the more exacting because of the anthropologist's discovery that the wet concrete had been fine-grained and liquid enough to form an excellent mold of the body's contours. This suggested that, although the remains were now skeletal, the mold's reverse impression might be detailed enough to help in identifying the body.

As a result, the more relevant chunks holding the victim fast were as delicately cataloged and packaged as the bones themselves, for latex casting later.

Even Kunkle was impressed by the careful unveiling's end results. "Jesus. I'm half waiting for him to sit up."

Joe crouched near the exposed cranium, studying it as if seeking a whispered explanation. "I think you're safe," he said.

CHAPTER THREE

Beverly Hillstrom was impressed, as well. "I've never seen a case quite like it."

For Joe, that was quite an admission, coming from not just the state's chief medical examiner, but one with vast experience. A confession of surprise from Beverly—given her erudition—was a rarity few had witnessed.

Joe, however, was among them. Over two decades, he'd earned her respect through his own dependable work ethic, and had recently graduated from colleague to romantic partner. That time—and now this new proximity—had allowed him insights into Beverly that generally escaped others—a development that had made him the happiest he'd been in a very long time.

At the moment, they—and Beverly's diener, Todd—were standing over what had been nicknamed CONCRETE MAN—pending a more permanent identity. He lay faceup, not on one of the morgue's two examination tables, but off to one side, on something more like a draped conference table. This was because Concrete Man was in pieces, each of which Hillstrom and Todd had spent an hour meticulously arranging in anatomical order, following their subject's return from the radiologist, who was busy studying the results elsewhere in the building.

The tidy array of bones reminded Joe of Wile E. Coyote, of Road Runner fame, after yet another encounter with a steamroller.

They were standing in the Office of the Chief Medical Examiner, or the OCME, located in the basement of the University of Vermont Medical Center in Burlington. It was the only place in Vermont where the state's roughly five hundred forensic autopsies were conducted every year.

"When you said you were sending me a case that had been entombed for forty years," she continued, "I imagined a much more damaged skeleton." She spread her gloved hands out, as if introducing a work of art. "But this is remarkable. I may have let popular prejudice override my scientific expectations."

"How so?" he asked, surprised.

"This means of disposal is a cliché of early-twentieth-century fiction," she said. "Usually in the context of the famous 'overshoes' of Prohibition fame. I'd always assumed that the stories played on a mere handful of actual cases. But concrete encapsulations are not uncommon currency—to the point where they were addressed in the *Journal of Forensic Sciences* a while ago. I've never seen it in Vermont, however. Also, for some reason, I thought that the acid in the concrete would be much more destructive of the skeletal calcium. I forgot that concrete has a high level of calcium, inhibiting the very leaching of bony matter I was anticipating."

Joe was amused. He always enjoyed it when she got nerdy on him, ramping up her already fancy prose style. "This was a special mix," he offered. "I don't know about the chemistry, but the quality and consistency of concrete was above and beyond the norm."

"I thought it was a warehouse floor."

"Yes and no. Every aspect of construction was so closely supervised that we were told they applied the same standards across the board, whether it was the reactor building or a slab off to one side. Plus, given the amount of material called for over the whole four-year project, they set up their own manufacturing on-site, where it could be pumped or trucked around at their convenience. Anyhow, that's why this guy's final resting place wasn't your run-of-the-mill garage floor."

She nodded. "Well, our good fortune. And I gather that they salvaged molds from around his face and one hand. That might prove helpful if they decide to make latex impressions later on, to help in identifying him."

Joe agreed. "Fingers crossed. There's probably not much out there for comparison, like dental records and X-rays. All this happened pre–computer filing."

She shrugged, still taking inventory. "It's a trade-off. They're making such inroads with DNA and the like, we may be able to get more out of this poor fellow than you think. Anyhow, let's see what he can tell us."

As she bent over her work, he asked, "So it is a male? The anthropologist at the scene said so, too."

"Oh, yes," she confirmed. "I'd say a six-foot male Caucasoid of approximately thirty years of age, based on the skull and pelvic synthesis."

"You don't have his name?" He laughed.

She looked up and smiled back. "That's where you earn your keep, I'm afraid. But, knowing you, I'm sure you will." She touched a small blue stain high on the pelvic girdle and announced, "He was wearing blue jeans. Did you find rivets at the scene?"

Joe had color photographs laid out along the table's edge. There were more than a hundred of them, taken as the body emerged into view. He extracted a shot that clearly showed a small round metallic nubbin resting on a bony background.

"Like this?"

"Classic," she said. "The one part of a pair of jeans that never seems to completely disappear—that and the zipper. Belt buckles, boot grommets, jewelry, watches, eyeglasses, credit cards. All good stuff. I take it the killer wasn't accommodating enough to leave this man's wallet in his pocket."

"No such luck," Joe confirmed. "We did collect some of the other items you mentioned, though, including the ring here." He indicated another picture. "Sadly, the inscription inside only has initials. Nice confirmation—if and when we make an ID—but not too useful now."

The back door swung open to admit a bespectacled man in a white lab coat carrying a laptop. Beverly's face creased into a wide smile. "Dr. MacColin Stare. Gracing us with your presence, no less." She turned toward Joe. "Special Agent Gunther, of the VBI, Dr. Stare, from Radiology. Dr. Stare was kind enough to drop what he was doing to process our friend's scans, but I didn't expect such rapid and personal service."

MacColin Stare was melting under her praise, and bashfully gave Joe a limp, moist handshake, making Joe wonder how often the man ever stepped into the sunshine. The thought stopped him from commenting about how appropriately Stare's name was matched to his specialty— that and the fact that it was a foregone conclusion the poor guy had heard it before.

"Well, I thought you might appreciate it," Stare said, smiling, "especially given the circumstances. This is sounding like a modern Agatha Christie novel, although I doubt she would've used a nuclear reactor as a setting."

As he spoke, he cleared some room, with Todd's help, on a nearby counter and fired up his laptop. "I have a couple of things you might find interesting," he said, scanning through a series of detailed X-rays.

"I know, for instance, that he was muscular, hardworking, and right-handed—from his skeletal development—but I realize you'd like me to cut to the chase. I was going to take you up the body, section by section, but this'll be worth it anyway."

To Joe's untrained eye, the set of images Stare selected appeared to show a shoulder.

"Ta-dah," the radiologist announced, moving aside.

Beverly leaned forward. "Is that a Hill–Sachs?"

Of course it is, Joe told himself silently.

"Very good, Doctor," Stare congratulated her. "The classic cortical depression in the posterolateral head of the humerus, along with—" He interrupted himself to scroll down the image slightly until he reached a visible aberration in the long bone hanging from the same shoulder. "—this," he added.

Beverly had returned to the table and fetched the body's upper right arm bone. "A healing fracture to the humeral shaft," she said, at last showing Joe something he could recognize. "Incurred close to the time of death," she added, studying it closely.

Stare's face brightened. "Exactly. And just to show off a little, look at the comparison between both upper limbs. The right is grossly hypertrophied, which would fit a man conditioned by swinging a hammer for most of his life—like a carpenter. I've seen it before."

"So what happened here?" Joe asked, returning to the humerus.

"That's why I consulted with orthopedics before I came down," Stare admitted. "It had me going—the combination of it. I mean, it had to have hurt. And no kidding around. It's a double whammy, after all—a fracture/dislocation."

"What did you learn?" Beverly coaxed.

"One of the orthopods recognized it right off—typical ladder-fall injury, he said, and I can totally see it. Look here. You're heading down, maybe carrying something, and all of a sudden, you slip, your feet go out from under you, and your arm gets tangled up between the rungs. Twist and snap. Slam-bam. A Hill–Sachs and a fracture, combined."

"Ouch," Beverly sympathized.

"He definitely went to the hospital for this," Stare confirmed. "Not that they did any surgery. But the way the humerus is healing, you can tell he must've been in a wrap-and-sling rig."

"Could this mean he was bound up when he died?" Joe asked.

"That's what I'd guess," Beverly confirmed as Stare nodded enthusiastically. "This bone fusion looks to be only two weeks old or so."

"Making him all the easier to overpower," Joe mused. He thought back to an observation Beverly had made, prior to Stare's arrival. "You said earlier that the killer wasn't accommodating enough to leave this man's wallet in his pocket. Is that your way of saying it's definitely a homicide?"

In response, she led them both to the display table and pointed to a spot high and slightly off center of the skeleton's chest. "This rib is positioned directly over the heart. See that small furrow? It's a typical tool mark for a knife. I noticed it when we were laying this out. There's another, right next to it, indicating at least two separate thrusts, both sharp-edged and perimortem. If there was any doubt about this being a homicide, those little scratches put an end to it."

Sally Kravitz glanced at her father's profile, just visible in the night. "I can't believe we're doing this," she whispered.

He took his eyes off the darkened house opposite the bushes concealing them to gaze at her with concern. "We can stop immediately," he offered.

She touched his forearm reassuringly. "No, no. That's not what I meant. I'm really happy you invited me. It's just that it's so . . . you know . . . private. In all sorts of ways. You're sure I'm not invading your space?"

He chuckled. "Are you kidding? I feel like I'm handing you the keys to the family business."

She shook her head, beaming with pleasure. Her father was a certified nut. She knew that. But he was the smartest, kindest, most sensitive and devoted nut she'd ever known, and the center of her universe, which probably made her a bit odd, too.

And she was in this with him, whatever the outcome. She wasn't exactly sure what "this" was, of course. When it came to job descriptions, her father's was hard to pin down. On the surface, he was a Brattleboro character—Dan Kravitz, the invisible everyman everyone seemed to know, if not necessarily by name. The man without a home; without a fixed job; who could do everything; who said nothing; who'd worked at more jobs—from washing dishes to cleaning gas station garages to unplugging culverts—than any twelve people she could think of. She'd seen a beer commercial featuring a bearded guy with two bimbos, claiming to be the most interesting man in the world.

They had no clue.

Because to her, Dan Kravitz would forever be his own alter ego: not the menial everyman with an eerie ability to keep clean, but rather what the papers had coined "the Tag Man" a couple of years ago. He was the never-identified burglar who for a while had committed a rash of illegal entries in which he'd deposited a Post-it note marked, "You're it," and made a point of eating a little of each upscale home's fanciest tidbits before leaving—like a literate mouse, visiting in the night.

At the time, it had caused a sensation—and a boost in the upper crust's demands for better security systems.

Of course, her father's nocturnal visits had been more than that. And—she could admit on a purely disengaged intellectual level—a little creepy. But not where it applied to Dan. For reasons no doubt entirely genetic, she had never once shaded him with any hint of creepiness. He was a researcher, an archaeologist, the Boswell of Brattleboro's human heart.

Okay—a slight overstatement. He broke into rich people's homes and studied their habits, collecting facts as others might scoop up the silver, and entered what he learned into a filing system the NSA might envy—if on an entirely local level. And—truth be told—he had left those sticky notes on the homeowners' night tables while they were sleeping.

But somehow, through Sally's skewed view of it, Dan had managed to make his outings at once beguiling and scientific. Her self-acknowledged delusion was encouraged by her realization that the police knew of his activities. Her father had actually stumbled upon proof of a crime, and helped the police—or at least Willy Kunkle—bring it to a successful conclusion. He had also sworn off the high-visibility Tag Man role— officially—and had sunk from judicial sight.

Less officially, he had merely stopped leaving the Post-it notes. Whatever boastful impishness had prompted him to plant them in the first place had apparently been placated. Either that, or he had taken his daughter's nascent interest in his covert life as reason enough to dial back the showmanship while he ramped up his role as a mentor.

Either way, she was grateful. An original thinker herself, hitched to this single parent and his withdrawn, nomadic personality since her birth, she'd been wondering what to do after high school, while finding no joy in the conventional choices before her, which partially explained why she was taking a "gap year" before college.

"What do you think?" she whispered, studying the house across the lawn.

He'd been here earlier, prepping the field. She knew that. Her apprenticeship wasn't to be rushed. He'd already sprung the locks and made sure the house was empty, to minimize the risks. Later, he would train her in security breaching, and expose her to the thrill of drifting through a house where the inhabitants were present, if asleep—or not.

But for the moment, she would shadow his moves, get used to the feel of the work, and discover if she was willing and able to inherit the mantle. There would be plenty of time, and her training would be thorough and carefully administered. She knew herself to be in tutelage to a master, though of what, she still wasn't sure.

CHAPTER FOUR

"My God, David. That's eerie."

Joe held the off-white death mask in his hands gingerly, as if cradling an ailing child. Its pale, sightless eyes stared past his shoulder, seemingly transfixed by something behind him. Joe almost turned to double-check.

Instead, he returned it to David Hawke, the state crime lab's director. "I had no idea the mold would turn out so well."

Hawke placed the mask on his desk. "Me, neither. Lucky break. For what it's worth, we also managed to get this." He shoved over a plastic hand with two perfect fingers and three crude extremities, making it look like an abandoned sculpture project. Next to it was a fingerprint card with two readable impressions in black ink.

"Not bad," Joe complimented him. "And speedy, too. I didn't expect this so fast."

It was early in the day, the morning after Joe's visit to the morgue. He'd spent the night with Beverly, who lived just south of Burlington, and had been surprised to get a call from David on the drive back to Brattleboro—convenient, given the lab's location along the way, in Waterbury.

"You caught us at a good time," Hawke told him. "Plus, who could resist jumping on this one? Way too cool. Unfortunately, I ran the prints through the system and got nothing, but you can't have everything. What did you learn from Hillstrom? I take it you went up there for the so-called autopsy."

"I did," Joe confirmed. "It's definitely a homicide—a knife to the heart. Although she stressed that an additional cause may have played a part, too—like a bullet that left no evidence on the bone. She's leaving that part undetermined."

"Careful woman," Hawke said. He indicated the mask. "He look like you imagined?"

"Hillstrom and the radiologist—and the anthropologist before them, for that matter—all said he'd be a white guy, maybe in his thirties. So this looks right. I like the mustache and sideburns, too. Very '60s and Ringo Starr, if a little fatter in the cheeks. I keep forgetting how much hair people wore back then."

Hawke picked up the facsimile and admired it. "It's still a little rough, as befits the medium, but better than the first example of this technique I ever saw. You hear about the statues of the dead in that Pompeii museum? A dozen or so bodies they found during the excavation, frozen in place by Mount Vesuvius's volcanic ash?"

"I've seen pictures," Joe said.

"That's what I thought we'd get when I worked on this last night," David explained. "Kind of the same circumstances—ash and concrete, both poured over bodies like caramel. But this is so much sharper.

"We got the DNA sample by courier, by the way, from the teeth. I sent it to CODIS for comparison. I'll run it through our in-state system, too, just to see if we get lucky. Course CODIS'll probably take months, it being a national database. Too bad we're not a TV show."

"A hit in-state would sure be convenient," Joe said hopefully.

"Would be," David agreed. " 'Cept you said on the phone that the

Yankee project involved over a thousand workers, mostly from away. That right?"

Joe smiled at the reference to "away," which in Vermontese meant out of state. "True, and maybe he had nothing to do with Yankee. If you knocked off somebody within hailing distance of one of the biggest digs in Vermont history, wouldn't you consider dumping your handiwork into the hole and having somebody else cover it up?"

David Hawke nodded. "Guess I might. Didn't they do that in a *Columbo* episode?"

Joe laughed. "If we catch him, I'll be sure to ask the killer what his favorite TV show was." He paused a moment before adding, "I hate to admit knowing this, but didn't that show start in the early '70s—after this guy died?"

Hawke raised his eyebrows. "So much for that theory, then." He pushed both the hand and the mask over to Gunther. "Take 'em. They're yours—they're 3-D printer copies of the original latex molds."

"Dad, you have any shirt stays I can borrow?"

Lester Spinney stepped out of the bathroom, removed his toothbrush from his mouth, and peered at his son: a deputy sheriff from the waist up, complete with badge, clip-on tie, and pen-and-pencil set; and—down to the floor—a pantsless, knobbly-kneed teenager in tighty-whities and athletic socks.

"You don't want to go out like that? Just stay in your car—nobody'll notice."

"*Dad.* C'mon. I'm running late."

Lester relented, knowing the commute time from their home in Springfield, at the top edge of Windham County. "I haven't worn a pair of those in years, but they used to be in my top left-hand drawer. Dig around in the back, and ignore the condoms."

"God, that's gross."

Lester laughed and returned to the bathroom, skirting by his wife at her sink and pinching her bottom through her nurse's scrubs.

"*Ow.* What did he want?" she asked, applying a hint of eyeliner.

"Shirt stays. You remember: those upside-down suspenders that connect your shirt to your socks. Make you look like a squared-away recruitment poster at all times."

Susan Spinney laughed. "You used to tell me you were terrified you'd get shot someday and they'd find those in the ER when they cut off your pants. God forbid."

He brushed a few more times and spat into his own sink. "They work, but they are dorky. I always felt like a Ken doll, putting them on."

"I thought they looked cute," she said. "And I can never look at a cop without thinking he has those things on underneath."

"Bet that does wonders for your respect for the uniform," he guessed.

She chortled, still intent on her task. "You kidding? With all the cops I know? Believe me, what they got under their clothes is the least of their problems when it comes to earning my respect."

"*Hey.*"

She broke away long enough to kiss him quickly. "Hey, yourself. How many cops do you want me to have in my life, anyhow? I already got two. Wendy'll probably want to sign up next."

That brought him up short. He looked at her closely. "She tell you that?"

Susan snorted. "Gotcha. She's a teenager, Les. You don't want to know what she's got on her mind." She then added seriously, "But don't be surprised if she does someday. Your kids happen to like you."

He smiled, pleased and a little embarrassed.

"I do, too, goofball," she said. "Go help your son. I can hear him still scratching around in there."

He kissed her neck on the way back out.

* * *

"You take her in," Willy said shortly, from behind the wheel. "Can't stand that knucklehead teacher."

Smiling, Sammie got out of the car to uncouple their child from the backseat, saying evenly, "*You* think she's a knucklehead, which, in your world, makes her one of ninety percent of the world's population. Also, she's not a teacher, and she's good people."

"I'll have you know I'm lowering my standards," he told her. "I'll be hugging people next."

Laughing, Sam gathered up Emma and carried her along the walkway to the day care, toward the woman standing at the door. Ten feet shy, however, Sam put her daughter down and, holding her by one hand only, slowly walked her the rest of the way, enjoying the child's ear-to-ear grin at her own success.

"Oh, look at you," the aforementioned knucklehead exclaimed, clapping her hands, squatting down, and opening her arms. "What a performance. Nice job, Emma."

Willy watched from the car, his window rolled down, waiting for Sam to return so they could continue to the office.

"Give her a Milk-Bone, while you're at it," he groused, disguising his pride.

"This our guy?" Lester Spinney asked, picking up the 3-D copy of the Concrete Man's death mask.

"Nice sideburns," Willy commented from behind his desk, adjusting his limp arm to settle more comfortably into his chair.

"I had a pair like that," Joe admitted.

Everyone in the small office laughed at the image.

"Jesus, boss. You must've looked like a French poodle."

Joe's eyes widened. "I beg your pardon. More like a dashing Vegas lounge lizard."

"Wow," Sam joined in. "There's an image I'll have to work to forget."

They were on the second floor of one of Brattleboro's landmark buildings, the municipal center, built on a hill in 1884 as the town high school and appropriated seventy years later for what it was now. Huge, brooding, clad in dark brick and marble, and topped off to look like a horror movie set, it housed a scattering of town offices, including the police department—the old stomping ground of three of the four current VBI squad members, excepting Lester.

"Okay," Joe announced, taking a perch on the windowsill behind his desk. "Let's figure out who this groovy dude is and why he ended up where he did."

He picked up a printout and waved it before them. "I came in early this morning and updated the case file. In a nutshell, it now tells us what we've got so far: a married, white, right-handed carpenter or roofer—maybe thirty years old—whose last name probably starts with M, since the inscription inside the wedding band reads 'HM and SM forever.'"

"Always wondered how long forever was," Willy said in a low voice.

"The most solid information comes from the medical examiner's office. At the time of death, our victim most likely had his right arm in a sling because of a combination dislocation/fracture. There's a high probability this was fixed at a hospital, and the radiologist at the UVM Medical Center told me it'll probably stand out, since it's a rare double whammy of an injury."

"Start by going through records at Bratt Memorial?" Lester asked.

"Sounds right to me," Joe answered.

"You sure about the carpenter/roofer background?" Willy asked.

"It's a reasonable fit only, given the injuries and the physical findings.

His bone structure indicates strenuous activity for most of his life, involving heavy use of the right arm."

"Like swinging a framing hammer," Willy filled in.

"Yup." Joe paused before resuming. "So, checking the hospital records for 1970 looks like our first priority. If we come up blank locally, we'll put the word out to an ever-expanding ring of medical facilities in Vermont, New Hampshire, and Massachusetts. VCIC in Waterbury ran the prints from the latex cast through the Vermont database, with no success, and the lab is doing the same with the collected DNA. The hope is that, if nothing else, we might at least get some familial hits that'll point us in the right direction to do a few interviews.

"Last but not least," he continued, standing up, "we need to do a records search. Vermont Yankee paperwork has to be combed through for anything unusual—reported fights, unexplained employee departures, unusual events—around the time of the burial. And let's not forget William Neathawk, the owner of the van that caught fire. Also, all missing persons complaints need to be reviewed. A lot of this is going to involve old-fashioned legwork. Most of the relevant material's going to be in filing cabinets. Some of it may be computer indexed—if we're lucky."

Joe crossed over to the coffee machine and refreshed his cup, adding the maple syrup and artificial creamer that made his colleagues cringe. "An additional historical note, since I'm the dinosaur in the room. Vermont in the late '60s, early '70s was going through a transformation no one would guess nowadays. In 1967 and '68, homicides jumped from four a year to around twenty. The hippie counterculture, the Vietnam War protests, the interstate coming through, unemployment . . . The population jumped sixty thousand, because of urban flight, at the same time about twenty-five hundred farms went belly-up. This state was reeling, and I'm barely touching the surface."

Joe saw Willy roll his eyes and quickly reached his conclusion. "I remember some of those killings—a baby left to freeze to death; an old woman cut open, Jack the Ripper–style; a teenager shooting his parents 'cause they'd pissed him off. Keep that stuff in mind. We're going to be hunting ghosts. You need to know what times were like when this guy caught a knife in the chest. It was a different world—not all love and peace like people think."

CHAPTER FIVE

Elizabeth Pace looked up from her computer screen and tilted her head to one side. "Joe Gunther. Good Lord. How many years has it been?"

He was leaning against her office doorjamb. "Too many. My fault. No excuse."

She saved what she'd been writing and sat back. "Pretty good excuse, from what I've heard. You're a bigwig now—major crimes. Far cry from when you used to drop by the ER and ask for favors." She chuckled at his expression. "I'm kidding. I was always happy to help. I don't say this about all cops, but you are one of the good guys. You always have been."

"Thank you. Takes one to know one." He indicated the office. "And talk about bigwigs. From night nurse to director of the whole department."

She pursed her lips dismissively. "I just outlived the competition. And now that I'm here, I'm not sure I wasn't happier working nights. Nobody told me that all the jackasses pulled the day shifts. Doesn't seem fair."

"Getting away from the jackasses is one reason I took the new job," he told her.

She nodded sympathetically. "So what're you after now? Must be a biggie for you to renew old acquaintances."

He shook his head. "You are becoming cynical, Elizabeth." He patted his jacket pocket. "This time, I actually have a warrant. I was hoping to mix a drive-by hello with some help managing the system. What I'm after may be a little offbeat."

She pointed to her guest chair. "You were never a dull visitor, Joe. Tell me."

He took up her offer as he spoke. "Nineteen seventy. A man may have come here to be treated for a combination dislocated shoulder–fractured humerus. We need to take a look at his records."

Her white hair spoke of Elizabeth Pace's years of experience and ability to catch what counted. She thought a moment before responding, "May have?"

"He was disposed of locally right after," Joe partially explained. "So we're hoping he was treated locally, too."

She laughed outright. "Listen to you. Do you think we all live under a rock? It was front-page news in the paper—'Skeleton Dug Up at Vermont Yankee.' Trust me—I think I know where he was disposed of."

He gave an embarrassed shrug. "Force of habit. I haven't read the paper yet."

"It's all right. You're forgiven. But you don't have a name. Or do you?"

"Nope."

She rolled her chair back, stood up, and gestured at the door. "Let's go fishing, then."

It was late in the afternoon before Joe returned to the VBI office. Nevertheless, the rest of his crew was still there, including Emma, who was standing in a portacrib in one corner, supporting herself by the top rail, greeting him with a wide, drooly grin.

He crossed over, crouched down, and ran his fingers across her hands. "Hey, sweetie. How've you been?"

It wasn't unusual, seeing her suddenly appear. Her parents had good child care, but scheduling could be tricky, and neither Joe nor Lester minded the extra company.

Still, Sam asked, "Okay, boss?"

He glanced at her, sitting at her desk. "Of course. If she's going to replace you two, she'd better know how things work."

"I'd sooner she was a lion tamer," Willy groused.

"Phooey," Sam challenged him. "You love this job."

"It's not me we're talking about."

"No," Joe interrupted. "It's not." He slapped an old, yellowed file on his desk. "It's this guy."

"You found him?" Lester asked.

"Henry 'Hank' Mitchell," Joe said. "He looks right for it—the dates line up, injuries sound the same, but I need to see the X-rays Hillstrom generated."

He slipped a large negative out of the old file as Lester called up what they hoped would be the same image on his computer. The squad clustered around the screen at the same time Joe held Mitchell's old hospital X-ray up to the light.

"That the upper arm, boss?" Spinney asked.

"Yeah. Says 'right/anterior,' if that helps."

"There," Lester announced, hitting a few keys and sitting back so they could all compare the two pictures. All except Willy, of course, who hadn't moved from his desk.

"Broken arm's a broken arm," he told them. "Even if they look the same, it won't be a hundred percent proof, and I bet they don't—X-rays being the interpretive things they are, sometimes. Am I right?"

"I think they do," Sam argued.

Joe put the old X-ray back. "I agree, but Willy's right. Too many variables in the two shots. Doesn't matter—we weren't going to proceed any differently, X-ray or no X-ray."

"Woulda been fun if they'd matched perfectly," Lester said, disappointed. He cast a look at Willy. "You are such a buzzkill."

Willy enjoyed that. Nevertheless, almost as a peace offering, he said, "Hank Mitchell matches the HM inside the ring. That better?" He then asked Joe, "What's the address for Mitchell? And his emergency contact info?"

Joe had already read the file that the hospital retrieved from its crosstown storage site.

"On Greenhill Parkway, and—to your point about the ring—the contact name's Sharon Mitchell. SM. That being said, I'd be surprised if anyone's still living there."

"Why?" Sam asked.

"Forty years," Willy answered for him. "Long time."

"Actually," Joe said, "I was thinking about the location. Once upon a time, Greenhill Parkway might've had some appeal."

"Before the interstate chopped off everyone's backyard in the mid-'60s," Sam finished the thought. "Got it. Not a great place to call home anymore."

"Maybe, maybe not," Joe mused. "Whatever the case, it's a start, as is the name Sharon Mitchell."

"What else does the record say?" Willy wanted to know.

"Hank was a smoker, drank too much, was urged to lose some weight," Joe recited. "Not much beside the shoulder problem that brought him in."

"I didn't mean that stuff," Willy cut in. "He's dead. Who cares? Was it a workmen's comp deal? Who was the employer?"

"Lighten up, Willy," Sammie said softly.

Elsewhere, that would have elicited a comeback. Here, he merely mumbled, "Sorry." This group had been working together for so many years, they'd virtually become family—with all the attending allow-ances and shortcomings.

"Ridgeline Roofing," Joe answered. "I remember when they were bought out by Vermont Amalgamated a couple of decades ago. It was a big deal."

Lester cut in. Still staring at his computer screen, he announced, "I got a Sharon Mitchell out of DMV residing in Bratt on Chestnut Street."

"How old?" Willy asked.

"Sixty-six," Lester said, throwing in her birth date.

Sammie had also been typing rapidly, and now added, "Nothing popping up on the Spillman or Valcour databases, so she's either well behaved or never been caught."

"Let's hope for the second," Willy said. "I hate the boring ones."

Joe looked at them all. "Okay. One of you has Emma to care for; Les, you probably wouldn't mind getting home. Who's joining me to break the news to Mrs. Mitchell?"

Chestnut Street had also been victimized by the interstate's being laid out like a runway across Brattleboro's map. From a bird's-eye view, Chestnut now resembled a garden hose, severed by a lawn mower and abandoned on the grass. Homeowners giving directions to their address had to specify whether to approach from the east or the west.

The street's fate at the hands of town planners notwithstanding, it had become—perhaps as a result—a quiet, pleasantly ignored, almost suburban nook in the midst of a busy town. The houses were in the plain, postwar style of an old TV sitcom, but well maintained, mostly single-story, with paved driveways and nurtured lawns. Joe and Willy headed west—Sam had opted to stay with Emma—until they came to the address listed as Sharon Mitchell's, some six doors shy of where

Chestnut smacked into the embankment leading up to the interstate above.

With Joe carrying a small package, both men got out of the car, crossed a lawn decorated with a swing set and a few scattered toys, and stepped up onto the concrete stoop of a split-level home. Confirming their research, a copper plaque by the door read, MITCHELL.

Willy cocked his head at the sight of it. "Think we got the right place?" He rang the bell.

The door opened to reveal a slightly built woman with profession- ally dyed hair, carefully flattering clothes, and well-tended nails—all of which Joe took in with a glance as he and Willy swung back their jack- ets to reveal the badges clipped to their belts. Joe noticed a gold ring on her finger.

"Mrs. Mitchell?" he asked.

"Yes."

"We're from the police. I'm Joe Gunther and this is William Kunkle. Are we catching you at an okay time?"

"For what?" she asked evenly, her cool blue eyes moving from one of them to the other—and taking in the arm unnaturally anchored to Willy's left trouser pocket.

Joe smiled. "Good question. We're working on a case where your name came up. We just wanted to ask you a couple of things about that."

"Do I need a lawyer?" The question was asked peacefully.

Joe was used to it—not that it happened frequently—and instinc- tively summoned his default expression of surprise. "Goodness. Well, of course, you may call one if you'd like, but there's no need that I know of. We're just looking for information."

"There may be more," he was impressed to hear Willy add. "We might have some news for you."

Mitchell's face paled. "Is everyone all right? You're not here about any of the kids, are you?"

Joe held up his free hand. "No. Absolutely not. As far as we know, they're all fine. Could we come in?"

She stepped back without hesitation. "Of course."

She preceded them into an immaculate, fresh-smelling living room, saying, "This is pretty mysterious. I hope it's not *bad* news."

She sat on a couch, waving them to a pair of chairs opposite.

"To be honest," Joe began, "it might be. Do you know—or did you know—a man named Henry Mitchell? Hank?"

Her eyes narrowed. "What is this about?"

Willy's voice was unusually supportive. "Please, ma'am. Could you answer the question first?"

"He was my husband. Or he still is, unless you're going to tell me different."

"You haven't seen him recently?" Joe asked.

Her smile was sorrowful. "You could say that. He walked out on us forty years ago. What have you found out about him?"

"A couple of more details first, Mrs. Mitchell," Joe stalled her. "I know this is hard, and we appreciate your patience, but we've got to be sure that we're talking about the same person. Are you okay with that?"

"Of course I am."

Willy glanced at Joe, who produced a small recorder from his pocket and held it up. "This is important enough to us, Mrs. Mitchell, that I'd like your permission to record the conversation. Just so there're no misunderstandings later on."

The emotions crossing her face were beginning to pile into each other. "I suppose so."

"Thank you." Joe turned on the machine and placed it by his side. "Shortly before he disappeared, did your husband injure his right shoulder?"

She nodded, clearly distressed. Her hands were clasping and unclasping in her lap, seeking elusive comfort in one another. Finally, she settled for twisting the ring on her left hand.

Joe opened the small bag he'd brought along, speaking as he did so, "Mrs. Mitchell, I'm sorry to do this, but the circumstances are so unusual, I'm not sure how else to proceed. A couple of days ago, a man's body was discovered—a skeleton—who we're pretty sure was your husband. We had a latex mask made that shows what he looked like when he died, in 1970." He looked up at her, hesitating. "I have a copy of that in this bag. I know it's a lot to ask, but would you be willing to look at it?"

She didn't answer right away, staring at Joe's hand in the bag as if it might reappear with a snake—which, in a way, it was about to.

"All right," she said softly.

In one gesture, Joe brought out the ivory-colored mask and cradled it in his extended hands, as if ghoulishly offering her a head on a plate.

The face stared up at her, ghostly and expressionless, as she responded in kind.

After a prolonged silence, Joe asked, "Is this your late husband?"

She tore her eyes away, allowing him to banish the mask back into the bag. "Where did you find him?"

Joe hedged his response. "Some people were dismantling an old warehouse, tearing up the concrete floor—"

She straightened. "I heard that on the radio. The Yankee plant. That was Hank?"

"Yes."

Her hand fluttered by her cheek a moment. "What was he doing there?"

"Mrs. Mitchell," Willy spoke, "did he have anything to do with that project?"

She shook her head. "He was a roofer. He did some odd jobs on the side, but never there that I know of. How did he die?"

"We're still looking into that," Joe answered quickly, laying Hank's ring on the table and asking, "Is that his wedding band?"

She picked it up and read the inscription. "Yes."

"What were the circumstances of his disappearance?" Willy asked, his tone encouraging. "You must've explained his sudden absence to yourself somehow—in order to make sense of it. You never called the police?"

"No," she answered, her expression softening with reminiscence. "No. In a way, he was already missing." She replaced the ring and sank against the sofa cushions, looking as if she'd been dropped there from a height. Her hands had stopped fidgeting.

"Our marriage was having problems. When Hank disappeared, he wasn't living with us anymore. I'd asked him to move out."

"I'm sorry."

She was quiet for a while, and then crossed her arms across her stomach and began rocking slightly, back and forth. Joe realized that she was silently weeping.

"Can I get you anything, Mrs. Mitchell? A glass of water?" He looked around for at least a box of Kleenex.

But she looked up and wiped her eyes with both palms. She took a deep breath. "It's hard, even after so long."

Willy interpreted what she meant. "Hearing what really happened?"

She nodded. "I never would've guessed it. He was so restless; so hungry for something else. I figured he took off. Those were the days, after all—'free love.' I thought the kids and I made him feel trapped."

"I know this is painful," Joe said, "but we were hoping you could give us as many details as possible about Hank. We have to try to reconstruct what he was doing, who he was hanging out with . . . Things like that. How long before he went missing did you two split up, for example?"

"Not even a month," she answered, her voice stronger.

"Where was he living?" Willy asked.

"On Oak Street. A nice place. It was an apartment, on the top floor. I visited him there."

"Sounds fancy."

She gave him a surprised look. "Why not? We were doing pretty well."

Willy frowned. "I thought he was just a roofer."

"He was. Ridgeline Roofing. But he was the owner's right-hand man—a partner, I suppose, really. He mostly got on roofs because he liked to get his hands dirty. Like I said: restless. But it made sense, too. It saved money, having him be management and labor, combined. And BB loved it."

Both men looked at her until she explained, "Robert Barrett—everyone calls him BB. He later sold out to Vermont Amalgamated. Made a killing." She waved her hand around to indicate the room. "That's what paid for this."

Faced with their continued silence, she went on. "BB told me he'd put Hank's money in a trust for me and the kids. I never knew about it, and I'm not sure to this day if I really believed it. Hank never mentioned any money. I always thought BB made it up so I wouldn't feel like I was accepting charity."

"Very generous," Willy said leadingly.

"BB was in love with me," she said without affectation.

Joe felt Willy's reaction as if it were an electrical crackle.

"He was always a gentleman about it," she went on. "Never pressed too hard, but after Hank was gone, he made his interest clear."

"Did you accept his advances?" Joe asked delicately.

She smiled sadly. "Oh, no. BB was a nice man. Still is. He's not that much older than me. But Hank was my guy."

It was said simply, as if read from a fairy tale, and prompted Willy to comment, "That must've disappointed BB."

"It did and it didn't," she responded. "I wasn't the girl for him. I think he knew that, too. I was the dream he didn't want to become real. He married three different women after I told him I wasn't interested. None of them was even vaguely like me. I actually liked them—well, maybe not Doreen, the middle one. They were all funny and outspoken and daring. And each was like the next, so they obviously were his type, even if he couldn't stay married to two of them. That's what makes me think we would've been doomed in no time."

"What about other suitors?" Joe wanted to know. "You were a young woman when Hank left."

But again, she shook her head. "He and I had problems. Everybody does. But we were soul mates." She pointed to the bag at Joe's feet. "What you showed me today proves I was right all along. I never believed he just walked away, like people said."

"And your kids?" Willy asked. "How were they about all this?"

"They took it hard. Greg was nine and Julie seven. It was toughest on Greg, of course—the whole father–son thing was shattered, and it seemed to leave him hanging, for years. That was the most difficult part for me to forgive."

She sighed before continuing. "Julie? Hard to tell. What was caused by Hank leaving, what was me going to work again, and what was just old-fashioned, hormonal, teenage baggage? She may have always been fated to be my wild child. That's sure as heck how it turned out."

"What kind of work did you end up doing?" Joe asked.

"Backroom stuff for Dixon's Business Supply—filling orders, monitoring inventory, arranging contracts with local schools and businesses. I was the workforce behind the door that says 'Employees Only.' They were good to me, mostly left me alone, and helped me pay the bills—along with BB, like I said."

"Do you remember if BB made an extra effort to be friendly to Greg and Julie before Hank left?" Willy asked.

She furrowed her brow. "BB? Why?"

Willy tipped his hand with his next statement. "Mrs. Mitchell. Your husband didn't end up buried in concrete by accident."

Joe flinched at his bluntness.

She stared at both of them. "Are you saying . . . ?"

"Nothing," Joe said firmly. "We have to ask questions to find out what happened. This is how we do it. It's sometimes hard to hear, and it can make people think we're going places we're not. But if we don't check every possibility—no matter how potentially hurtful or unlikely— we're not doing our job. Can you understand that?"

"Of course."

He kept going. "This was all a long time ago, so we have a lot of catching up to do. We have to reconstruct a world even you've left behind. I mean, in your mind, Hank might as well've been living in Hawaii with a whole new family. If you ever thought of him at all anymore. I was married once. Same thing—love of a lifetime. She died of cancer, and I never remarried. Nevertheless, it fades with time, doesn't it? It becomes like the loss of a parent or a favorite relative. You move on."

She was nodding in agreement. "Yes. You do."

"Well, sadly, we've got to upset the applecart, and I'll guarantee you that it'll get confusing, and that your friends and relatives're going to get worked up. It's not anything we want, but we're stuck with it, or we'll never get to the truth."

"I guess so."

Joe gave her a supportive smile. "Fair enough. Now, let's step away from some of this emotional stuff for a while and get a few nuts and bolts squared away. Would that be okay?"

"All right."

"We're still not messing up your plans for the evening? Fixing dinner or going out or anything?"

"No. I'm fine. Thank you for asking."

Willy saw his chance to smooth out any ripples he might have caused. "The thanks are all ours, Mrs. Mitchell. You've been a big help."

Joe gave him a sideways glance. His rough-edged colleague was not famous for conciliatory comments.

"Let's start with Robert Barrett, then," Joe began. "BB—still living in the area?"

"Oh, yes," she replied, back in conversational mode. "He's retired, but hale and hardy. Married to Number Three."

"How old is he?" Willy asked.

She actually laughed, to Joe's relief. "He must be almost seventy. I have no idea how he does it, but he'd give most fifty-year-olds a run for their money."

"And presumably, he's doing well for himself," Joe surmised.

"Oh, you bet. He's rich. First he sold Ridgeline to Vermont Amalgamated, which was good enough—at least for this town—and he was put on the board. But then, in no time, he turned around and took over Vermont Amalgamated. It was amazing. In fifteen years, he doubled its business and then sold it to some national outfit with initials I can never remember. It doesn't matter, since they've left things alone. If you weren't on the inside, you'd never know Vermont Amalgamated isn't a local business anymore—it's kind of like Ben and Jerry's that way. Anyway, that deal made him millions, on top of what he already had. It's one reason I'm not too proud to accept his generosity now and then. He's rolling in dough."

"And where's he live?"

She gave them an address on Summit Circle, on the southern outskirts of Brattleboro—an upscale, newly developed area where the police were rarely summoned.

"And your kids?" Joe asked casually. "Still dropping by for the occasional home-cooked meal—maybe with kids of their own? I saw the swing set and toys outside."

She smiled again. "Well, my daughter does, but I don't get to see them very often. The swing set and the rest are mostly wishful thinking on my part. They do live around here. Greg's in Dummerston, I think, and Julie's in Vernon." She recited the latter's address, but then stopped, embarrassed. "This'll sound terrible," she said, "but I don't actually know where Greg is right now. He's going through a difficult phase. His sister knows."

"That's okay," Willy said offhandedly. "They both married?"

"Julie's on her second husband. Greg . . ." Sharon paused again, her expression wistful. "He's had girlfriends, but never married, and now . . . I guess I'm old-fashioned, but I think it helps a relationship to get married. Anyhow, he broke up with the last one. He's not seeing anyone, as far as I know. But, I probably wouldn't—know, that is. I really only hear about Greg through Julie, and she's too busy to spend much time with me. It's hard to keep all those balls in the air nowadays."

"Julie has more than one child?" Joe interpreted.

"Three," Sharon said, raising her eyebrows. "Two by her first husband, one by the second. And they are a handful."

"She work, too?"

"Oh, yes. Don't they all? She's a secretary at McGee, Conklin, here in town."

"That's great," Joe said. "You said they were relatively young when Hank went out of their lives, but they weren't infants. How would you have characterized their relationship with him?"

She shook her head thoughtfully. "He was great with them, and they loved him. They were hurt when he moved out. And when he disappeared, without leaving a word, things went downhill, like I said. To me, that just showed how attached they were to him."

"So no problems?"

"No. I always thought he was a good father, especially since he wasn't that great a husband."

Willy cleared his throat to ask, "Did your kids like BB coming around after Hank was gone?"

She frowned at the characterization. "Coming around? He wasn't a stray. BB was a family friend—always had been. Greg and Julie saw him all the time. His affection for me was private. The kids were never aware of it."

"Let's talk about you and Hank," Joe said. "What were your major problems?"

"He cheated on me, for one thing," she said quickly.

"Who with?" Willy wanted to know.

"I don't know. I asked him to give me at least that much respect— to tell me who it was. But he just denied it."

"There was no doubt about it?"

"No. I found a crumpled love note in his pocket once, when I was doing the laundry. Nothing specific. Just something like 'I love you,' or whatever; it's been too long and I was pretty upset. Then I began to pay attention, and there were other clues. He'd hang up the phone when I came into the room. I found a movie ticket in his truck for a night when he'd said he was working late. And one night, I even smelled her on him when he came home."

"But he never fessed up?"

"No. That made me so mad—to be taken for a fool. He said he'd never seen the note, hadn't gone to the movies, and that I was being paranoid about the phone. He wouldn't even talk about what I'd smelled."

"You said he drank, too."

She let out a long breath, heavier than a sigh. "Drank, hung out with friends, wouldn't keep his promises. I told him he reminded me of a dog, pulling on his leash all the time. To be honest, I wasn't surprised when I realized he was seeing someone else. It sort of became inevitable."

"Did he hang out with the same people?" Joe asked. "People we might be able to interview?"

"Oh, sure," she said. "BB was one of them. They were more like brothers than business partners that way. But I think even BB began to feel bad about how Hank was acting at the end, and BB was no saint."

"Do you think he knows who the other woman was?"

She frowned in response. "I don't. I asked him, when he was trying to get me to be with him, after Hank left. He suspected something was going on, like I did, but he swore he had no clue who it was, and I believed him."

"How 'bout Hank's other friends?"

She tilted her head thoughtfully. "Maybe. I only knew two or three of them, anyhow, and I know there were more. But he'd meet them at bars or the bowling alley or wherever, when I'd be home with the kids, so I never knew who they were."

Willy took a pad out and handed it to her, flipped open to a blank page. "Could you write down any names you can remember?" he asked. "And add anything else, like addresses or workplaces, even hometowns. Anything to help us find them."

"Of course," she said, picking up a pen from the coffee table and setting to work as the conversation continued. "It's going to be a pretty rough list. I hope you know that."

"Not a problem," Joe reassured her.

"By the way," Willy asked suddenly, "did you or your husband know anyone named William Neathawk in the late '60s? Worked on the VY project."

She shook her head, sticking to her writing. "No. Doesn't ring a bell."

"Tell us about your parents or any siblings," Joe requested. "They must've been saddened by the way your marriage was going."

Sharon paused in her task. "My mom was sad, but my dad was a drunk, so he didn't care."

"Did either of them express any anger toward Hank?"

"My mom figured that was the way all men acted, and my dad . . . I don't really remember. I think he probably said something like, 'I knew he was a loser when I met him.' That was how he was."

"They're both dead?"

"Years ago."

"And your siblings?"

"I have a brother and a sister. They haven't lived here in forever— couldn't get out of Vermont fast enough."

"Could you add their information to that list?" Willy requested.

"Of course." She'd resumed writing, but now looked up to ask, "Are you going to pester all these people?"

"Pester?" Joe came back. "Your husband may've been murdered. You do get that."

She gave him a level look, and finally spoke with some of the passion he imagined she prided herself on bottling up. "My husband's been dead to me for over forty years, Mr. Whatever-Your-Name-Is. You come in here and say you dug him up, and I'm doing what I can to help. And maybe one of these loser friends of his did hit him over the head with a shovel or a beer bottle. I don't know. But you're wasting your time and our taxpayer money if you think that my daughter or son—or my dead mother—killed him. That's a pile of baloney."

Joe placed a business card on the table between them. "It's Gunther," he answered calmly, "and I hear what you're saying, Mrs. Mitchell. And you're probably right. But if you *were* just another taxpayer, you'd want us to solve this thing as fast and as accurately as possible. We can't do that until we know as much about your husband's life as we can."

She was already waving her fingers at him apologetically, still holding the pen. "I know, I know. This has been a lot to take in, all at once."

"Don't worry about it," he quickly soothed her. "We unfortunately do this quite a bit, and believe me, you've been a terrific help. It's a hard thing to process."

"Thank you," she said, straightening and pushing the notepad toward Willy, asking, all of a sudden, "What happened to your arm?"

Joe looked at him, unsure of how this poster child for unpredictability would respond.

But Willy simply said, "It was a bullet wound—a line-of-duty thing."

She gave him a sympathetic smile. "Crazy world. Even up here in the backwoods. You never know what's going to happen."

"Not till the last second," he agreed.

CHAPTER SIX

"Those shirt stays work out for you?" Lester asked his son, entering the kitchen and tossing a grape into his mouth from a bowl on the counter.

"Yeah. Thanks. Mine kept letting go whenever I got out of the cruiser. I was starting to think I'd just live with tucking my shirt in whenever I had the chance."

"You boys," his sister, Wendy, addressed them, her head in the fridge. "It's all about underwear and looking good."

Her brother threw a piece of the popcorn he was eating at her, hitting her in the back. She withdrew from the fridge with a can of whipped cream in her hand. Dave, still in uniform, recoiled in horror.

"Don't, don't. I can't get this dirty."

She laughed at him. "I rest my case. You are such a coward."

"You can't say that. I'm armed."

She proffered the can threateningly. "And I'm not?"

"Where's Mom?" Lester asked, in part hoping to head off a food fight.

Wendy exchanged her weapon for a casserole dish, which she placed next to the stove. "Had to extend her shift. Someone called in sick at the hospital—there's irony for you. We're on our own tonight, with left-over lasagna."

"Okay," Spinney said, as Dave inquired of his father, "You work on that buried body case today?"

"Not much. Today was mostly putting all the pieces on the board—autopsy, background checks, who's who and what's what. The boss and Willy are interviewing the guy's wife right now."

Dave was beginning to set the kitchen table. "So you know who he is?"

"We think we do."

Wendy opened the microwave next to the stove and slid in their meal. "We were talking about it at school today. It's like a movie or something. A real whodunit."

Lester opened a cabinet and lined up three glasses for drinks. "Yeah, with the 'who' in this case maybe living in an old folks' home. Can you see us walking into some guy's room and trying not to get the cuffs tangled up with his oxygen tubing?"

"That would be awk," his daughter said.

"You think that's what's going to happen?" Dave asked.

"Beats me. Everyone involved has to be about sixty or older to have been there," Lester said. "For all we know, the doer's already dead and buried. You go around killing people in your twenties, it generally means you're not an exercise and health food nut."

"Live by the knife, die by the knife?" Dave said.

Wendy laughed. "Oh, please. Where'd you get that?"

Lester brought the drinks to the table as the microwave's dinger went off. "It may sound like an old radio show," he said. "But Dave's right. Most of the bad guys we deal with come from the same group of fifty to a hundred people, more or less. It's like they're on a merry-go-round. They just can't stop making all the wrong choices."

Wendy delivered the lasagna as they sat down to eat. "Sounds kind of hopeless, if you ask me."

"Dad," his son asked, "isn't it a fact that if you've got a tough case with no leads, sometimes the best thing to do is nothing, 'cause someone's going to blab and spill the beans?"

"Often, yeah."

Dave continued. "Well, then it sounds like you're stuck tween a rock and a hard place, 'cause that would've happened by now, right? Which means you're not dealing with the same bunch of losers who can't get out of their own way."

"Don't you sound like Sherlock Holmes," Wendy said.

"He's probably right, though," Lester confirmed, dishing out the food. "The killer could've been grabbed right after and put in jail for who-knows-what; he might've died robbing a bank, taking his secret with him; or just maybe, he got away with it because it was either a random act of violence, or very carefully planned."

"And he got lucky," Dave added.

Lester smiled and nodded. "And he got lucky."

Wendy raised her glass in a toast. "He or she—and here's to their luck turning, since Dad's on the job."

Lester accepted the toast, but he was quietly considering what—besides the body of Hank Mitchell—might have been festering for forty years, waiting to be uncovered. And at what cost.

Joe had borrowed a whiteboard from somewhere, and set it up that morning in the corner of the office, prompting Willy to stop on the threshold to comment, "We better get milk and cookies with this, or I'm goin' home."

"Do shut up for once," Sammie urged him, pushing him forward so she could enter.

Joe didn't care. "I have color markers," he said. "In case you get confused."

Lester laughed as Willy scowled and said, "I'll manage."

Joe waited for them to settle in, fix coffee, check e-mails—and in Willy's case, put his feet up on his desk—before writing HANK in the middle of the whiteboard, in red.

He circled it, saying, "This is our starting point. No telling what he did to get himself killed. He may have been a son of a bitch whose thirty-one-year life expectancy was up, or the perfect example of a wrong time–wrong place kind of guy. Whatever it was—big or small, illegal or not—somebody decided he was better off dead. What Willy and I got from his widow last night was a bunch of dominoes, one or all of which may have played a role in toppling this one over." He tapped on the name with the marker.

"Sharon Mitchell being the first," Willy said. "Always start with the wife."

"Usually a safe bet," Sam seconded.

Joe wrote the name SHARON above Hank's and drew a line between them. "Fair enough. She told us she tossed him out of the house a month before because he was cheating on her."

"BB Barrett," Lester read off the report that Joe had entered into the computer the night before.

Joe wrote down BARRETT, while explaining, "He had the hots for Sharon and wasted no time making his play after Hank disappeared."

"But got nowhere," Sam pointed out.

"Doesn't matter," Willy said. "Lust was in the mind of the beholder. Also, we only have her word she didn't go for it."

"Which suggests they knocked off Hank together," Sam filled in, "only to find out they weren't the perfect couple."

"The son, Greg Mitchell," Lester offered. "If you want to play tag team, your report says he was devastated by his old man abandoning them. Could be the kid knifed him, after which his mom, or BB, or both, covered it up and buried him to save the kid's hide."

"At nine years old?" Sam protested.

"Sure," Willy told her. "Two thousand eight—an eight-year-old in Arizona shot his father and another man with a .22. It happens."

Without comment, Joe wrote GREG on the board.

"If you're going to list the wife," Sam said, "fair play demands you write down the girlfriend—for the same reasons, more or less."

Joe marked down GF.

"Does the same logic apply to the daughter?" Lester asked before checking the report to add, "Julie? Her mom called her a wild child—with the same adult assistance?"

Willy protested. "A seven-year-old? I thought I was the cynical one. There are limits, even for me. Besides, she got wild afterwards."

"I agree," Joe said. "I think we can leave her off. Let's be practical and hopeful, for once."

"I got a practical wrinkle," Willy offered. "If BB Barrett was sniffing after Sharon, what better way to improve his odds than by introducing Hank to Tootsie, whoever she is? He might've even paid for her dedication."

"Eww," Sam said, but Joe nodded slightly, drew a connecting line between GF and Barrett, and balanced a red question mark on top of it.

He raised a questioning eyebrow at Willy, who responded with a thumbs-up and added, "It would explain why BB made his move so fast after Hank's disappearing act."

"Don't forget William Neathawk," Lester contributed. "And while we're at it, you should list . . . I don't know . . . Call him the 'Missing Man.' The guy who might've set Neathawk's van on fire to draw attention away from the warehouse site. I'm thinking Neathawk was a convenience anyhow—just the patsy whose vehicle was chosen."

"This might've been all one person," Willy mused. "A wireless detonator or a timer, planted under the van at any time, including in the middle of the night. Chances are Neathawk was living locally, to cut down on the commute, assuming he was from out of state."

Lester was shaking his head. "KISS, as they say—Keep It Simple, Stupid. My instinct tells me there were two of them—just makes it easier, and more realistic."

Willy, surprising Lester, didn't argue. "Maybe."

"Moving on," Joe said, turning to the board to list TOM, JIMMY, CARLO. He circled them as a group, explaining, "First names of the three drinking buddies Sharon could remember. When she got ticked off at us for suggesting her family members as possible suspects, she implied it was more likely that Hank had been killed by one of his pals."

"But she did say her old drunk dad pegged Hank as a loser from the get-go," Willy recalled. "Was that to make sure he wouldn't make our list, even though he's dead and buried?"

Joe shrugged. "He's already in the report. My vote is to leave him there, to be considered if and when everybody else drops out of contention."

Willy had no complaint.

"Same for Sharon's brother and sister?" Lester asked, for the sake of argument.

"I think so," Joe agreed. "Anyone disagree?"

There was no response. Joe therefore faced the board again, looking at the list. "That's ten. It's a start. We may get lucky—it's been known to happen, but before we're done, I wouldn't be surprised if we end up with twice that many."

"Cheery thought," Sam reacted.

Joe turned to face her. "I hope I'm wrong. Maybe it's because Hank's been dead so long, but I have a feeling we'll be digging deeper than usual with this one."

"The mere fact you just said so'll make it happen, oh fearless leader," Willy said resignedly. "That is the way it works."

CHAPTER SEVEN

Summit Circle, as befitted its name, was a hilltop road ending in a circular dead end, alternatively cloaked by trees and offering sweeping glimpses north, across Brattleboro township and the Connecticut Valley beyond. For owners with the right acreage—and who'd carefully chosen which trees to cut—the view encompassed a vision of New England approximating what the original inhabitants had enjoyed.

It was a far cry from Joe Gunther's standard field of operations.

This last point was driven home as he rounded the final curve in the access road to encounter a broad, paved driveway flanked by two enormous granite pillars supporting matched concrete vases.

He looked in vain for an overarching wrought iron sign declaring Xanadu, before he swept up the avenue, rounded a manicured copse of trees and a fountain, and found himself staring at what he imagined to be an undersized knockoff of a run-of-the-mill palace.

"Jesus," he whispered.

There was a cool breeze at this altitude, carrying the odor of new spring growth, reminiscent of what drifted out from a flower shop's refrigerator when a bouquet was being retrieved. Joe paused by his car and faced the view, letting the sensation of yearly renewal soak into his bones, along with the anemic but welcome sunshine. He wondered if bears underwent the same level of appreciation when they finally escaped their dens. Joe was a native-born son of the soil, descendant of a long line of stoic Vermont farmers, but he was hard-put to argue against this past winter as having challenged a man's patience.

"Perfect time of year, isn't it?" said a male voice from behind him. "Especially before the bugs wake up."

Joe turned to see a white-haired, unshaven man in old jeans and a soiled shirt round a corner of the elaborate house, a shovel in his hand.

"You had to bring them up, didn't you?" he asked.

The man shrugged, approaching. "That's why we live here, ain't it? Nine months of snow and three more of damned poor sledding, swattin' at flies."

The two men shook hands, in so doing recognizing a kinship in pedigree, and perhaps background.

"Joe Gunther—Vermont Bureau of Investigation."

"No shit? A lousy copper. You finally caught me; took you long enough. BB Barrett."

Joe smiled. "Thought you worked for the lord of the manor. Today casual Friday?"

Barrett laughed and turned to face his easily seven-thousand-square-foot home. "Yeah, right. Ridiculous, ain't it?" He hefted the shovel. "Nope. I'm the lord, and the gardener, and the master of all my goods and chattel. What the fuck is chattel anyhow?"

"Your personal belongings besides real estate."

Barrett stared at him. "Really? Then what're goods?"

"Merchandise."

The other man grunted. "Huh. Guess those days're behind me, then. No goods. Shitload of chattel, though. What do the cops want with me?

And the Bureau of Investigation? What the hell's that? I never heard of you guys. No offense."

"None taken. We're a major crimes unit. They invented us a few years back, supposedly to streamline things and ramp up the quality of work."

"You a state cop?"

"Yes and no. We're not state police, but most of us were recruited from them. Not me. I used to work for the local PD."

Barrett leaned forward slightly and peered at him intently. "Who did you say you were?"

"Joe Gunther."

"Holy shit. I remember you. You worked for Frank Murphy back when. Headed up the detective squad after he died."

"There's a name from the past. Yeah, that's me."

Barrett shook his hand a second time. "Jeezum, man. You been around forever."

Joe shrugged without comment.

Barrett placed a hand on his back and ushered him toward the huge house. "God. I know what that's like. Come on in. You wanna drink of something? I won't offer you a beer, unless you're real old school, but we got all sorts of other stuff here."

"You have a Coke?"

His host let out another guffaw. "Do we have a Coke? Christ, no, we don't. Black Death. That's what it's called around here. Rot your guts out. Oh, no. Our bodies are temples in this house. We only eat birch bark and drink lilac piss."

He stomped up the broad marble steps and threw his shoulder against one of the oversized cherry doors, bringing his shovel and Joe into a cathedral-sized front lobby with a chandelier the size of an upside-down parachute.

"But do *I* have a Coke?" he continued. "You bet your ass I do. I just keep that kind of so-called poison in the bar, far from inquiring eyes. The wife and I have an informal arrangement. If I mind my manners around her and her pals, and don't make cracks about their running outfits and spinning classes and bottled water and foofy food, then I get to eat and drink like I want on my own time."

He led the way down a hallway carpeted with thick Oriental rugs, under the gaze of a row of ponderous landscapes that looked like they should be famous—but just slightly missed the mark. "Come with me. This museum makes me uncomfortable."

Joe followed the man with his shovel, quietly noticing that one of his shoes was leaving clots of dirt in its wake. About halfway down the corridor, Barrett took them through a side door, down a set of stairs, and after several more turns, into a light-drenched, wood-lined, man cave of a room, complete with pool table, jukebox, leather furniture, stuffed animal heads, and a corner bar equipped with a neon sign advertising Budweiser.

"Ah," he said with evident relief, propping the shovel against a wall. "One Coke, coming up." He headed off for the bar.

Joe toured the large room, admiring the trophies, the racks of expensive rifles and shotguns, and the wall of French windows overlooking an enormous swimming pool. Evidently, the mansion had been built partially into the hillside, allowing for the grand entrance they'd used, while making room for this sheltered, less regal spot under one of the wings.

Joe estimated that his own home, a rented carriage house behind an old Victorian in Brattleboro, had about the same square footage as this one room.

"Take a load off," Barrett offered, clumsily waving a hand filled with one drink toward a semicircle of seats near the window. Joe chose a leather armchair and received his Coke, still in its can, before Barrett settled into a corner of the sofa at right angles to him.

"Ahhh," the big man sighed, taking a long swig of what looked like a gin and tonic. "The rewards of life."

Joe took a sip of his drink, waiting for his host to say more.

"Okay," it finally came, as Barrett fixed him with a pair of cold, calculating eyes and said without a smile, "Enough of this. What'd you want?"

"Whatever you can tell me about Hank Mitchell," Joe said, watching for the reaction.

It grew slowly, by degrees. Barrett's face didn't change at first, which Joe ascribed to pure calculation. He'd appreciated the man's earlier lack of pretense. But questions about the meaning of "goods" aside, this house spoke of someone with brains and probably no small amount of ruthlessness.

And there was another possible factor. Had Sharon Mitchell already called her old friend—or coconspirator, if Sam was right—to give him an early warning?

Barrett took a thoughtful sip before placing his glass on the coffee table, to be ignored thereafter.

"There's a name I haven't heard in a while," he said with none of his former bluster. "Where'd you dig him up?"

"Interesting choice of words," Joe reflected, struck by either the coincidence if Barrett was ignorant, or the arrogance if, indeed, he'd been tipped off. "Can you tell me anything about when you last saw him?"

Barrett's eyes narrowed slightly. "All right. I'll play. About forty years ago, when he dumped his wife and family, and left without a word."

"You were friends and business partners," Joe said. "Sharon told us you were close to her and Greg and Julie. I was hoping for more than just, 'He left.' What were the circumstances of your last meeting with him?"

Barrett pursed his lips before answering, "It was decades ago."

Joe remained silent, watching him.

"We were drinking, probably," he finally said grudgingly.

"At a bar or someone's house?"

"Probably a house. That's what we usually did. We'd mix in a card game."

"Your place? Or maybe Carlo's? Jimmy's?" Joe prompted.

Barrett's face hardened. "You seem to know all about us. Why don't you tell me, so it'll refresh my memory?"

Joe returned the attitude. "Because I'm here investigating a murder."

Surprise replaced irritation, to BB's credit. "Murder? What're you talking about?"

"Sharon didn't call you?"

"I haven't talked to Sharon in years. What the hell's happened?"

"You don't listen to the news or read the paper?" Joe asked, incredulous.

Barrett blinked, hesitating, and then asked, "Are you talking about that thing at Vermont Yankee?"

"That's the one."

He sat back and stared out the window at the pool and the New Hampshire mountains in the distance. "Holy cow."

"Yeah," Joe prompted him.

Barrett looked back at him. "You can't think I had anything to do with that. Fuck, man. You said it: We were friends."

"You were even friendlier with his wife. You asked her to marry you."

"That doesn't mean I killed Hank. We were beyond partners. Did you know that? And I kept her and the kids above water afterwards, because none of this would've happened without him." He indicated their surroundings.

He slid forward in his seat and leaned toward Joe for emphasis, even touching his knee with one stubby finger. "I told her it was a return on Hank's initial investment in the business. That's a crock. Hank never had any money. But he knew his stuff when it came to pricing a project, and the guy worked like a machine. He was the face of Ridgeline in the early years, and he got us through the door. After he took off—died, I guess—it was a struggle, but the momentum was there, and that was all his doing."

He paused to rub his forehead. "Damn."

"What?"

"I was just thinking back. The biggest reason we succeeded was the Yankee project. It drained the whole area of labor for years, from something like '69 forward. Projects all over southern Vermont suffered. We helped fill the gap. We were handling more jobs than we knew what to do with 'cause of Hank's hustle and my conning the banks so we could overpay our guys and keep them from leaving. It was a wing and a prayer time, and it was working, when—just like that—" He snapped his fingers. "—Hank was gone."

He shook his head vigorously. "No fucking way I knocked him off. He was my goddamn golden goose. Yeah, I loved Sharon. I even admit I told her that before he disappeared. But I'm not suicidal." His shoulders slumped before he conceded, "Besides, she'll tell you herself—if she hasn't already—we wouldn't have pulled it off. She really loved that peckerhead, and he would've been there between us, forever, like a ghost. Besides, if you knew any of my ex-wives, you'd know Sharon is way classier than what I always end up with."

"I gather she and Doreen didn't hit it off," Joe said, recalling a statement from his interview of Sharon.

Barrett cut him a look. "Yeah, well, she's in good company there. Doreen's a psycho. If I wasn't drunk at the altar, I sure as hell was for as long as that marriage lasted."

Joe let a moment slide by before he asked again, "Tell me about the last time you saw Hank."

Barrett sighed. "It was at Jimmy Stringer's, and it *was* a card game. That was no lie. And I do remember it. What's not to remember? I didn't know it at the time, but it turned out to be the end of one life and the start of another. But until Hank came up missing the next day, it was a night like any other."

"Who else was around the table?"

"Jimmy, of course, me, Hank, Johnny Lucas . . . I can't . . . I don't know about Carlo."

"Johnny Lucas?"

"Another of the guys. He ended up replacing Hank. Half the man, but I had to have somebody after I got dumped—or thought I'd been dumped."

"No women?"

"Women?" He laughed. "You kidding? We must travel in different circles, Gunther. Not even Doreen would've been at one of those games."

"But there were women," Joe guided him gently.

"Meaning what?" Barrett became watchful again.

"Meaning it was the '70s. Pretty frustrating to be married with the sexual revolution in full swing. And Hank had moved out of his home. Supposedly, he was chafing at the bit, wanting some action."

"Yeah, yeah, yeah," he said dismissively. "Sharon gave me that, too. Look, I know about women's intuition and all that crap, but if Hank was screwing around, he didn't tell me, and he sure didn't act it."

Joe tilted his head slightly. "Would've made things easier for you with Sharon, if he did have someone on the side."

"Well, he didn't, as far as I knew."

"Sharon thought he did, and she told us you agreed with her."

"Yeah . . . Well, maybe I led her on a little. I mean, he'd left, as far as we knew." He suddenly burst out, "What're you after, Gunther? You think I'm lying about this?"

"I think it's an interesting detail—some mysterious woman neither Hank's wife nor his best friend know anything about. And yet, there she is, supposedly hanging around in the background. Why doesn't anyone know her, unless she was a convenient piece of fiction?"

"That's why you're the detective, isn't it?" Barrett hesitated before adding, "Look, maybe their marriage was rocky, and maybe I did have feelings for Sharon, and maybe I have no clue if there was another woman. But Hank loved Sharon just like she loved him. That much I can tell you. Who the hell knows what happened that got him killed? But you're barking up the wrong tree if you think it had anything to do with their squabbling. That was just . . . I don't know . . . married couple shit."

"All right," Joe accommodated him. "Let's put that to one side. Tell me about Hank's buddies. So far, of the ones still alive, I think, I have you, Jimmy Stringer, Carlo Fuentes, Johnny Lucas, Tom Capsen. That's according to you and Sharon, both. There any others?"

BB shook his head. "Not really. He had more friends, but people've moved or died or dropped out of sight over the years. I guess that list's pretty much what's left."

"Where's Lucas nowadays? He still alive?"

Barrett laughed. "Alive? Hell yeah. I told you I made him Hank's replacement. He did fine for himself. Rode my coattails straight to the bank, along with a bunch of others. He's around."

"You don't keep up?"

He looked a little wistful. "Hard to keep those friendships alive. Too many years." He laughed. "And too many disapproving wives." He rubbed one eye with his finger. "I kept in touch with a couple of 'em, kind of. Johnny and I were never that close. He did the work and he did an okay job of it, but it was guys like Carlo and Jimmy—and Hank, of course—that made those nights worthwhile."

"How 'bout the bars you frequented, or restaurants? Places like Zero's, or the Quarter Moon, or the Village Barn? Can you think of anyone who might have regularly seen you all hanging out—barkeeps or waitresses?"

"Oh, no. Those've all disappeared. Jesus, man. This is wicked old news."

"Not anymore," Joe corrected him.

Barrett gazed out at his view of New Hampshire again. "No," he agreed after a moment's reflection. "I guess it's all gonna come back now."

Joe studied his profile, wondering if what he'd just heard was truly history, or simply one man's version of it, as was so often the case. Either way, he was pretty sure this wasn't going to be his last conversation with Robert "BB" Barrett.

"How're things going with Mr. Mitchell?" Beverly asked on the phone as Joe reached Summit Circle from BB Barrett's extravagant driveway.

He pulled the car over to speak more comfortably. Recently, Vermont had passed a "hands-off only" driving law regarding cell phone usage, but even when it had been okay to handle a phone and steer, he'd generally avoided it. Plus, in this instance, he wanted to savor the moment. Chats with Beverly—given their schedules and the distance separating them—were akin to the watering stations he'd seen lining the Boston Marathon.

"I'm reminded of when I was a kid," he told her, "when I used to think twice about dipping my foot into the pond on the farm—something about the time I saw a snapping turtle grab a frog off a twig. Still makes me nervous, even now."

"Murky waters, eh?"

"I've done two interviews so far, and I've already got so many more to do, I'm almost hesitant to keep going."

"He was that unpopular?"

"No—that's almost the worst of it. Everybody *loved* him, including the wife who threw him out. I'm starting to wonder if the guy had any pets who hated his guts. According to every source I can find, he was hardworking, a good father, a nice guy, and a hell of a drinking buddy. I should probably just arrest the first person who thought he was only so-so."

She was laughing by now, which prompted him to say, "So much for my Loony Tunes. How 'bout you? You call with a question?"

"No, no," she said. "I was doing paperwork. I thought I'd take a break and hear your voice if I got lucky."

"You are a sweetheart. Never hesitate to call. If I'm in the middle of a gunfight or something, I'll phone you right back."

"You better," she half scolded him. "And do not hesitate to have Mr. Kunkle kick down doors ahead of you. I don't wish him ill, but I certainly don't want to lose you now that I know you so much better."

She stretched out the "so," which naturally stirred his imagination. "Hey," he proposed, "as today winds down, you want to compare notes, and see which one of us can drive up or down the interstate to visit the other?"

"Or meet partway," she countered. "We haven't enjoyed the hospitality of a motel in a while."

"Oh God," he moaned theatrically. "Now I really do have to go. Keep that thought. Talk to you later."

"Count on it."

CHAPTER EIGHT

Even Willy was struck by days like this—warm, bright, shifting from brown hues to green. Some of the older locals referred to this time as the "unlocking," a term Willy found all too apt. As he drove past a small park and over a tumbling stream in Brattleboro, he was struck more by a sense of relief—as if the entire winter had been spent during one deep breath, held to bursting.

Not that the notion lifted his spirits any. He'd traveled his entire conscious life anticipating the misfortunes lurking inevitably around every corner. Discovering otherwise—even concerning good weather—always came as a surprise, and with surprises, he knew stubbornly, you usually get bad news. For him, life was a guaranteed layering of suspicion, mistrust, and dreaded anticipation.

So, spring—hopeful, temperate, and sunny—especially following a winter this harsh—became an ironic metaphor for his inner turmoil. Whatever enjoyment it provided he'd keep private.

Willy knew his outlook to be dire. Years ago, he met a man who'd confessed to never having suffered from a headache—had no clue what one felt like. Willy was fully aware of how many people didn't share his afflicted view of the world—and even how the happy ones perhaps weren't simply idiots. In truth, it was on the off chance that they might be right that he had slowly opened up to Joe and Lester and—crucially—to Sam and finally Emma.

But there was the rub. As much as he recognized this development as healthy, he struggled against it for its inherent promise of inevitable loss and grief.

Willy drove up Main Street and pulled over to the curb, at the heart of Brattleboro's downtown. For all the changes this town had undergone through the decades—from fires and floods to ebbs and flows in population and prosperity—Brattleboro had remained largely unchanged for almost 150 years. Kunkle had studied photographs of this section that were taken in the late 1800s and sometimes trotted out by the town's historical society, and he'd easily seen past the striped awnings and rickety, ornate balconies to recognize the Brattleboro of today. It was as if, while fashions had changed, and clothing styles evolved, the body beneath had remained as familiar as ever.

He wouldn't have voiced any of this, of course. He had a taciturn image to preserve. But there was a permanence to such revelations that provided a comfort, even for him.

He ignored the parking meter and entered the first-floor lobby of a narrow, three-story, granite block building labeled MCGEE, CONKLIN over the door.

"Hi, there," said the receptionist, facing the entrance. "How may we help you?"

He smiled, the bland greeting transforming the hard lines of his face into something unexpectedly pleasant. "I was hoping to have a quick word with Julie Washburn," he said. "I was just talking with her mom and wanted to ask her about something that came up."

The shared implication of a minor intimacy—nothing in itself—routinely gained him access past a sentry of this sort. That and the damaged arm.

Her face brightened further. "Oh, sure. Go straight up. She's at her desk on the second-floor landing. You can't miss it."

The scene upstairs resembled the one below, if with more desks, more young women sitting at them, and the wall lined with office doors—brass plated with the names of their occupants. McGee, Conklin was Brattleboro's largest law firm, and accordingly stuck-up in appearances—at least to Willy's eye.

A severely coiffed, pinched-faced blond woman—a pale, unhappy facsimile of Sharon Mitchell—looked up at him as he reached the landing.

"Yes?" she asked.

"You Julie Washburn?" he inquired quietly, approaching her desk.

Her face shadowed slightly. "Do I know you?"

None of the other legal aides or secretaries were paying attention to them, but he only discreetly showed his badge. "I was hoping we could have a very quick chat, somewhere quiet. Just take a minute," he said.

"What's this about?"

"Your father."

The set of her mouth told him this was no more to her than a second shoe dropping, and Willy imagined the phone call from mother to daughter that had preceded his appearance.

Julie Washburn rose and gestured to him to follow her down a corridor to a small conference room. She shut the door behind them.

"My mom told me," she said immediately, facing him without further explanation. Sharon had implied that Julie weathered life unhappily following Hank's disappearance. That much was apparent in her watchful, suspicious eyes.

He decided to match her blunt tone. "Yeah. Sorry to drag this back up. You remember your dad?"

"Of course I do."

"Well?"

"I liked him. He was fun."

"Greg's older. He probably remembers more. I want to talk with him, too. We're having to dig pretty deep after all these years. You have any memories about when your dad dropped out of the picture? Any impressions that've stayed with you?"

She paused for a moment, but her response was merely, "Not really."

"What about your mom? How did she change afterward?"

Again, Julie appeared to consider a response, before settling for, "It was years ago. How would I know?"

Willy conceded her point, and asked, "Where's your brother hanging his hat?"

"Greg?" she asked, caught off guard.

"You got another?"

A small crease appeared between her brows. "Why do you want to talk with him? He was a kid then."

Willy had consulted a couple of law enforcement databases after Sharon failed to supply an address. They had yielded a recent address of one of Brattleboro's more decrepit flophouses. Greg had been a passenger in a vehicle pulled over for erratic operation, two months earlier. The driver had been arrested for a criminally suspended license, while the other occupants had been required to show their IDs, as was standard good police practice. To Willy, Greg's presence in the computer had implied that while he hadn't done anything illegal yet—or at least been caught at it—he was likely treading on precarious ground. In any case, Willy had checked the place out and found that Greg had moved on.

Julie Washburn picked up a pad from the conference table behind her and wrote down the address of a little-known cluster of cabins on the Brattleboro—Dummerston line, tucked away in the wooded hills.

Without much further ado, Willy thanked her and took his leave, having registered the turmoil behind her tightly controlled veneer.

Not that he was surprised—or even cared all that much. He'd spent a professional lifetime looking into the faces of youngsters who'd been stepped on by adults—sometimes literally. After a few years, the pain had virtually ceased to impress. What did the bumper sticker say? LIFE IS SHIT AND THEN YOU DIE. Worked for him.

Most of the time.

Willy didn't know it for a fact, but he suspected the cabins Julie had identified might have found their origins either during the early car-camping days of the late '20s, or from the need to house Roosevelt-era CCC crews. Whatever the truth, they had that vintage appearance, although updated and modernized, and had become a little-known and cherished Brattleboro hideaway. There were some four separate, single-story buildings, all told—the larger two of which had been partitioned into small apartments—scattered along a steep, twisting, dead-end dirt lane that had been cut through the trees and into a rolling, grass-covered, south-facing meadow.

It was quiet, peaceful, pretty, isolated, and so far off the beaten track as to leave the track behind. In truth, as he rolled to a stop, Willy was at a loss about where to park—the road having simply petered out beneath him.

He got out and looked around, absorbing the sounds of birds, a soft breeze, and the warmth of a weak spring sun. The most distant cabin was his destination, one of its doors numbered 3.

It was midday, in the middle of the week. Not a good time—most would imagine—to find anyone at home. Cops in Vermont, however, rarely paid heed to such conventions, since their primary clientele didn't either.

Sure enough, as he approached the door in question, it opened to reveal a heavy, middle-aged bearded man in a T-shirt and jeans.

"Who're you?" he asked, neither friendly nor hostile. He looked vaguely as if he'd just woken up, although Willy suspected the effect was permanent.

"I'm a cop," Willy told him, not bothering to show his badge. "That okay?"

"Depends. What've I done?"

"Nothing I know about."

The man pointed his chin at Willy's left side. "What's wrong with your arm? You okay?"

What was it with this family? Willy wondered, but he was impressed by the care he heard in the question. "Yeah," he said. "Old injury. Thanks for asking."

"No biggie. What's up?"

"Are you Greg Mitchell?"

"Yeah."

Willy considered his options and chose to go straight to the point. "You talk with your mother lately?"

The man's mouth opened slightly. "She all right?"

"Fine. Perfect. I just wanted to know if you'd talked."

"No."

"Then I guess I've got some news for you. Not sure if you'd call it bad, exactly, since it's kind of ancient, but you might find it helpful."

The man instinctively touched the doorframe, as if for possible support. "What is it?"

"We found a body a couple of days ago. You mighta heard about it in the news. It was your father."

The tradition among cops was to add, "Sorry for your loss," but Willy didn't truck with that. He wasn't sorry, and he wasn't always sure when a survivor might not agree with him.

So he stayed silent, as did Greg Mitchell, who continued staring at him for several seconds before asking, "My mom know?"

"Yeah."

"And Julie?"

"Yeah. Your mother told her, but she didn't know how to reach you. Julie gave me this address."

Greg dropped his chin to look at the dirt patch between them. "Yeah. Things've slid a little between me and Mom."

"Bad feelings?" Willy asked.

"Not really. More disappointment," Mitchell acknowledged. "I been a letdown to her my whole life. I figured maybe I'd just . . . I don't know . . . drift away somehow."

"You chose a good spot for it."

Willy let the silence swell between them—an old interviewer's gambit.

"You wanna come in?" Mitchell finally asked. "I got coffee."

"Sure."

The cabin's interior came as a surprise, given Willy's knowledge of Mitchell's previous digs. Blond pine walls and vaulted ceiling; broad, double-glass doors overlooking a small deck—all of it flooded with sunlight. It was modern, bright, cheery, and in startling contrast to its hulking slow-moving denizen. It made Willy think of a local bear breaking in and calling it home—Goldilocks in reverse.

It was tiny—a single room, half of it filled with a bed, the other half by a kitchenette and a closet. A small bathroom was at the end. There were about as many possessions lying about as in a standard abandoned motel room. Greg Mitchell was not making a big dent on the world.

"Nice place," Willy complimented him, as Mitchell led him to the counter holding a coffeemaker and poured him a mug taken from an overhead cabinet in which only two mugs resided. "How can you afford it?"

Mitchell didn't take umbrage. "I cleaned up," he said with a ready frankness common to many twelve-step program attendees. "Stopped drinking and doing drugs. Don't know if it'll stick this time, but I'm tryin'. Means more money in the bank. I got a job at the Cumbie in West B. You want sugar or something?"

Willy chose not to further stress the man's resources. "I'm good."

Near the bed was a small table with one chair. Mitchell sat on the edge of the bed and indicated the chair. "Have a seat."

Willy did so, asking, "Did you miss your dad?"

Mitchell let his large, blunt, workingman's hands dangle between his knees. "Been a long time."

"Still. It can be hard having a ghost as a father."

Mitchell looked up at him. "You, too?"

Willy considered that. He had been born in New York City, and sometimes wished more of his family had been ghosts—instead of what they were. "Something like that," was all he said.

"I did miss him," Mitchell recalled. "I look back now, I realize he filled my life when I was a kid. I'd sit in school, looking forward to getting home and seeing him after work." He spread his hands apart, as if detailing the length of a large fish, and added, "He was like a huge presence—more of a feeling than a man." He paused before saying, "Course, that's just how I remember it. He was probably just a dad, and I was a bratty kid."

"But he went into thin air," Willy suggested. "Like a puff of smoke."

Mitchell was studying the floor and nodded several times. "Yeah—he did."

"You remember that happening?"

"Sure."

"Tell me."

Again, Mitchell was quiet, either drifting again, or gathering his thoughts. "It wasn't like a puff of smoke, like you said."

"Okay."

"There was a sort of buildup. My folks fighting. That was hard. Julie and I would talk about it. Or I guess she would ask me and I would try to answer. But we were small. I didn't really understand, and I felt I was supposed to make her feel better, if I could."

"What were they fighting about?" Willy asked, pulling him back. He was a cop, after all—not a shrink.

Mitchell seemed to get the message. "Right," he said. "Well, my dad moved out, if that tells you anything."

"You think there was another woman?"

Mitchell shrugged. "There musta been, but that's not what I picked up. What I got was that my dad was unhappy, and I felt I was probably the reason. You know how kids do. I wasn't doing great in school, and I was nowhere near the athlete he'd been, and I was useless helping him with chores. I mean, I know now that they were most likely on the outs 'cause of their own baggage. But back then? I felt caught. Nobody was happy anymore, including Julie, and I couldn't fix it."

Willy tried again. "Children sometimes overhear what their parents are fighting about. How 'bout you?"

He nodded. "There was one night. She yelled at him. She never did that—she's pretty buttoned down. Julie gets that from her. But she yelled that he smelled. I couldn't figure it out. 'I can smell it on you,' or something like that. I can guess what she meant now, but I never knew for sure."

Willy changed his approach. "Let's look at the broader picture. Who do you remember of their friends?"

Mitchell's face cleared somewhat. "BB was the one we saw the most. He was over all the time, like an uncle."

"How did he act?"

"Fun. He played with us and horsed around, and made my mom laugh. He used to tickle her, which amazed me, 'cause she wasn't big on being touched."

"You think he was maybe doing more than tickling?" Willy risked asking.

But Mitchell just laughed shortly. "I wondered about that. After Dad disappeared, BB was over a bunch for a while, and I was pretty sure he was after what you mean."

"How did she react?"

"She didn't hate it. I never heard her yell at *him*. And I thought I interrupted them kissing once. But right after, he stopped coming over, so I don't know what happened."

There was another pause, after which Mitchell asked, almost shyly, "How did my dad die?"

Willy didn't think he had much to lose. "Somebody killed him."

Mitchell's face went slack and his body sagged. "I thought it might've been an accident. He'd just hurt himself when I saw him last—had his arm in a sling." He passed his hand across his forehead. "Who killed him? Why?"

"That's what I'm looking for from you," Willy told him.

Mitchell was nonplussed. "Me? What would I know?"

"You hang out with your dad much? Drive around with him, seeing his pals?"

"Sure. I loved doing that."

"Who do you remember? You stopped with BB. Weren't there others?"

"Oh, yeah. There was Johnny. He was always around."

"Lucas?"

"He worked with Dad and BB. They had a company together. Roofing. You probably knew that."

"That's okay. Where was Johnny in the pecking order?"

"Dad and BB ran things—at least that's what I thought. Johnny didn't become a partner till later."

Willy was interested in that. "Would you say Johnny moved into your dad's spot?"

But Greg wouldn't go that far. "Not really. What I remember is BB managed the company on his own for a year or so. Johnny worked for him, along with a bunch of others, but it wasn't till later that he became management. I guess he deserved it. Not that I'd know much about it, but he's high on the hog now, so he musta done something right."

"Rich?"

"Not BB's kind of rich. That's crazy. But Johnny did fine."

"How did your dad and Johnny get along?"

"Fine. They were buddies."

"Were there others?"

Greg gazed into the distance, trying to recall. "Jimmy Stringer was one of them, and a guy named Carlo. Don't know his last name."

"Anyone else?" Willy pressed him.

"That's pretty much all I know. Dad was a popular guy, but names . . . ?"

"Tell me about Stringer. He keeps coming up."

Greg smiled slightly. "It's probably that last name—sounds like a kid's book. I don't know. My dad liked him well enough, but he never paid much attention to me—not like BB. He seemed kind of rough. I think my spider sense told me he could be mean."

"You ever witness that side of him?"

"Nope. It was just a feeling. You know what they're worth."

"A lot, sometimes," Willy told him. This brought him around to one of the primary reasons he'd come here.

"Greg, let's go back to when your parents were having their problems. I understand you felt guilty—that you were to blame somehow, even though you weren't. I get that. But you told me how big a presence Hank was in your life. How he filled the room, so to speak. That's a big hole to leave behind. How did you feel when he moved out?"

Mitchell's eyes wandered to the view beyond the deck. "It's hard to separate how I felt then to later. I guess numb. And lost. I was pretty confused."

"How'd you feel about the old man's vanishing act?"

"Hurt. Angry. And—again—confused. Julie's reaction didn't help. She wigged out—smashing stuff and throwing fits. She started hitting people, too."

"What was her relationship like with your father?"

"Cool," Greg replied. "Like mine. He was a good dad—read to us, played ball, went on hikes. All the dad stuff."

Willy waited for more, but that was it. He asked, "Who do you think did him in?"

Greg stared at him. "How would I know?"

"Kids know all sorts of things," Willy said.

The other man blinked a couple of times before resuming his contemplation of the scenery.

"You're not telling me something," Willy told him.

"I told you everything."

Willy saw Greg's expression harden. "Your life went into the toilet after your dad left," he said. "And here you are, decades later, doing no better. At that time, your mom stayed the course, money wasn't a problem, you had a roof over your head. Children have one of their parents walk out on them all the time. It may mess with their heads a little, crank 'em up and make 'em act out. But it doesn't usually do what it did to you."

"Guess I'm special that way," Greg said tersely.

Willy was quiet again. But this time, Greg Mitchell had reached his limit. In the end, Willy rose, left his business card on the table, and left without saying another word.

But he was convinced there was more to be said—what it was, and who would utter it, remained to be seen.

CHAPTER NINE

Another night, a different house, and Sally Kravitz was still reliving a teenager's excitement about her inaugural outing, twenty-four hours earlier. That place had been empty, like this one, and her father—whom she always called Dan—had disconnected the alarm beforehand. But the adrenaline rush of going from room to room, feeling the presence of occupants who had stepped out for the evening, had been addicting. She'd loved it.

And it hadn't been a pointless ramble. Dan had made it a lesson of component parts—how to move, what to look and listen for, what could be touched and what was best avoided. He was wonderful—patient, supportive, even funny when she'd needed it.

Just as important for her, it also cast a light onto her father's tightly controlled personality. In contrast to their currently gloomy surroundings, he had blossomed before her—his step becoming quick, his mood playful, his focus fully engaged. He'd no longer been the social enigma who spoke like a scholar to her and to others in monosyllabic grunts. In the midst of someone else's environment, and the blackness of night, he'd ironically ceased to be invisible and restrained. He'd moved decisively, smoothly, and as quietly as a cat. He'd gone through closets, cabinets, drawers, and desks; he'd moved items about, opening them for examination, going through their contents. And yet, when he finished— with her watching every motion—everything appeared as it had before. She could have sworn that not even the dust had been disturbed. Dan had made her think of an artist in peak form. If her father had shucked off his overalls and taken flight like Mikhail Baryshnikov, Sally Kravitz couldn't have been more surprised or charmed.

And now, here they were again, across town, breaching the envelope of another oversized, luxurious home.

Because that was Dan's practice: He pursued only high-end houses, never removed conventional valuables, and always made sure to pause long enough to fully enjoy his theft of others' presumed privacy.

Also, when not tutoring Sally, he only broke into homes in which the occupants were present and sleeping. That last bit had led to the hubris of leaving Post-its, which, he'd since admitted, he came to rue as a mistake. As you push at the edges, he'd counseled her, never fall prey to overconfidence.

True, he hadn't actually suffered as a result, thanks to Willy, for whom he'd been an informant for years. Kunkle hadn't known of Dan's secret back then, of course, but he'd always valued Dan's being so well informed.

Which he was, even if it wasn't just knowledge that he sought. He collected information, and with it, he served Willy Kunkle. But he also garnered a tidy income via insider trading. He was good with computers, comfortable reading financial records—sitting late at night at other people's desks—and happy to later make stock choices and investments based on what he'd learned.

Sally didn't know the intimate details of that, or see herself as the Artful Dodger to her father's Fagin. To her, Dan better represented Robin Hood, with the additional rationalization that he merely stole data and did no one any harm. Her own ambitions for joining him were more emotional. Put simply, she wanted to know Dan Kravitz in his heart. Bonding with him at his happiest seemed the best means to achieve it.

The fringe benefit, she was now happily finding out, was discovering not only how good she was at acquiring his set of skills, but also how much fun it was to do.

Tonight, they were in West B, on Orchard Street, predictably not far from the country club. The house, as was often the case, had begun life humbly enough, a century and a half earlier, probably as a farmer's home. That was before the industrial revolution, the growth of urbanization, and the sprawling of suburbia—all of which had transformed this building from shelter to status symbol. As a result, a once functional home had become a clapboarded, manicured mansion, tricked up with dark green shutters, entryway roofs and quaint weathervanes, bricked walkways, a nearby tennis court, and the obligatory, seldom-used Jacuzzi.

It was a foreign world to Sally, who'd spent her life following Dan from pillar to post around town, once even—for a while—calling a converted school bus home. Dan, for all his education and secret funds, was a man who lived upon the earth as a fog lingers among trees. He drifted—watching, absorbing, and learning—and she'd adapted to drifting with him. Moving attentively from room to room in this house so thick with possessions was like roaming through a museum to her— interesting and informative, but in the long run, alien from her own reality. Thanks to Dan, Sally's life had become the study of humanity's joys and sorrows, generosity and mean-spiritedness, and finally, its ability to endure—not the practice of keeping score with baubles.

Her inaugural wanderings through these houses were therefore extensions of that homeschooling—another way to palpate society's heartbeat from the inside. They were autopsies of a sort, conducted out of sight and in private, dedicated to enlightenment.

They were also scary, and the most exciting aspect of her education so far.

The textbook ideal for law enforcement field interviews is to put two investigators onto each assignment. It's safer, better for later corroboration, and allows the two cops to compare notes and buddy up if the interviewee proves a tough nut to crack.

In rural policing, there wasn't much opportunity for the ideal. There weren't enough people, not enough money, and too much territory to cover. Teams of two simply weren't practical.

There were exceptions. When the person of interest had proved dangerous in the past, or when there were several people to be interviewed at once, budget and manpower concerns were overridden.

Which explained why Sam and Lester were sharing a car late that afternoon. Following a discussion on best approaches, they'd chosen to tag-team Jimmy Stringer and Carlo Fuentes at the same time, in the same place.

Fair to say, it was the location of that place that had prompted the strategy. Lester had been told by the Brattleboro PD's patrol division that, even decades later, the two men remained best friends, and had maintained a habit of regularly hanging out together, five days a week—bonded by habit, televised sports, and beer. Fuentes was the semiretired co-owner of a downtown watering hole, where Stringer might as well have had a brass plaque attached to his favorite stool.

Why not, the two detectives had reasoned, approach the two in their comfort zone, although early enough to find them sober?

It was dark when the cops entered, despite it being shortly after noon, and following the bright sunshine outside, they had to stop just inside the door and adjust to the gloom.

"Come on in," a man's voice called out from the back of the cave, followed by the laughing recommendation, "Walk straight ahead. When you're about to bump into your first chair, you'll just be able to see it. Trust me."

Lester was game, and quickly discovered that about ten feet in, the soft neon glow did begin asserting itself. He made out two men by the row of taps—one seated, and one tending on the far side.

"Gentlemen," he said, Sam following from close behind. "How're you doing today?"

"Feeling no pain," the bartender confessed. "What can we do for you? It can't be a drink—you two look too fancy for that, unless it's turned into a bad day at the office."

By this time, what lighting there was had allowed the newcomers to take in their surroundings. Not that there was much to see. The tavern was one of Brattleboro's older such establishments—stolid, static, and resistant to trendiness. It was strictly working-class, complete with a minimalist décor of stacked beer cans, stained posters, and grimy neon signs—along with a few battered, scarred, and much-repaired furnishings. Aside from the two before them, the room was empty.

"Thin crowd," Spinney commented, reaching the bar and pulling out a couple of stools.

The barkeep smiled. "It is now. Come back later—then we're good till closing."

"Good to know," Lester said, noticing that both men had barely glanced at him, preferring instead his far more attractive partner. Sam had placed her canvas bag on the bar and was rummaging around inside it.

Lester revealed his badge. "Lester Spinney, gents. This is Samantha Martens. We're from the VBI."

The bartender reached over to shake hands. "Carlo Fuentes. I thought you looked out of place. Have I got a nose, or what?"

The other man said guardedly, "Yeah, you got one of those."

Lester turned to face him, hand extended. "And you are?"

"I gotta answer that?"

Spinney laughed, unfazed. "Yep, you do. But I can help. Jimmy Stringer, am I right?"

"If you knew, what d'ya ask for?" Put in an awkward position by Lester's refusal to drop his hand, Stringer gave it a quick and reluctant shake.

"What's on your mind, officers?" the friendlier Fuentes asked.

Sam spoke for the first time, the recorder she'd been searching for in hand. "A name from the distant past," she said, matching her friendly tone to Lester's, despite her instinctive distaste for a couple of men who seemed convinced that her face had slipped to the center of her chest. "Hank Mitchell."

Stringer and Fuentes each reacted with surprise. "Hank?" Stringer said first. "What the fuck you care 'bout him? He's been gone like half a century."

Sam hit Record on her machine and placed it on the bar. "You don't mind if I record this, do you? Saves on getting the details wrong."

"Sure I mind," Stringer predictably shot back.

But Fuentes overrode him. "Oh, for Chrissake, Jimmy. Lighten up." He gave a wide smile to Sam and nodded. "You go ahead."

"Mr. Stringer?" she asked.

"Yeah," was the answer.

For the record, therefore, Sam quickly stated the time, date, and location of the conversation, along with who was present. She also inquired of both men if they'd been drinking enough to be inebriated, which they both vehemently denied. This last was a frequently awkward formality, ignored by many cops. More often than not, however, Sam had reaped the rewards in court later.

Fuentes remained affable through it all. "Why you wanna know 'bout Hank?"

"You knew him back when?" Lester asked.

"Sure. We all did. He was one of us."

Sam kept the mood going. "How so?"

Jimmy lifted the beer bottle before him. "That's how."

"Drinking buddies?"

"That we were," Carlo confirmed, adding, "Jimmy and I are the only two left."

"The rest all dead?" Lester asked, surprised.

"Might as well be," Jimmy said unhappily.

"No," his friend corrected him. "They moved on. Well, some of them died, for sure. Tom Capsen turned toes up a month ago. But BB's still around."

"BB's too good for losers like us," Jimmy growled, taking a swig from his bottle.

"Who else?" Sam asked Carlo, the talker of the two.

"I don't know. Johnny was part of it. Fred, Nicky, Dwayne Matteson. 'Member him, Jimmy? He was a character."

"Long gone," Jimmy said.

"Really?"

Carlo shrugged. "Yeah, actually. He's right. When you look at it, there weren't that many of us to start with. Johnny Lucas and BB may be all that's left." He shook his head in wonder. "Kind of amazing, when you think of it. Time flies."

"What was Hank like?" Sam asked.

"I liked him," Carlo predictably said. "Definitely one of the gang. He was BB's right-hand man—kind of the brains, if you ask me. He could price a project like nobody I knew. Had the eye for it. But he didn't put on airs like BB could."

"He didn't have an eye for other people's wives," Stringer said in a low voice. "That was BB's specialty."

"Oh, come on, Jimmy," Carlo reprimanded him.

"Ouch," Lester reacted. "That doesn't sound good."

"It's nothing," Carlo tried saying.

"Bullshit," Jimmy interrupted. "You know goddamn well he had the hots for her."

"BB had the hots for Hank's wife?" Sammie asked.

"We don't know that for sure," Carlo protested.

"Spare me," Jimmy complained. "Maybe we didn't know if they got it on. I'll give you that. But his tongue fell out of his head every time he looked at her. Hank might as well've not even been in the room. It was so obvious."

Takes one to know one, Sam thought, watching Jimmy still checking her out.

The front door opened to hit them with a blinding bolt of sunlight, outlining the figure of someone tall and slim.

"Hey, darlin'," Carlo called out. "Come on over. We got guests."

Repeating their own entrance ritual, Lester and Sam blinked to regain their night vision, gradually recognizing the newcomer as an older woman fashionably dressed in tight jeans and a bright tank top, with a sharp-angled, worn face that struck Sammie as having been once quite beautiful.

"Lacey Stringer," Carlo introduced her. "This is Lester Spinney and Samantha Martens. They're cops, asking about Hank Mitchell."

Lester watched Stringer's expression as she took them in, noticing a tension in her eyes that didn't seem born of the moment.

"Lacey," Carlo continued, "is Jimmy's far, far, far better half."

"Up yours," Jimmy said, drinking again.

"She also helps out around here from time to time, waiting tables. I didn't tell you folks," Carlo said, "that I'm part-owner of this place. I'm not really the bartender, in case you were wondering. He's due in a while. I just open up and shoot the shit a little with Jimmy here. When things get hot, they don't want me gumming up the works. Too old and too slow."

He'd slid back into social mode with Lacey's arrival, but not even she was buying it.

"Why d'you want to know about Hank?" she asked bluntly, skipping any amenities.

Lester regretted the timing of her arrival, since he'd been interested in hearing about BB and Sharon. Now he was further put off by Lacey's husband adding, "Yeah. You never told us: Who gives a shit about Hank? What's going on?"

This was the downside to conducting group interviews. Sammie glanced at her partner, who gave her a barely perceptible nod of acquiescence.

"He's been found dead," she said. "Somebody killed him."

Carlo reacted with, "Wow. You don't say?" while Jimmy growled, "I knew it." But Lacey's face drained, her mouth tightened, and she took a step back before saying, "Fuck you." She then abruptly headed toward the back and presumably to the kitchen beyond.

Neither of the men at the bar took note.

"Damn," Carlo said. "What does that mean? Was he living around here and nobody knew it? Like a hermit? Doesn't sound like him at all."

"Jesus H. Christ, Carlo," Jimmy castigated him. "Sometimes your head is so far up your ass, I'm amazed you can breathe."

"What?" the bar owner asked, baffled by his friend's attitude.

"It's all over the news," Jimmy said tiredly. "They found a skeleton at VY—been buried in concrete for decades." He eyed Lester. "Right? That's Hank, ain't it?"

Sammie quietly eased away, leaving Lester to continue the conversation, and followed Lacey into the bar's nether regions. Predictably, this back section of the establishment made the front look ritzy. Sam didn't focus much on Vermont public health laws, but she assumed from what she saw that no health inspectors had been here in recorded history.

She found Lacey standing before an ancient open fridge, pulling out limes and lemons and slapping them down hard onto a worn and filthy cutting board.

"Lacey?" she said quietly, so as not to startle her.

The other woman stopped, her shoulders slumping. Sam circled around, glanced at her tearstained face, and led her to a nearby stool, closing the fridge door as she went.

She leaned her hip against the counter and gently stroked Lacey's shoulder. "Sorry you had to hear it that way. We had no idea you were close to him."

The older woman wiped her eyes with the back of one hand, her head still bowed.

"I heard he was a good guy," Sam said.

"Yeah." Lacey's voice was almost inaudibly soft against the background noise of old and ailing kitchen appliances.

"When did you last see him?"

Lacey looked up. Her makeup was smeared. The harsh overhead lighting made her look haggard beyond her years. "He was here one minute and gone the next," she said. "No warning. I didn't know what had happened to him."

"You were living together at the time?"

Her responding smile was sad. "Don't I wish. That's what I wanted." She jerked a thumb toward the front of the bar. "I was ready to dump that prick and move in with Hank. In a heartbeat."

"You were already married to Jimmy?"

"He knocked me up at sixteen. Yeah, we were married, not that it ever mattered."

"Okay," Sam said, hoping to keep her on track. "So why didn't it happen with Hank? Hadn't he left his wife by then?"

"Sure, but not for me. I loved him; not the other way around. He was still mooning for that stuck-up bitch. What he ever saw in her is beyond me, but it was always Sharon, Sharon, Sharon."

Sam scratched her forehead. "So you two were never lovers?"

Lacey sighed. "I tried. Believe me. I did everything but pull his pants down. He wasn't interested."

"Tell me what happened, the last day you saw him."

"Nothin' to tell. I was at his place, on Oak Street. I tried to go there every day, just to prove I was stickin' to it. That day, I went by, and he wasn't there. And that was it. Never saw him again."

"There must've been talk," Sam said leadingly.

"There was, but because he'd already moved out of the house, everybody was thinkin' he'd just blown town, headed for the wild blue yonder."

"Did that make sense to you?"

"Not really," she conceded. "But it didn't *not* make sense, either, if you know what I mean. He was restless and he could be a little crazy sometimes. It's not like it was the class loser suddenly becoming a movie star."

"How were things between him and everybody else?" Sam inquired. "His colleagues, buddies, even Sharon, for that matter. Were there any animosities?"

"Any what?"

"Bad feelings. Was anybody particularly mad at him, or vice-versa?"

"Sharon probably wasn't too happy with him. She'd thrown him out of the house."

"What was that about?" Sam asked.

"She likes things neat and tidy and predictable," Lacey explained.

"That's why I thought we'd be good together. I don't go around looking like I got a prybar up my ass."

"Did Hank talk about their splitting up?"

Lacey made a face. "Yeah. Again and again, and I had to pretend like I gave a damn."

Sam's brow was furrowed by now. "Let me get this straight, just so I'm solid—I heard she threw him out 'cause he was cheating on her, but you're saying he kept talking about their getting back together."

"That's what I said."

"I just don't want to make any wrong assumptions. Lacey, is it possible he was seeing someone besides you?"

The older woman took it like a pragmatist. "Anything's possible. But I seriously doubt it. What I do know is that he pissed and moaned about his marriage, and I had to hold his hand."

"But you kept at it," Sam encouraged her. "You musta done that 'cause you felt you were getting somewhere."

"I was just being stupid," Lacey said dismissively. She again glanced toward the front of the building, adding, "Being married to an asshole can do that to you."

"Okay," Sam moved on, feeling she'd exhausted the matter. "Apart from Sharon, who else might've been unhappy with him? How 'bout Jimmy? Did he know of your interest in Hank?"

"He's never given a shit."

"That wasn't the question."

Lacey gave a frustrated toss of her head. "He puts on a 'tude, but it never goes anywhere."

"So he knew," Sam pressed her.

"I told him nothing was goin' on. After Hank took off—well, after we thought he took off—that was the end of it."

Sam said nothing, letting the silence speak for her.

"No frigging way," Lacey finally said. "Jimmy may be a douche bag, but he's not a killer. Plus, he didn't really care back then—any more than he does now."

"So, even at the time Hank went missing, you had no suspicions that maybe Jimmy had done him dirt?"

She was shaking her head partway through the question. "No way. Like I said. Never crossed my mind, and it woulda, otherwise, 'cause I can read that dope like a book. But about Hank, Jimmy was all bark and no bite. I mean, shit, you don't think I would'na known?" Lacey waved her hand. "No, no, no. There's nothin' to that."

"Okay," Sammie soothed her. "I got it. So that's Sharon and Jimmy crossed off. Anyone else?"

Lacey ran her hand through her hair. "Jeez. This is all so long ago. BB wasn't real happy."

Sam frowned. "Why?"

"The business," Lacey told her. "BB's hot stuff now, and he was always a smooth talker, but everybody knew it was Hank that brought in the business and made Ridgeline a profit in those days. I think BB figured he was up shit creek when Hank did a Houdini."

"What about Johnny Lucas?" Sam asked. "I heard he came in and saved the day."

Lacey smiled. "Damn, you been pokin' around, haven't you? Well, you're right—sort of. Johnny joined up, but he only saved the day afterwards. I guess BB had to check him out, or get used to him, or somethin'. BB probably had enough money on hand to tide him over till Johnny got going."

"Tell me about Johnny," Sam requested. "I haven't met him yet."

"He was okay," Lacey said. "Kinda kept to himself. I haven't seen him in years—ever since he and BB went separate ways after Ridgeline sold to Vermont Amalgamated. But in the early days, he and BB, both, used to hang out with the rest of us."

"He get along with Hank?"

"Damn," Lacey said. "You're like a broken record. I don't know. I guess so. Forty years is forty years, lady. I'm not gonna remember shit like that. Were people sayin' that Johnny killed Hank after Hank disappeared? No. No more than they were saying that about anyone, 'cause we all thought Hank had moved to California to become a hippie or something."

She checked her watch with an irritated jerk of the wrist. "Are we done? I gotta get to work and I'm sick of this, anyhow."

Sam nodded, smiling. "I appreciate the time, Lacey." She took a business card from her pocket and put it on the counter between them. "If you think of something later, don't hesitate to call me."

Lacey ignored the card, turning back toward the limes and lemons. "Whatever."

Sam caught up with Lester outside, where he was sitting in the car with the window down, peacefully waiting for her and enjoying the cool, late afternoon sun.

"How'd it go?" he asked as she slid into the passenger seat.

"According to Lacey, she had a serious hankering for Mr. Mitchell but his love was reserved for the wife. One difference is that Joe and Willy reported that Sharon said it was Hank who was yearning to be free when she chucked him out. Lacey just said he felt wronged and was pining to be let back in. Who knows what the truth is? She also denies Jimmy might've whacked Hank out of jealousy."

"She and Jimmy were a couple even back then?" Lester asked, surprised.

"Yup—teenagers in lust, I guess. She calls him a douche bag now, though, and claims that's what he was back when he got her pregnant. Although," she added thoughtfully, "she did seem to rally to his defense when I asked if Jimmy might've gone after Hank. How 'bout you?" she asked. "How did things end with Carlo and Jimmy?"

Lester leaned forward and started the engine. "Pretty much what you'd expect: know nothing, see nothing, hear nothing. So much time has gone under the bridge that there're no twitches or tics to work with. They could stare at you all night with those old, tired-out, alcoholic eyes and lie their asses off. We'd never know the difference."

He drove to the edge of the parking lot and waited for a hole in the traffic. "*Something* happened back then," Lester continued. "And it got somebody worked up enough to knife a guy and have him paved over. What we're stuck with are a bunch of shifty geriatrics and a bucketful of questions."

Sammie eyed him questioningly. "Which leads you to what, exactly?"

He saw his chance and entered the road. "Absolutely nothing. Hell of a case."

CHAPTER TEN

For Vermonters living east of the Green Mountains, the Connecticut River is as iconic a reference as is a major boulevard to a city dweller—say, Fifth Avenue to a Manhattanite. To some, the Connecticut is a strict divider between New Hampshire and Vermont—with all the prejudice that might entail. To others, it is either a long, powerful, historically laden symbol of old Yankee capitalism, or a playground for modern sports enthusiasts—or both.

But whoever is consulted, and regardless of their response, there is an opinion. Everyone, it seems, has an association with the river—despite the rarely discussed fact that legally, New Hampshire owns the water right up to Vermont's shoreline.

That notwithstanding, Joe always viewed it as part of his New England birthright. It was his body of water, as Lake Champlain is to northwestern Vermonters, Lake Michigan to Chicago, or San Francisco Bay to its town. It lay claim to a corner of his permanent memory—like the bedroom closet he had as a child.

He unconsciously considered that now, as he drove along its bank, watching the birds skimming over the gleaming, muscular, undulating water in the day's ebbing light in search of whatever food was available just beneath the surface.

Joe was in New Hampshire on this drive. For all of Vermont's references to the river, few of its towns were actually perched on its edge, or many houses—at least compared to New Hampshire—largely as a result of the railroad having purchased so much of Vermont's shorefront property.

A little less sentimentally, what he knew most about the river concerned dead bodies: Anyone found floating in it automatically belonged to the Granite State. There was no telling how many one-liners had been uttered at a death scene, where some Vermont cop had proposed pushing a newly discovered floater into the current, in order to make it someone else's jurisdictional problem.

Not that anyone had ever done such a thing.

Joe was on the River Road, north of West Chesterfield—a meandering, little-traveled, well-maintained favorite among motorcyclists and bicycle lovers that steadfastly lived up to its name by hugging the river as closely as was practical.

Along its length—unlike what appeared to be wilderness over in Vermont—were snug and quiet homes lined up at peaceable distances from each other, like respectful fishermen enjoying a little isolation from a busy world.

It was next to one of these—although a larger, newer, more modernized and fortified version—where Joe eventually pulled over and parked.

In fact, the house was not attractive. While its setting spoke for itself in soft and budding shades of green, interspersed with the river's alluring openness, the building—sharp-edged, blank-faced, modern, and jarring—had the same brutal feeling to it as a concrete bunker overlooking a beach.

He approached the heavy front door, aware of a beady camera lens suspended to one side, and rang the bell.

"Hello?" a man answered.

Joe took a step back, as if to give room to the disembodied voice. "Hello?" he reacted, caught by surprise. He was no stranger to security systems, but cameras and speakers were rare this far from urban America.

"What do you want?"

"Is that Mr. Lucas?" Joe asked. "Johnny Lucas?"

"What do you want?" the voice repeated.

Joe revealed his credentials to the camera. "I'm a police officer, Mr. Lucas. No one's in trouble. I just want to ask you a couple of questions— dating way back. I was hoping you could help me out."

"That's a Vermont badge."

"That's correct," Joe affirmed, returning it to his pocket. "Vermont Bureau of Investigation."

He was about to expand on that, but was cut off by, "You have no jurisdiction here."

"True," Joe said pleasantly. "Which is why I mentioned I was just looking to chat."

"I don't have to talk to you."

"You certainly don't, Mr. Lucas. I'm not quite sure why you wouldn't be willing to help a police officer, though."

There was a pause before the voice announced, "Mr. Lucas isn't here. Leave."

Joe nodded and took out a business card, which he also held up for viewing. "Got it. Well, if you could do me a big favor and give him my card when you see him, I would sure appreciate it. I'd like to pick his brains."

Another pause. "What about?"

Joe smiled. "Open the door and I'll tell you. As you said, I have no authority here. It's just a conversation I'm after."

But there was no response. Joe stood with his card in his hand for a few moments, feeling increasingly ludicrous, wondering if he was looking at a dead camera lens or being studied by someone who might just as well be in Detroit. Certainly, there had been no sign of life from inside the house during this exchange.

He resisted the extra humiliation of speaking further to an inanimate structure, and poked his card under the edge of the front door—half expecting the house to spit it back out.

Willy pulled over to the curb and lowered his passenger-side window to address two people he'd recognized walking on the sidewalk, just shy of the Arch Street drop-off from Main.

"*Hey.* Kravitz."

They turned to face him. Dan Kravitz—tall, gaunt, immaculately dressed in clean and pressed Goodwill togs—and a teenage girl with blond hair, whom Willy knew to be his daughter.

Dan leaned into the window's opening and gave Willy a gentle smile. "Detective."

"Haven't seen you in a while," Willy stated. "You been staying out of trouble?"

"You would know."

"Been staying out of other people's homes?"

"Isn't that our agreement?"

"You are so full of it." Willy bent forward to include Sally. "Hey, there. You still in school?"

Sally knew Willy, if only slightly, and although Dan had tempered her impression with his own more nuanced insight, she still considered him as someone best to be avoided.

Nevertheless, she got close enough to say, "I graduated."

"Hangin' with Dad, then?"

"I guess. Taking a year off."

"Watch out for him," Willy said seriously. "One of the smartest men

I know, but he's got some wild hairs. You wanna think about that. He's not as invisible as he thinks he is."

"Okay."

Dan's face was impassive. "What can I do for you, Detective?"

"That's my question for you, Dan. We still have our arrangement, like you said—you let me know if there's anything cooking I should hear about?"

"We do. Are you inquiring about anything specific?"

"You heard about the body at VY?" Willy asked.

"Just that one had been found."

"Nothing else?"

"Not yet. I'll keep my eyes peeled."

Satisfied, Willy gestured for Sally to get closer, so that she could hear him without any passersby catching a word.

"I know you don't like me—that's the longest line in history. But I like your dad, and I trust him, which I can say for about five people in the world. I wasn't just busting your chops about what he does. If you know what I'm talking about—which would mean he's taken you into his confidence—then pay attention. I'm your friend, as weird as you think that sounds. Everybody else'll toss you to the dogs in a heartbeat."

He paused long enough to study their faces, after which he smiled, if barely. "That tells me I'm right—or you'd be telling me to fuck off. That being the case, do me a favor? Please?"

Sally was scowling, at once alarmed, confused, and angry. Dan remained imperturbable.

"What would that be, Mr. Kunkle?"

"Take care of each other. Watch each other's back. It's a tricky world."

Sally's eyes widened slightly as Dan acknowledged, "Always. Thank you."

Willy pulled into traffic and drove away. Sally looked up at her father. "That was random."

Dan draped his arm across her shoulders and smiled. "And kind of wonderful."

Now that spring had replaced winter, the days were longer, so there was still light coming through the office window when most of the squad assembled to compare notes. All except Sammie, who'd asked Lester to represent her while she went by the day care to pick up Emma.

Throughout their daily routine, as befitted operational protocols, each squad member filed his or her activities electronically, so that the others always knew, from hour to hour, of any new developments. Surprisingly to Joe, who'd originated this practice long ago, Willy had complied without complaint. Only later, feeling slightly foolish, had Joe conceded that one primary reason for that easy acquiescence was that Willy was as prone to entering fiction as fact, depending on his needs and moods.

In any case, the older, more traditional habit also remained—of regularly gathering to discuss the day's work—thereby giving Joe the additional value of a Socratic exchange.

"You read today's dailies?" Joe asked them after Spinney had settled down with his last cup of coffee for the day.

"Yes, Dad," Willy said in a bored monotone.

"Not yours, though," Lester added with a smile.

"Fair enough," Joe conceded. "I just got back from Johnny Lucas's in West Chesterfield, where I had an unenlightening conversation with a talking house."

Lester laughed. "They only spoke over the speaker?" he interpreted correctly.

"Was it Lucas, at least?" Willy asked.

"I think so," Joe told them. "He could totally deny it if he wanted to."

"You say why you were there?" Willy followed up.

"Nope," Joe said. "Which I found interesting, too. He's either a complete paranoid, had his pants around his ankles at the time, or already knew what we're up to. Has the paper put a name on the Vermont Yankee body yet? I haven't read it today."

"The radio did," Lester said. "A few hours ago. Somebody talked."

"We been blabbing it all over town ourselves," Willy observed. "Twitter and Facebook have done the rest, I bet."

"Regardless," said Joe, "Lucas is pretty high on my list. Why would you avoid the police, unless you had something to hide?"

"'Cause you have a girlfriend in bed when your wife's out shopping?" Willy proposed. "Could be any reason better than an ancient homicide. Just sayin'."

"Okay," Joe agreed, reading off his computer screen. "What else? Sam writes that she and you, Les, found something out of whack with what Sharon Mitchell told Willy and me."

"Yeah," Lester explained. "Either Hank was yearning to be free or Sharon thought he'd already overstepped in that department, and threw him out. I could see that happening between a couple—both spinning their own version. It didn't really set up who might've wanted him dead, though."

"You believe Lacey that she and Hank were never an item?" Joe asked.

"Sam did, from what she told me in the car," Lester said. "Plus, Lacey did a real stand-by-your-man imitation when Sam asked if maybe Jimmy killed Hank.

"One thing rattled around my head afterwards, though," Les added. "Lacey implied that BB could've resented Hank for being so good at drumming up business. It was subtle, but it's kind of what I got from my interview with Jimmy and Carlo, too: Hank was Ridgeline's ace in the hole. If you combine that with BB's obsession with Sharon, then suddenly, BB has two reasons to see Hank gone."

"Talk about shooting yourself in the foot," Willy said.

"Except he didn't, did he?" Lester asked generally. "Not in the long run."

"Not financially," Joe agreed. "But what about the time delay between Hank leaving and Johnny taking his place? How did BB survive if he was so bad at bringing in business? Lacey told Sam she figured he had deep pockets, but that's not what I heard. It would be interesting to somehow take a closer look at that time slot."

"Did Ridgeline have a bookkeeper?" Lester asked.

The three men exchanged looks.

"Okay," Joe said. "Tack that onto our to-do list." He took his eyes off the screen and consulted several notes he had scattered across his desk. "What's our progress with Vermont Yankee's old records? Reported fights, unexplained employee departures, unusual events—around the time of the burial? We get anything there? And any leads on Mr. Neathawk?"

Willy didn't deign to respond, so Lester answered, "We're all sharing that load, between interviews. Nothing's standing out. You were right about those records being less than God's gift to organization. On paper, there was a single umbrella contractor, but there were also so many jobbers responsible for their own people—some of which left no footprint—that a small army of people could've worked there nobody knew about. Until the nuke stuff arrived, it was just a construction job, with pretty basic accountability. Everybody was focused on the integrity of the containment vessel and the reactor building—not on who was or wasn't coming in to do the peripheral stuff."

"I found Neathawk listed here and there," Willy contributed. "But no special mentions."

"Did any of those entries postdate the torching of his van?" Joe asked.

"Yup," Willy confirmed. "So he definitely stuck around afterwards. Looks like he left with the rest of the high iron guys."

Joe reflected a moment and then checked his watch. "All right. Why don't we call it a day? If this damn thing ever catches fire, we'll be putting in overtime like usual. No point driving the bean counters crazy prematurely." He looked up at them. "Anyone got big plans tonight?"

Both men laughed, and Lester answered for the two of them, "Right—home to pass out in front of the tube after a plate of mac 'n' cheese." He quickly held up a hand, as if in protest, adding, "Not that I'm complaining."

It wasn't mac 'n' cheese for Joe that night, although it might have been under normal circumstances, along with a book and his cat for company. Instead, it was a nice dinner halfway to Burlington, early retirement to a motel room, and an hour and a half of much-anticipated and utterly satisfying lovemaking with Beverly Hillstrom.

Then there was a little TV watching, with the sound turned off, featuring the silenced struggles of a series of young men competing to conquer a watery obstacle course featuring a climbing wall and several ropes—all against the background of an oversized clock.

Joe, his arm around Beverly's bare shoulders, and with her head on his chest, asked, "Are we good?"

She chuckled, making her shoulders shake. "Are we worried?"

He shook his head. "Not me. I want to make sure you're happy, though."

After a thoughtful pause, she said, "I am. Utterly." She raised and twisted her head around to give him a kiss before resuming her position. "I will confess, however, that if you'd posited a few years ago that you and I would be sharing a motel bed with our clothes off, I'd have laughed you out of the room." She squeezed his waist and added, "I am delighted to have been proved wrong."

He smiled. "You could've just said, 'Yup.'"

She laughed. "Then you wouldn't have known who you had in your arms."

Good point, he thought. She was an original. And her words rang truer than perhaps she knew. Getting to this point romantically—to this particular woman—had not been without trial and loss, which might have had a lot to do with Joe's self-confidence. With Beverly, at last, he felt as if he'd found a place from which he could build.

It also wasn't an evening at home for Willy Kunkle—at least not yet. He was parked in his car in Brattleboro, across the street from an Argentine restaurant named Bariloche, waiting for all but the antiburglar lights to be turned off. Upon that happening, he crossed the street, climbed the two steps to the locked glass door, and tapped on the glass.

Dan Kravitz finished putting a chair upside down on one of the tables, crossed to the door, and opened it without protest or hesitation.

"Mr. Kunkle," he said amicably, letting Willy inside. "Would you like me to fix you something?"

"I'm good," Willy told him, sliding into a booth where he wouldn't be seen from the street.

It was becoming a familiar setting for them, which was unusual for an urban nomad like Kravitz, who had variously called home other people's trailers, abandoned houses, corners of empty warehouses, and now—for the past several years—a large room above this restaurant, which the owner had made available to him in exchange for Dan's helping out now and then.

Willy alluded to this sedentary abnormality. "You running out of gas in your old age, Dan?"

Kravitz slid into the booth opposite him. "Because I'm still calling this place home?"

"You gotta admit—it's not your style."

Dan reflected before responding. For a long time, Willy had thought him mentally delayed. Their first conversations had consisted of Dan's uttering little more than grunts, single words, or extremely short sentences, painfully doled out. In the end, the truth had proved to be the exact opposite. Dan was articulate, highly educated, and perhaps even a genius—if an unconventional one. He was also a watcher—at once removed from society while obsessed with analyzing and cataloging its every tic and twitch.

Willy, of course, couldn't have cared less about what drove him. He just liked him for what he could dig up, and at that, Dan was the best Willy had ever known.

"I am making adjustments now that Sally has grown older," Kravitz said at last. "Among them being some sense of domestic stability."

Willy didn't comment. The floor overhead wasn't actually legally inhabitable, due to its restricted access—a narrow, ladderlike staircase behind the bar—and its lack of amenities, which the restaurant itself supplied for after-hours use. But it was a high-ceilinged, bare, single room overlooking the street, with separate sleeping alcoves for father and daughter, and kept compulsively clean and tidy. That was another striking attribute of the man seated before him: No matter what the task or the environment, Dan Kravitz always managed to stay as scrubbed clean as an operating room technician. Kunkle was a neat-freak—Sam never had to touch a vacuum cleaner or wash a dish at home. Kravitz made Willy look like a slob.

"I don't usually see so much of you as I have lately, Mr. Kunkle," Dan said in his oddly canted English.

"Yeah," Willy conceded. "Well, I have a job for you. Maybe seeing you earlier today reminded me of your talents."

Dan waited patiently.

"You were lying your ass off about breaking into people's houses, weren't you?"

"Have you received complaints?" Dan asked, his concern clearly more directed at having been detected than at committing an illegal act. Dan prided himself on leaving no evidence of his visits behind, nowadays.

Willy understood that. "No. And I'll take that as a yes, since you're being cagey. Let me rephrase: If I happened to know a nutcase who loved to break into houses and snoop around, there's an address I'd like him to check out. How's that?"

Kravitz smiled demurely. "That's excellent. What might be the address and the reason for a curiosity that clearly doesn't amount to legal probable cause?"

"Very clever," Willy growled. "No, it doesn't. It ties into that body at VY."

"Yes. The long-missing Henry Mitchell. I read about that online."

"One of his ex-pals, Johnny Lucas, lives—"

"On River Road, across the Connecticut," Dan interrupted—an unusual breach of manners for him.

Willy stared at him, struck by exactly that point. "Showoff," he said. "You been there?"

But Kravitz shook his head, looking slightly embarrassed. "I'm not inclined to cross the river—or leave town, for that matter. I'm simply aware of Mr. Lucas and his residence, because he used to work in Brattleboro, and because of his unusual path to wealth. I apologize for speaking out. You were explaining your interest in Mr. Lucas." Dan seemed eager to move past his misstep.

"What do you know about him?" Willy asked pointedly.

"Nothing, which I find very interesting." Dan left it at that.

"Right." Willy dragged out the word, still amused. "So one of our guys stopped by Lucas's place and was told to get lost over the security speaker. We find that interesting, too."

A lifted eyebrow betrayed Dan's piqued curiosity. "You suspect Mr. Lucas of a specific malfeasance? Perhaps killing Mr. Mitchell?"

"Perhaps," Willy agreed. "But it's vaguer than that. All we know for sure is that Lucas was a grunt until Mitchell bit the dust—or left the stage, as people thought in 1970. Then, like you said, it was life on the fast track. Johnny got into BB Barrett's good graces—I'm sure you know him—became his number two man, made the business a big hit, and eventually retired, fat, rich, and happy."

"You have no indication that Mr. Lucas willfully removed his rival?"

Willy sighed. "You're making it sound like a soap opera. No, we do not. In fact, there was a hiccup in time between when Hank disappeared and Johnny replaced him, which makes it look like BB was hoping to run things on his own for a while—till he realized he needed help."

"I take it that you've conducted a background check on Mr. Lucas," Dan guessed.

"You take it right," Willy reassured him. "As part of our normal routine. I seriously doubt we can do the kind of high-tech snooping you can, though. Our methods are legal, so nobody shows up much unless they've stepped in the shit. We have the fusion center in Burlington, but they feed off public records. I'd bet that what you collect and how you collect it would land us in jail." He then added quickly, "Assuming you ever did anything crooked, which of course we know you don't."

"As you also know, Mr. Kunkle," Dan said disingenuously, "I have a personal moral code. You are assuring me that your request is founded on some real concerns about Mr. Lucas's being a bad person. Is that correct?"

Willy made a face. "I think he's a dirtbag who's hiding something—yeah."

Dan nodded once and sat back. "May I get back to you about this, perhaps in a couple of days?"

Willy slid out and stood up, automatically adjusting his arm. "You know how to find me."

*   *   *

Dan Kravitz finished closing up the restaurant and climbed the narrow stairs to the room above, where his daughter was ensconced in an armchair, reading a book.

"You have company?" she asked, looking up as he appeared. "I heard voices."

"You did," he replied. "The same police officer who spoke to us on the street."

"The famous Willy Kunkle," she said with a small scowl. "He was weird."

"He is," her father agreed, adding, "But lucky for me, a righteous man. More important, he's given us an assignment, with which—after I do some preliminary advance work—I may ask for your help. Would that be of interest?"

Her face beamed as she imitated his speaking style. "Surely, Father, you jest."

CHAPTER ELEVEN

Sally Kravitz was completely focused, standing outside the house, watching, as her father put it, for "anything that moves." Despite his easy manner and the surrounding stillness, her concentration was sharpened by a neophyte's conviction that whatever could go wrong was about to, and that it would be her fault.

"You in?" she asked over the throat mic he'd given her—a tactical model that needed a mere whisper to function.

Her father's voice was light and comforting. "Almost, sweetheart. I'll let you know—promise."

She pressed her lips together angrily. She'd sworn to herself that her coolheadedness would leave him astonished, and already she was acting like a kid. Dumb, dumb, dumb.

Dan had let her select her observation post outside Johnny Lucas's house, and she'd chosen the low limb of a tree across the street. Here, she'd congratulated herself. Not only had her father approved with a nod of the head—high praise from him—but, now that she was in place, she also found that she had a near perfect view of all approaches, including the river beyond. This was made easier by Dan's having given her a pair of night vision goggles, which she loved. Also—and this had truly surprised her—he had planted a pair of motion detectors down the road, in both directions, programmed to signal them over their headphones should anything come near.

"All right," he whispered laconically over her earpiece. "Home sweet home. Now for the internal security system. You happy out there?"

"Very," she assured him.

She'd been pleased to be invited. Dan had made it clear from the start that her apprenticeship would take a long time and many "house calls," as he termed them, before he'd take her on his kind of visitation— the ones with the residents still inside.

In fact, the building was empty now. Nevertheless, Sally recognized this to be a higher-level target than her father might normally have chosen for her, had Willy Kunkle not assigned it to him. Dan's preference—as he'd explained—would have been another simple, non-alarmed, one-story building. Perhaps even a weekend or seasonal home, to further ensure that they wouldn't be disturbed.

This, however, was no such situation. The house was modern, multi-level, wired with both audio and video defenses, and owned by someone with a questionable enough past to have stimulated Kunkle's interest. This was no starter project, and Sally had been flattered by Dan's trust in her.

He had done his homework beforehand, even if he hadn't spent the time he preferred—including several visits over the previous couple of days—"casing the joint," as was the phrase in the old movies they enjoyed watching together. What he learned had given him the confidence to involve Sally. Lucas lived here with his wife only. There were no children, only fish for pets, and—apparently—the type of security that Dan felt he could readily defeat.

That being said, he hadn't entered the house until tonight, which raised the question about whether she'd be invited inside or not. And

truthfully, her excitement about that prospect was about evenly counter-
balanced by old-fashioned fear. If Mr. Lucas was a bad apple, what
might be his reaction upon finding two strangers snooping around his
place?

"Okay," Dan said after what seemed a very long time. "You interested in a little exploring?"

"Really?" she answered, again immediately regretting her childish
glee.

But he didn't laugh at her. He never did. "Yup, if you feel up for it.
You have to listen to your inner voice, as we discussed."

She tried hesitating, to show she was actually making a choice. "I'm
ready," she then said. "How do you want me to come in?"

He gave her directions. She nimbly climbed down from her tree,
crossed the road, and—picking her footsteps carefully, as she'd been
taught—worked her way around to the riverside aspect of the house.

There, she discovered her father leaning out of a window, proffering
his gloved hand.

The house he helped her enter was dark, emotionally cold, and reminiscent of an overly architected rat maze. She even glanced up quickly,
upon getting her bearings, to check if the ceiling hadn't been removed
for easier viewing from above.

The moon was full and the night sky cloudless, the openness of the
nearby river allowing for additional illumination through the windows.
The night vision equipment supplied the needed edge, however, giving them near perfect visibility.

Nevertheless, the place remained remote and distant and every inch
of decoration was clearly and aggressively expensive. Each item she saw
broadcast the fact that price rather than appearance had dictated its
selection. The result was like entering the green-tinged frozen hologram
of a high-end cocktail party—accessorized with trendy and costly
possessions—and minus all the guests.

Sally wasn't alone in her evaluation. "Very homey," her father said. "If you're a polar bear."

But while she was once more absorbing the novelty of standing on trespassed ground, Dan was on task, hoping to fulfill his obligation to Willy Kunkle by finding something more revealing than Johnny Lucas's shortcomings as an interior decorator.

He began in the office, after they'd completely surveyed the building's interior, noting every door, window, light switch, and staircase—as was Dan's normal pattern. Sally stood by, at once learning and taking in the feel of the place. They'd discussed how his search of Lucas's possessions would be more of a raid than a training session, and therefore more given to speed and results than to instruction.

That being so, she couldn't but admire Dan's concentration and economy. With the precision of a surgeon, she imagined, he used gloves and a miniature flashlight attached to a headband to help him forage through drawers, files, an assortment of cabinets, and a laptop computer—using his cell phone camera to photograph items he thought might be relevant.

Twice, the motion detector was triggered on their radios, and they gathered at the window to see if the oncoming vehicle might be Lucas's, but both times proved to be false alarms.

From the office, Dan led them to the bedroom, where he quickly identified Johnny's side of the bed and his half of the closet. He noted the man's personal details, from the kind of book he had on the nightstand to his bottled prescriptions and taste in shoes, clothes, and even shampoo.

And in contrast to his calm and peaceful tone of voice, Dan maintained an impressive, sure-handed speed.

This turned out to be a good thing, since the third alarm led to them watching the Lucas vehicle slowing down, about to enter the short driveway.

"Oh, shit," Sally moaned.

"Not to worry," Dan reassured her, politely gesturing toward the bedroom door. "Just head for the window we entered by. You remember the way."

It was said as a statement, and gave her the confidence to proceed without misstep. As she went, she mimicked Dan's habit of replacing everything as he'd found it—from the angle of an open door to the way a small carpet corner had been flipped up. "Leave no trace" went beyond mantra here—in instances like this, it contributed to survival.

As she was instructed, Sally exited the building quickly and carefully, leaving no footprints in soft soil and putting the rubber-soled slippers they both wore to their quietest use. She crouched by a bush on the periphery of the lawn and waited nervously for her partner in crime to follow her out.

The lights went on at the front of the house, spreading across the lawn in a semicircular stain. The shadows of two people began to drift across the curtains.

And still, there was no sign of Dan.

Sally began to consider her options. Create a distraction? Throw a stone through a far window? Phone the house to immobilize at least one of the occupants? She'd been given the home's number just in case, thinking the gesture absurd at the time. Maybe she should knock on the door, pretending to seek directions, or report a fire up the road. The one thing she didn't consider was to use the throat mic to consult her dad. She was too worried about distracting him just enough to throw off his game.

She rose tentatively, on the verge of acting on any of these choices, when his shape appeared briefly at the window. He shut it behind him as if in a graceful afterthought and soundlessly slid up beside her, just as the same window popped into harsh relief via a hallway light behind it.

"Did you enjoy yourself?" he asked, slipping his arm around her shoulder, the canvas bag he'd stuffed with documents in his other hand.

She nodded, confessing, "But this is definitely going to take getting used to."

Sheriff's deputies in Vermont walk a parallel line alongside most other police officers. They go to the same academy for their training and end up with the same certificates, but once on the job, they discover—if they weren't already aware of it—that their boss, and thus their agency, is a form of law enforcement doppelgänger. A Vermont sheriff is not a hired chief or a pulled-from-the-ranks state police colonel—he or she is a politician and business owner, and not even required to be a certified cop, even though they all are. Each county's sheriff is paid by the state, and expected to perform such duties as civil process, court security, and prisoner transportation, but the actual requirements of the office are flexible. If a sheriff—elected for a four-year term—chose to simply sit back, do nothing, employ no deputies, and collect his or her salary— they could do so legally. It might turn out to be a short career, but at almost seventy-five thousand dollars per year, not an unprofitable one.

No Vermont sheriff acted this way, but David Spinney had done his homework, and discovering this enormous degree of latitude had been helpful in understanding why some sheriffs stuck their necks out to create virtually full-service agencies, and others were far less ambitious, merely working to stay employed.

The core of the dilemma, as David had found out, was that sheriffs, regardless of their aspirations, had to be profit-minded, first and foremost. Unlike the state police or municipal departments, sheriff's offices ran on contracts—to stand by road construction projects, secure facilities such as Vermont Yankee in the old days, enforce traffic for a particular town, or supply the school resource officer at the local high school. In other words, despite the fact that they existed by edict of Vermont's constitution, and not by statute, sheriff's offices nevertheless had to fund their operations in an assortment of inventive ways.

As in verifying VINs—or vehicle identification numbers—which is what David was on his way to do that morning when he found himself meditating on all this.

He wasn't unhappy being employed within this unconventional, often versatile framework. He liked his colleagues, enjoyed the autonomy of working from his cruiser for most of the day, and was becoming increasingly self-confident through every day's string of spontaneous interactions. As he saw it, this job was an excellent training ground for discovering if he wanted to stay in law enforcement, and in what capacity.

But right now, he had to document an automobile's provenance, as part of its being transferred from one owner to another. Not glamorous, but necessary, and certainly an opportunity for a nice drive in the country.

He wasn't crazy about how this particular road was turning out, however. This was his first time in this corner of the county, and from a well-maintained, well-traveled dirt road—if a little spongy because of mud season—this one was rapidly disintegrating into little better than a greasy rutted goat path. Still, his GPS urged him onward, insistent that the address he sought lay ahead.

Which it did, finally. Through his mud-spattered windshield, Dave made out a sad-looking trailer tucked under a row of ancient hardwoods, with a blighted front yard spread out like a soiled apron. He pulled up next to a battered pickup truck, swung out of the cruiser, and looked around.

"Hello?" he shouted, at least expecting the obligatory Heinz 57 dog.

But there was no response.

He reached through his vehicle's open window for the radio mic, to inform Dispatch of his arrival and confirm the address, when he felt a rough hand yank him back outside. Something hard jabbed him in the back, and a harsh voice ordered, "Move one muscle and you die. Do not turn around."

Of course, instinct dictated otherwise. Dave did twist slightly, quickly enough to catch a glance of his assailant's shoulder, before a thick cloth sack was dropped over his head, obscuring his vision.

"What the hell?" he yelled. "I'm a cop."

"No shit," was the response, as Dave felt multiple hands seize his arms and legs and yank him free of the ground.

"Put me down," he ordered, kicking and struggling as best he could.

They did, dropping him hard on his face. The wind knocked out of him, he heard several people laughing and felt one of them use his own handcuffs to secure his wrists behind his back.

"Can't believe it was so simple," someone said, his voice tense with excitement.

"Guys think they're so fucking great," said another. "Wait till this gets around. Got the camera?"

Dave was fighting panic, his own rapid breathing making him light-headed in the bag. "Stop this," he said. "Stop it now. What you're doing isn't worth it. This is a major felony. You will be caught."

"Use the tape," ordered one of the voices. "Shut this asshole up."

The familiar screech of ripping duct tape preceded Dave's head being wrenched to one side and a tight band clamping the bag's fabric against his mouth. Breathing became even more challenging, and speaking impossible.

"That oughta do it."

More tape was then used around his ankles and knees, severing his last vestige of independence. With that piece of tape applied, David felt his heart sag, and he stopped resisting.

Instead, he altered strategies—trying to make out how many of them there were. Identify them via their voices, he told himself. Link them to a cause, or a purpose, or a locale by some carelessly dropped reference. And listen for any names that might be mentioned.

And try not to think of what they're planning.

As they manhandled him across the yard—presumably to another vehicle hidden behind the trailer—he thought that he could distinguish three voices, which fit the number of hands he felt on his body. They sounded young, as if in their twenties or late teens, like himself, and high-strung—nervous about what they were doing. From odd snatches of conversation, the entire enterprise was starting to sound like an absurdist prank of some sort, rather than a lethally intended kidnapping.

Whatever it was, David's ability to listen in on it vanished as he was dumped into the trunk of a car, and all sensory input was reduced to darkness and a muffled orchestra of indistinguishable voices, engine noise, and a string of thumps and bangs as the car traveled down the same rough road he'd used to get here. He remembered TV shows where the victim cataloged any and all passing sounds—factory whistles, train noises, the echoing rattle of a car passing over a wooden bridge, and so on—to be relayed in perfect order to investigators later. All he was aware of were his aches and pains, his rising panic, his increasingly labored breathing, and a sense of impotent rage.

It ended, seemingly a long time later, when all motion stopped, fresh air poured into the trunk, and David was lugged back outside to the accompaniment of his captors' laughter, to be unceremoniously dumped onto a thick patch of grass. In the background, he could hear the sound of rushing water.

"Okay, asshole, end of the road. Smile for the camera."

He heard them arguing about the best angle for their shot, before another voice asked, "You ever been on the receiving end of a Glock, Mr. Deputy?"

David felt what he assumed to be the hard, metallic pressure of a gun barrel against his head.

"This is what it feels like. Before everything goes dark."

He waited, not breathing, not moving a muscle, his eyes squeezed shut.

And then, as suddenly as it had begun, it ended. The gun was removed, the laughter faded, the car drove off, and David Spinney was left alone, listening to the water passing by.

CHAPTER TWELVE

Joe hung up the office phone and addressed Lester Spinney. "Technically, that call was for you. We're going to the ER."

Joe was slipping on his jacket as he spoke. "Everything's okay—a hundred percent, from what I was just told—but your son was just transported there to be checked out."

Lester stood up quickly enough to send his chair skittering into Sam's desk. They were alone. "What the hell?"

Joe placed his hand on Lester's shoulder. "He's fine. They're following protocol—same process you've been through a dozen times. I'm coming with you, and," he added with emphasis, "I'm driving."

"What'd they tell you?" Lester asked as they left the parking lot shortly thereafter.

"Essentially, nothing," Joe said. "The sheriff got an anonymous call, telling him to pick up one of his deputies by the side of Stickney Brook, right off Route 30."

"What?" Lester exclaimed. "He was standing there with his thumb out?"

Joe kept his eyes on the traffic. He was taking backstreets to the hospital, hoping to reduce the trip to no more than five minutes. "I don't know, Les, but I doubt it." He suddenly flashed on a case he'd investigated over twenty years earlier, and added, "Maybe someone handcuffed him to a tree or something. Weirder things have happened."

The ER wasn't busy, it being only midmorning, and one of the nurses at the long counter lining the central passageway looked up from her paperwork, took them in at a glance, and directed simply, "Room Three."

There, they found a doctor and another nurse, the first a woman and the second a tall bearded man, tending to David Spinney, who was sitting upright on a gurney in his undershorts. His face fell at the sight of his father.

"I don't believe it. Dad, who called you?"

Lester gave him a lopsided grin. "Like I needed calling. Don't you know you're part of the biggest gang in the country?"

Despite his son's obvious unhappiness at being found so exposed, Lester walked up to him and tousled, if not his hair, there being so little of it, at least his son's closely cropped head.

"Dad," Dave protested.

Lester ignored him, addressing the doctor. "Any damage?"

She shook her head. "Minor abrasions and bruises. We conducted scans of his head and neck to be on the safe side, but he appears to be in perfect shape."

She turned to the nurse, said something unintelligible, signed a clipboarded form, shook David's hand in farewell, and left, taking the nurse with her.

Lester and Joe waited for the door to close.

"So, spill," Lester told the young man.

"Mind if I eavesdrop?" a male voice said from the reopened door.

Jeffery Wallace, the county sheriff, stood before them in uniform. "It took me longer than I hoped to get here." He spoke directly to David. "You okay?"

"Perfectly, sir," David answered, straightening awkwardly on the gurney. "They're all just making a fuss. I'm really sorry about this."

"It's not a fuss. It's what should be done." Wallace glanced at the other two men and added, "I'm only sorry I wasn't the first one here."

Only then did they all exchange handshakes. Jeff Wallace was a no-frills, hardworking, well-regarded cop. Trained for over a decade by the state police, he'd opted to run for office when the old sheriff announced his retirement. Throughout most of New England, throwing your hat in for sheriff barely rippled the local political waters. As a result, keeping the post often boiled down to not making a mess of things.

As far as Joe was concerned, Jeff had done much better than that, and he'd been happy to hear of David's signing on with Wallace for his first job in law enforcement.

Following the niceties, Jeff took a small recorder from his pocket and laid it on the metal table adjacent to the gurney. "Sorry to do this, but I need to be sure everything's recorded. Who knows what may be waiting down the line, huh?"

Nobody argued the point. They'd all been around too long for that. But a coolness had been injected into the air.

"You want us to step out?" Lester asked, his expression clearly demonstrating his lack of enthusiasm.

But Jeff remained reasonable. "Not at all. I want this to be friendly and supportive. I also don't want it to be used against any of us later."

He faced David again. "You good with this?" He nodded toward the recorder.

"Yes, sir."

"And do you swear under penalty of law to tell the truth to the best of your knowledge?"

"I do, sir."

Jeff then rattled off who was in the room with him, the date, and the location before saying, "Okay. Back to what I so rudely interrupted when I walked in. What happened, Dave?"

Dave ran his hand across the top of his head, clearly embarrassed. "I guess I was mugged, sir. I went to that VIN, as instructed by Dispatch, and got jumped when I leaned into the EQ to radio in my twenty-three. To be honest, I was also going to ask for confirmation that I was at the right place, 'cause there was nobody there when I drove up."

"Where were you?" Jeff asked.

David gave him the address, adding, "It's a trailer, in the middle of nowhere, which is what got me wondering."

"Go on."

"Not much more to it. Somebody grabbed me from behind, put a hood over my head, trussed me up like a turkey with duct tape, and chucked me into the trunk of a car I never saw. There were three males, as far as I could figure. They sounded young. They never mentioned any names or places that I heard. One of them talked about taking a picture, which means it'll probably go up on Facebook or somewhere pretty soon, if it isn't already there."

He paused before adding hesitantly, "One of them also put my gun against my head, as if he was gonna shoot."

The young deputy looked pleadingly at his boss, the recorder forgotten, as was usually the case. "Am I going to be fired, sir?"

Jeff almost cut him off. "Whoa, whoa. Let's not get ahead of ourselves. And let's get something straight. Word gets out fast about these things, like you said. Assuming there are reporters in the parking lot—which I'm not saying there are—you and I will be getting into my vehicle in a while, and you will be wearing your full uniform, including my weapon in your holster, and we will drive away from this facility with you sitting in the front seat of that car. This conversation is obviously going to continue, but if what you just said is confirmed—and I have no reason to think it won't be—then you were a victim here, son, and bear no culpability whatsoever. Is that clear?"

David nodded. "Yes, sir. Thank you, sir."

"It's just the way these things ought to be done," Jeff said flatly. "Back to your narrative: Was there anything that sticks in your memory? Especially in the few seconds before the hood was put on? Maybe a movement from the trailer. Was there another vehicle in the dooryard, for example, besides the car you didn't see?"

"An old pickup," Dave told them. "But it didn't look drivable." He then said, "There was one thing. The guy behind me—who grabbed me by the collar and jabbed the gun in my back—he told me not to turn around, just before he covered my head. But I did anyhow, and I saw his left shoulder. He was wearing a shirt with the sleeves cut off, and I saw a tatt, high on that shoulder."

"Can you describe it?"

"No, sir. I'm really sorry." He stopped, his expression blank, before adding, "I know it's pretty lame, but that's all I can think of. I tried to remember the tones of voices, or if anything smelled funny, or even if there was something I could pick up in the trunk. All I could get was this." He held out both his hands, looking apologetic.

They all three stared at what looked like nothing at all, until Joe tumbled to what he'd meant.

"You scratched into the trunk's carpeting," he said. "Good man. Smart."

Jeff had already moved to the door. He opened it, caught a nurse walking by, and asked, "Could we have a rape kit in here, please? I gotta collect some evidence from under my deputy's fingernails."

The sheriff returned to the bed, announced the termination of the interview to the recorder, hit the Off button, and said, "Okay. Enough of that. We'll pick through the details later. You did good, Dave. I didn't tell you, but we collected your EQ at the scene, along with your cell phone, which was on the ground next to it. As far as I've been told, there doesn't seem to be anything missing. We'll issue a BOL on your gun, of course. But right now, I want you to go home to your family and let some of this sink in. I know you're feeling fine and probably just want to get back on the road. But you need a breather. And I'm going to set up a meeting with a counselor. No arguments. That's an order. Crap like this can run deeper than you know."

Jeff pocketed the recorder. "I'll step out so you and your dad can have a little private time. But I'll be ready to get you out of here when you're done."

Joe accompanied him into the hallway, where the sheriff immediately said, "Hope I didn't come across too strong in there. I was just picking up vibes that he thought he was to blame. In the meantime, assuming I can confirm what I can of his story, I'm already thinking of something that ought to make the media happy without actually spilling the beans. Fingers crossed, we catch the bastards fast."

"What did you get from the trailer?" Joe asked.

"Nuthin'. It was a blind. Nobody's lived there for over a year. They just gave that address to draw him out."

"Him meaning Dave, specifically?" Joe asked.

"No. The call came in for a VIN check. That was it. Plain and simple."

"They might've known Dave's schedule and coverage area," Joe argued.

Jeff nodded. "Could be—he was on his assigned route, which is probably as well known to the public as it is to us. You thinking this was personal?"

"Not necessarily," Joe admitted. "Just keeping my options open."

The nurse that Jeff had stopped earlier appeared with the requested rape kit.

"Would you do the honors?" he asked of her. "Just the fingernails. I wouldn't want to mess it up."

* * *

Inside the room, Les and Dave stopped talking as the nurse entered. They silently watched her collect her evidence, package it up, and disappear, virtually without saying a word.

Dave glanced at his fingernails, as if judging a manicure. "Well, that was painless. Hope it'll do some good."

"We've cracked cases with less," his father said optimistically.

Dave dropped his hands dejectedly. "Yeah. Good luck with that. Be a little late to save my career."

Lester burst out laughing. "Are you kidding me? Look at Willy Kunkle, for crying out loud. After all the shit he pulls, and stays employed, you'll likely get a promotion. Jeff wasn't bent out of shape."

"Not in public, he wasn't."

Lester realized that his son was not going to be cheered up so easily. He reached out and massaged Dave's shoulder briefly. "Come on, kiddo, let's wrap up here and take the rest of the day off. Maybe go fishing or something. Let some of this drain out, like Jeff said. I mean, it ended up fine, but you must've been scared out of your mind, not knowing what they had planned."

Dave didn't make eye contact as he quietly conceded, "Yeah."

"No way that was random."

Joe looked at Willy, not surprised at the paranoia, and intrigued to hear the reasoning behind it.

Sammie, by contrast, merely rolled her eyes.

"Do tell," Joe urged him.

They were in the squad room, minus Lester, who'd taken his son home for the rest of the day.

But Willy remained silent, causing each colleague to react in turn.

"That's it?" Sam prodded. "No conspiracy theory?"

"Hey," he responded. "I'm usually right about that shit. Don't shoot the messenger."

"Why's David being grabbed not random?" Joe asked quietly, actually shopping for a valid theory.

Willy approached his answer indirectly. "All we ever do in this job is say how much we hate coincidences. So, why would the kidnapping of one of our kids be a coincidence, just as we're looking into this long-lost secret homicide? Cops don't get grabbed like he was. Somebody's making a point."

"But they didn't," Sammie argued, more conditioned than Joe to take issue with Willy's pronouncements. "From what it sounds like, they scared him, took pictures, stole a gun, and beat feet. And he said they were kids. It was probably a double-dare. What've you got that says otherwise?"

Willy patted his stomach with his right hand. "Instinct." He dropped his feet from his desktop and leaned forward to make his point. "Look, could it be a bunch of losers? Sure. But what if that was the whole point? If you grab a cop's kid solely to make Dad lay off the case, that's not gonna work. Everyone's gonna go apeshit. But if you're subtle, and just introduce the idea that the same kid—and everyone else who's near and dear to this squad—is at risk, but for no clearly defined reason, what do you think that's gonna do to the squad's effectiveness and morale? On that level, you gotta admit, it's brilliant."

"Only if you buy into it," Sam pushed back. "Right now, you're the only one making the point, so you're bumming us out all on your own."

Willy held up his hand. "Okay. I wasn't doing it for that. I just don't believe for a second that Lester's brat was taken by a bunch of teenagers. I think we ought to keep our eyes open for an alternate theory. Let's not forget that by requesting a VIN at that time and for that address, they were almost guaranteed to get Dave Spinney." He suddenly looked at his boss. "Speaking of all this, please do not tell me that the sheriff's office is the primary investigator. Why the hell don't we have it?"

"Same answer to both questions," Joe told him. "Conflict of interest. David's family to us, and on the sheriff's payroll. The state police are handling it. They'll keep us in the loop."

"Yeah, I bet," Kunkle grumbled.

He was silent from then on, but what kept gnawing at him was the conviction that David Spinney's kidnapping was not isolated.

Only Willy knew about Dan Kravitz's covert visit to Johnny Lucas's house, and the resulting findings struck him now as only part of a sequence of developments. The discovery of Mitchell's body, a main suspect's elusiveness, and the kidnapping of one of the investigators' children—as Willy was interpreting them—were starting to look more and more neatly aligned.

There was something here darker, more current, and truly danger-ous going on, he thought, than the ancient murder of a long-forgotten roofer.

CHAPTER THIRTEEN

"You were seen, dipwad."

Willy and Dan were in the restaurant, again after hours, again in one of the booths.

"I don't believe so," Dan said. "On what evidence are you basing that opinion?"

Willy rubbed his eyes. "I think I liked it better when all you said was Yup and Nope. Now, half the time, I feel like swatting you just because you sound like a fucking professor."

Dan smiled apologetically. "I'm sorry. We could return to that."

Willy sat back abruptly. "Forget it. How're you so sure you weren't?"

"The house was empty. I checked it thoroughly. I located the security and alarm systems and bypassed them. I was confident enough that there were no remaining cameras to proceed."

"Cameras? Plural? Meaning there were more, beyond the one at the front door?"

"Oh, yes. A pretty standard array."

"Couldn't there've been another set, separately wired?"

"Yes," Dan readily agreed. "My standard, pre-entry assessment of these situations normally relies on multiple sources of intelligence, such as background checks, past social history, and other indices, to guide me in my approach. Your time constraints with this assignment did not allow me to reach that comfort zone, as I made clear at the time."

"For Chrissake," Willy complained, essentially to himself.

Dan, however, was not simply being academic. He was worried, if privately. He hadn't told Willy of Sally's involvement, and she was of paramount concern to him now.

"Could we step back a few paces, Mr. Kunkle? What's making you think that I might have been observed?"

"You heard about the kerfuffle at the sheriff's office today?"

"I heard a news release reporting that a couple of deputies had misbehaved at the expense of one of their colleagues, resulting in their being disciplined. It sounded like a fraternity prank that got out of hand."

Willy grunted. That had been the sheriff's doing, making Dave's abduction sound vague and sophomoric and restricted to fellow deputies. High jinks duly reprimanded, with no names given. Not built to withstand much scrutiny, it was likely to work, given the lack of fallout and the waning keenness of the local journalistic cutting edge.

"That was the cover story," he partially explained. "People are saying I'm being paranoid, but I'm not sure it wasn't payback for your little visit."

"Why would something involving the sheriff be directed at you?"

"The deputy who got ambushed is a colleague's kid. And nobody got disciplined—no other deputies were involved. Somebody else grabbed the young man, tossed him into the puckerbrush, and stole his gun."

"Was he harmed?"

"Not a scratch. That's the beauty of it. If it was a threat, the damage is all in the mind of the beholder."

Dan maintained his composure, not wanting to reveal the nature of his own fear. "If you're right, the target was frighteningly close to home."

"That's my point," Willy said darkly, his violent nature coloring his voice. "Which means I want to get my hands on the asshole behind this, ASAP." He stared at Kravitz. "Which brings me to the subject at hand—what did you get?"

Dan pulled the canvas bag up from the seat beside him and placed it on the table. "I've included a thumb drive containing photographs and documents. There's a fair amount of material in there—financial, personal, miscellaneous. Having no idea what you were after, I collected probably more than you need."

"Anything jump out?" Willy asked, foraging through the bag.

"Nothing like the last time we worked together," Dan said wryly, alluding to a photo album he'd found and brought to Willy years earlier, containing what the latter had referred to as "snuff pictures."

Willy looked up. "Yeah—well, that was over the top." He slid out of the booth and slipped the bag over his shoulder. "Keep your eyes open, Danny Boy. Let me know if I'm right, or just seeing bad guys where there are none."

Dan usually saw his guest to the door on these occasions, but not this time. In fact, he was too angry to do more than sit and watch Kunkle leave.

A careful man, not given to spontaneity, Dan had been put in an awkward position by Willy Kunkle, who didn't share his self-control. As Dan saw it, Kunkle had pressured him into breaking and entering a target not of his choosing and in violation of his protocols, and, in the process, exposed Dan and—more importantly, Sally—to an unknown threat.

It was time, Dan thought, to take some independent action, albeit for his own self-interest.

"He asleep?" Sue Spinney asked her husband.

"Yeah," Lester said, settling onto the couch beside her. "I finally forced him to take a swig of scotch. He didn't like it, but I think it'll help. It was all, 'I'm fine, I'm fine,' while he was bouncing off the walls."

Sue kept her professional nursing demeanor, being fresh from her shift at Springfield Hospital. "Meaning what?"

He caught her tone and became more focused. "Meaning pretty standard post-event adrenaline, nothing worse. Totally within the spectrum of a winning football team, or a pumped-up skydiver, or anyone else who's just been in a high-stress situation. I've seen it more times than I can count." He slipped his arm across her shoulders and drew her nearer, feeling bad about omitting the detail concerning the gun that had been held against her son's head. "I'm not bullshitting you, Sue. You've seen it, too—probably more than I have. Obviously, we'll watch for more, like PTSD, but that's not what I'm getting so far."

She reached up and squeezed his fingers. "What the hell happened out there?"

"Sounds like what he told us—three hyped-up morons in search of a rush. And it seemed totally out of the blue—they couldn't've known who'd be responding to a VIN call. And nobody called him by name, either. I hope it's not the start of a trend, but I don't think there was much real threat involved."

She craned her neck to kiss his cheek. "That's very sweet, honey, but it's a crock. You do what they did to a cop, it's a fine line to using his gun on him next time."

He looked at her, startled by her unsettling accuracy. "Susie," he protested, "I may've been sugarcoating a little, but from what I heard, there was more male posturing going on than anything else."

"Cops are shooting people and people are shooting back," she said. "It's in the news every week."

He wasn't sure what to say. His wife had never been a shrinking violet, but this was harder language than he was used to—as if she were at once reading his mind and beating him at his own game.

But he was a deliberate man, if under a carefree, joke-cracking sur-face, and—as with his son earlier—he was willing to let his wife sort through her feelings before returning to the subject later.

So, for the moment, he returned her kiss, got up, and announced, "I'm gonna head up. You want to join me? We could watch some TV, if you want to put your brain on hold. Couldn't hurt."

She smiled up at him. "In a bit. I want to decompress first. I won't be long."

She listened to him, first tidying up in the kitchen, and then tromp-ing up the stairs.

She had a good life—good kids, good husband, a job she still found challenging and worthwhile after so many years. Lester was in a great place, finally doing what he loved best, with people he respected. The change that overtook him upon joining the VBI had been transforma-tive, and had turned the final trick in giving them all the sense of peace and accomplishment that she had always dreamed about.

It was in that spirit that she'd wished her son well when he announced a desire to follow in his father's footsteps and attend the police acad-emy. Lester so clearly loved the job that she was reluctant to deny her son the same opportunity—although she well knew of its risks. Lester had never been a foolish man, but even so, he'd had the occasional close call. Plus, she wasn't a fawn in the wilderness. Being an ER nurse for so long had exposed her to every kind of carnage and mishap this neck of the woods had to offer.

All of which made hearing of Dave's misadventure that much more disturbing.

Perhaps it was the aimless nature of it that had frightened her—what she'd been telling Lester about the world's encroaching violence. She thought that had Dave known the young men who'd mugged him, it might have made his ordeal at least partially comprehensible.

Or maybe it was that he'd barely been given a chance to grow into the job before undergoing an experience that, as far as she knew, had never happened to another cop in Vermont's history.

Whatever its source, Sue now understood being the victim of a terrorist act. No one might have been hurt, and, as Les was hoping, the aftereffects for Dave might even be transient, but the end result was that she was now in fear for her son's life, and—for his sake—forced to keep that distress under wraps.

The mother in her raged at being put in such a position, and her anger made her want to lash out.

But it was an emotion without outlet, forced to either die of its own accord—or fester.

Willy Kunkle didn't have a home office. Sammie had once suggested one, safely isolated toward the rear of the house, and he'd tried it briefly. But among his idiosyncrasies was a distrust of anything habitual. He would often sleep in odd spots around the house, enter through the front or back doors on a whim, or variously park in the garage, in the drive, on the street, or a block away. He also preferred moving about with his computer and files, setting up shop at the dining table, the guest bedroom, the living room, or even on the floor of his daughter's room, sometimes in the middle of the night.

He'd been a lethal loner in the military, and had put his skills to repeated use. Now he'd absorbed many of the sniper's quirks as his own in civilian life—moving restlessly and unpredictably, rarely acting the same way twice, staying completely still and silent for hours on end. Sam saw his mobile office routine as another extension of the same grab-bag of eccentricities.

She was therefore not surprised to find him in the living room, quasi-pinched between the wall and the back of the couch, sitting on the floor with the sofa's end lamp twisted around to give him light.

She kneeled on the couch, rested her arms along its back, and peered over the edge. "Whatcha doin', hunny-bunny?"

He looked up at her, openly astonished by her greeting. "You drunk?"

She chuckled. "Nah. Just lightening you up." She tilted her head at his spread-out paperwork. "Cramming for finals?"

"Could say that," he said. "I had Dan Kravitz steal a bunch of stuff from Johnny Lucas's house. I'm trying to see what he's up to."

She poised her chin on the backs of her hands. "You are a piece of work. You know that?"

"You're not gonna give me the your-illegal-shit-becomes-my-shit speech, are you? How the hell else're we gonna find out what makes him tick?"

"Like everyone else in law enforcement?" she proposed as a question. "Through old-fashioned, court-sanctioned police work?"

"Waste of time," he grumbled, back to sorting through Dan's research.

"Okay," she said. "Then, for the sake of form, and implying that I give a damn anymore, I will repeat that your fondness for breaking and entering—however you go about it—will in fact eventually cost us both our jobs and possibly our freedom and put Emma in foster care. Just for the record."

"Point taken," he said, not looking up.

"Now that that's over," she continued in a lighter tone, "did you find anything interesting?"

"Not so far," he told her. "But I am just starting."

"Why him?" she asked. "Why not the rich guy? BB? Or the bar crawlers?"

"Johnny's rich, too. And he acts like he has something to hide," Willy stated. "I might sic Dan on the rest of them next."

"What're you thinking?" she wanted to know. "At the staff meeting, you sounded bored by Lucas."

"I wasn't thinking much of anything, at first," he said. "Now I'm wondering if finding Hank maybe didn't kick up a wasps' nest."

Sammie made a quick calculation. "Because of what happened to Dave Spinney?" she asked, her voice incredulous.

He gave her an appreciative gaze. "You're good. Yeah. In part. I don't like things that happen for no reason, so I'm not buying the whole teenagers-on-a-dare fantasy the rest of you're so happy with. Also, I like Lucas 'cause he came outta nowhere, and wouldn't open his door to a cop. Seemed way too hinky to me. Last but not least, if I didn't get the lowdown on him this way, how else d'you think we'd learn anything?"

"How do you mean, he came outta nowhere?"

"*Aha*," Willy exclaimed in a discovery-moment parody. "You didn't read the fine print. In all those piles we're collecting at the office, there's background material we got from the fusion center on some of our players—what they were up to back when Hank was put underground. Most of 'em were either local or came up for the VY job, and then stuck around after—like the late Tom Capsen. But not Johnny Lucas. Lucas is just there, like Scotty beamed him down—the man without a past."

Sammie was trying to fit together the pieces. "Dave Spinney was trussed up and dumped because of something that happened *before* Hank got killed forty years ago?" she asked. "Aren't there about fifty easier theories?"

"Not if you line up the latest ducks," Willy said. "We find Hank; we start poking around; I get Dan to snoop on Lucas, who was tipped off by Joe's knocking on his door; and Dave gets grabbed. To me, it's not much of a reach to suppose that Lucas caught wind of Dan's visit—maybe through a video system Dan missed—and that Lucas, or whatever his name really is, then decided to issue a subtle threat by informing us all that he knows who we are, where we live, and who our kids are."

Sam was skeptical. "I don't know, Willy—"

He didn't care. "Tell you one thing: It'll make you a believer if another cop's relative gets grabbed—or worse."

She scowled at him. "You better not be saying you want to set Emma up as bait."

He reached up and grabbed her hand, a virtually unheard-of show of emotion. "Babe, you know better. Maybe I am being paranoid. Fine. What I'm saying is that if I am right, I don't want Emma in harm's way. I don't give a rat's ass what everybody else thinks, or if and how they want to watch their backs. I want our kid safe."

As far-fetched as the conversation had become, especially given the little evidence Willy had to offer, Sam shared his belief that preparation trumped regrets later on. "What do you want to do?" she asked.

"Having said what I did," he said, "I don't wanna go crazy. Louise is an ex-cop. That's one of the reasons we picked her as a babysitter. So, instead of shipping Emma off somewhere, I say we restrict her to quarters, bring Louise up to speed, make sure she's armed, and invoke a no-one-in, no-one-out policy for a few days. We'll supply food and anything else she needs, and figure out a way for Louise to reach at least one of us at the drop of a hat, in case something comes up."

He paused to look around. "As you know, when I got this place, I made sure of its defenses. It's not a bunker, but it's got stuff even Dan might have trouble with."

In another first, he gave Sam a slightly embarrassed expression. "Too much? Too crazy, even for me?"

She leaned way over and kissed him. "Not a bit, sweetie. It's all good."

Of course, it wasn't. As she left him to pursue his studies into Johnny Lucas, she couldn't help considering the blurry line between any rational theory they were trying to establish in the Hank Mitchell case, and the possibly deranged conclusions that Willy was reaching in the current void.

CHAPTER FOURTEEN

BB Barrett put down his newspaper and rose from the lawn chair with a grunt, his 260-pound frame resisting all the way. Hank Mitchell, he reflected, shaking his head and gazing at his deep blue swimming pool, its surface rippling in the breeze from the valley below. Who would've thought that name would ever crop up again? Gone and forgotten for damn near a half century. Incredible.

He moved to the edge of the pool and examined the bottom, where remnants of winter's passage stubbornly clung as a faint but noticeable streak of pale brown sediment. He'd always loved the notion of an in-ground pool, and enjoyed reading within proximity of its shimmer and soft slapping sound. But he rarely got into the damn thing, and he hated the constant maintenance it required. He'd even mentioned to his wife that they let it go wild, maintaining his enjoyment while eliminating the pool's need for care and feeding. Needless to say, she wasn't amused—even though he hadn't been kidding.

He shuffled over to the shed in the corner of the low fence encircling the area and extracted the vacuum, hose, and long, ungainly pole he needed to reach the pool's lowest depths. Lugging it to the water's edge, he unceremoniously dumped most of it overboard, keeping a hand on the pole's far end.

Then he hooked the hose to the suction pipe under a small hinged plate and began pacing back and forth, working the vacuum head below across the brown stain on the bottom. There was at least that small reward: The results were clear to see.

He had entered a state of repetitive-motion dreaminess when something abruptly snapped him back to the present. He paused, looked up at the distant horizon, and listened. There was the nearly inaudible hum of the distant town, an equally subtle chirping of distant birds, and, of course, the breeze. But that was it.

Shaking his head, he crooked his arm to prepare for another sweep across the pool, when he felt a sharp jab in his side, accompanied by a muted pop.

"Ouch," he said gently. "What the fuck?"

He reached back under his right arm to feel for what had hit him, expecting either a small bird or a large bug. Instead, he felt a hole, and discovered blood on his hand when he looked at it.

"Holy shit," he said, now alarmed.

Still holding the pole, he turned to see behind him, his eyes widening in amazement as he did.

He never said another word. A second pop resulted in another hole, this one in the center of his chest. He dropped the pole at last and tentatively touched the leaking hole, as if it were the most delicate of orchids—which it faintly resembled.

And then, as he watched, a third hole appeared, not an inch from his fingertip. There was a humming in his ears now, and a strange light-headedness, as if he might be on the verge of levitating.

The coolness of the water closing over him came as a soothing and delightful contrast to this confusion. Why haven't I done this more often, he wondered?

* * *

"Wow," Willy said, gazing into the pool. "Fat does float."

Joe frowned, not that he could argue the point. BB Barrett's body looked like a cresting pink jellyfish, his arms and legs suspended in the blue water like bulbous tentacles. Mostly blue water, that was, given the reddish tinge extending from the body like a blush.

Bonnie Barrett, the wife whom BB had rarely referred to by name, had called it in, coming home to find her husband faceup in the pool.

Joe had thought it noteworthy that she'd made no effort to reel him in. On the other hand, the recorded 911 call had sounded suitably hysterical. And the man had been—and remained—a whale.

He sensed she'd recover. For the preliminary interview, he'd offered her a seat in BB's old den off the pool. "I always hated this room," she'd said dismissively, leading him elsewhere. Redecorating was evidently already seeping into her thoughts.

She'd had nothing to offer. Married only a few years, they hadn't had much to do with each other. She'd referred to herself as a trophy wife, sounding content with the role. As she'd pointed out, waving her hand around, the benefits were nothing to sneeze at.

Reemerging into the sunshine, Joe found most of the component parts of a homicide investigation in place and at work. The medical examiner, the crime lab folks, the rest of the VBI team, support troops from the Brattleboro PD—all accounted for. It was the muggings, the burglaries, the penny-ante dope deals that often suffered from sloppy procedure—felony murder cases tended to work like the proverbial well-oiled machine.

Which didn't preclude some being more challenging than others. After the assistant medical examiner, a young man named Jerry Senturia, had fished BB out of the drink, the first surprise was delivered as a small group of investigators crouched around the sodden remains and Senturia pointed out the two holes in Barrett's chest.

"That's small caliber, like a .22," he said, lifting the body's right arm. "And there's a third one here."

"Huh," Lester grunted. "Not what I'd use."

Willy was still standing, looking down. "Worked, though. And it's quiet. That type of ammo is all over the place, and a .22 is probably the most common firearm in the country. Maybe you should learn how to aim better and rethink your next murder."

Lester didn't disagree. "Clearly."

"All right," Joe cautioned them, sensitive of too many ears in proximity—not to mention the widow, somewhere in the house. "What was used will still be in the body, judging from the lack of exit wounds. Multiple shots implies multiple shell casings, if we're lucky, so let's cover every square inch around here, reaching out to the tree line."

"You're assuming it was a semi-auto," Willy said. "Shooter coulda policed his rounds or used a revolver." He glanced at Lester. "Like I woulda done."

Joe stood up. "Well, we won't know till we root around."

That process took many people many hours, even with additional manpower coming in from the state police and the sheriff's office, and the crime lab techs laying out a search grid and orchestrating things. By the end of it, they had precisely what they'd started with—nothing.

As Lester put it tiredly, late in the afternoon, "No shells, no footprints, no cigarette butts, no dropped pens. It's like this dude was shot by a flock of birds."

"Nope," Willy argued. "No bird shit, either."

Joe arrived at the medical examiner's office after hours. He'd called ahead, out of courtesy, but he knew his kindred spirit well—Beverly was still there, wrapping up stray ends.

He punched in the door's combination number, went straight

through the darkened facility to her inner sanctum, and received her embrace at the door, wrapping her in a bear hug.

"I know it hasn't been very long," he told her, savoring the warmth of her in his arms. "But this really feels good."

She kissed his earlobe.

As was their style, however, five minutes later, they were standing side by side before a wall-mounted computer display, looking at X-rays of BB Barrett's corpulent remains.

"Just a nerdy observation," Beverly was saying, "but I rarely see a pattern quite like this, where all the projectiles end up approximately in the same place, despite having entered from three different portals. It's almost as if Mr. Barrett were made entirely of ballistic jelly, rather than bone, organs, and tissue like the rest of us."

"To be fair," Joe said. "There was a lot of jelly. Were the slugs .22s?"

"Yes, they were," she said, "and their penetration was consistent. That doesn't tell us much, of course, since we have no idea of either the grain load of the cartridges or the type of weapon used. That is correct, no?"

"Yeah," Joe said mournfully. "Sadly true. We're instinctively thinking it was a handgun, but we found less than nothing to corroborate it."

"And no casings," she confirmed.

He shook his head.

"Does that tell you anything?"

He laughed. "On TV, it would. I love it whenever the hardened but beautiful detectives immediately say, 'Clearly a professional hit.' I've actually worked a couple of professional hits, and neither one of them used a .22."

"For what it's worth"—Beverly pointed at one of the X-rays—"I can tell you that the first shot was the most counterintuitive. It was this one—entering Mr. Barrett's back, posterior to his right armpit. The wound track was intersected by one of the later ones, indicating that it was administered first. It stands to reason that he turned after receiving it, and was then struck twice in the chest."

"Which was the lethal one?" Joe asked.

"I don't know which of the two chest wounds was fired before the other," she answered precisely. "But this one pierced his heart, shredding half the aorta at this juncture. The other would have proved lethal on its own, but taken longer. Even the very first one was effective—it's doubtful he would have survived it had the other two never been fired. It was a very effective cluster."

"Could you tell anything from the slugs themselves?" Joe asked.

"I measured them for caliber, but that's where I stop. I leave all the right-twist, left-twist analyses to the experts. Know your limitations, is my credo. You'll have to consult with your friends at the lab."

"Easily done," he said, slipping his arm around her waist. "You had dinner yet?"

She twisted around and smiled. "I do have an appetite, but let's eat after we've satisfied it. Would that suit you?"

"I believe it would," he said.

David Spinney scrutinized his computer before adding a name to the list on his pad. He hadn't been completely forthcoming at the ER. He blamed his fragmented memory for only now being able to recall the details of that one attacker's tattoo. But that didn't excuse his then keeping the information to himself.

In truth, Dave had been swamped by mixed emotions since the kidnapping two days ago. The intense focus he'd seized upon at the time, and the purpose he'd put it to—trying to remember voices and times and events—had collapsed into a jumble of less useful feelings. Variably fearful, angry, resentful, embarrassed, guilty, and plagued by self-doubt, he hadn't been able to absorb reassurances from parents and colleagues. In the end, sleepless and frustrated, he'd resorted to a long, thoughtful walk around town in the middle of the night, before retreating to where he was now—in front of the office's computer, digging through every law enforcement database available, in search of the one visual snapshot he'd retained of the entire traumatic episode.

The tattoo, he now recalled in clear detail, was of the dragon Smaug, from the Hobbit movies. And tattoos were one of the many distinguishing marks that police records had been preserving with ever more accuracy for years. Dragons, unsurprisingly, had become about as common a tattoo as MOM, decades earlier. But Dave was hopeful that the people entering the data nowadays were—like him—more cognizant of newer popular icons than older cops like his father, who wouldn't have distinguished Smaug from Puff the Magic Dragon.

So far, Dave was proving his instincts right. By entering the gender of his attacker, an approximate age range, the location of the tattoo, and its precise identity, he'd already hit on three possibles.

One of which resided in southeastern Vermont.

Dave knew that he was still on an uphill climb. For everyone entered into the computer, there were legions of tattooed people out there who'd never been stopped by a cop, or—if so—hadn't had their body art documented. Nevertheless, it was a start, and more than what he'd given Lester and Joe.

And why hadn't he? Because to right the wrong done to him, he needed to solve his own case, by himself.

It was shortly before eight the next morning when the squad reconvened at the office. Since BB Barrett was found floating in his pool, they had spent hours, late into the night, scouring through his life, trying to identify whoever had fired three bullets into him. The results had not been rewarding, and the political and media pressure—unlike when

Hank Mitchell had resurfaced—had been proportional to the town's losing one of its wealthiest and most prominent citizens.

As was becoming a habit, now that the VBI was so frequently associated with high-profile investigations, Joe had set up a media hotline directing all press inquiries to a response desk in Waterbury, where the organization was headquartered and where its director, Bill Allard, could personally manage the party line. The move didn't stop those reporters who had the local cops' cell phone numbers, but at least it had reduced a flood to a manageable trickle of distractions.

Joe sat back in his desk chair and placed his feet on the edge of a half-open drawer, letting out a sigh of relief.

"Hell of a day. I've read what I could of your updates—including last night's—so thank you all for keeping the information flowing. It's been a big help. Unless I missed anything, I think I got that we've interviewed or reinterviewed the wife—Bonnie—the newspaper delivery guy, the UPS driver who dropped off a package at ten, and the mailman who did his own thing about three hours later. Also, everyone whose number showed up on BB's cell phone, a few of the same people we talked to about Hank days ago, and everybody Bonnie Barrett listed as an alibi for yesterday morning. Last but not least, the crime scene was processed, BB shipped north for autopsy, his house searched, the house's alarm service checked, and—" He paused before wrapping up. "—I don't know what else. Anything?"

"Nothing that matters," Willy said. "Just like everything else on your list. Waste of time."

"Maybe," Joe came back. "Maybe not. Who knows what we've set in motion? There's a chance BB got himself whacked because we stirred up some old memories after Hank was dug up. Could be we hit a sore spot."

"You think he was killed because Hank came back to haunt, so to speak?" Lester asked.

Joe raised his eyebrows suggestively.

"Why?" Lester pressed him. "Hank was no Jimmy Hoffa. It didn't make a splash when he disappeared—same as when we found him."

"Willy said it after Dave was grabbed," Joe explained. "It's one of those coincidences we've learned to distrust. And if we're not ruling out Dave's kidnapping as being possibly connected to the Hank case, why rule out BB's killing? Especially since—unlike with Dave—BB and Hank actually knew each other."

Joe dropped his feet to the floor and sat forward to make his point. "I'm not saying this is all interconnected. But we should absolutely keep it on the table."

Sammie was doubtful, recalling her conversation with Willy earlier. "Even his nearest and dearest figured he'd pulled up stakes for a life-style change. Why would all this be happening over some nobody who's been dead for forty years?"

Willy, however, took a different view. "It would if someone didn't know he'd *been* dead all that time."

"Far out," Spinney said under his breath, after a moment's consideration.

Sammie frowned. "Then that would turn it into a revenge on BB by somebody like Greg or Sharon."

"Or one of Hank's drinking buddies," Willy added. "Hank was a well-loved man, which suggests Lacey Stringer, as well."

Sam rubbed her temples for a couple of seconds. "Hold on. That maybe covers BB. But where's Dave fit in? Assuming that's still a warning to us to back off looking into Hank."

"'Assuming' is the operative word," Joe told her. "Just as we don't want to miss a possible connection between the BB and Hank killings, we also don't want to mess ourselves up by saying they're definitely related. That's even truer for Dave."

Her eyes widened. "What? Which is it, then?"

"Right now?" Willy said, amusing himself. "Both."

"Or neither," Joe added.

Willy laughed. "Let's not forget the holy quartet, after all." He held up one finger at a time. "Lust, lucre, liquor, and lunacy—the four corners of ninety percent of all homicides. Chances are good Bonnie Barrett whacked her hubby so she could redecorate his den."

"Or not," Joe emphasized once more. "In medicine, the old saying is, if you hear the sound of hoofbeats—"

"Yeah, yeah, yeah," Sammie interrupted. "Chances are it's horses. But it may be zebras. The way this is going, it's sounding like everything's a zebra. How do we run not one, but two homicides based on that? And a kidnapping? We have to have at least a couple of theories to run with, don't we?"

Her frustration showed on her face, stirring Joe's sympathy. Sammie Martens did not like ambiguity. There was right and wrong, and a bunch of crap in-between mucking everything up.

"We've barely started," he pointed out, hoping to help her out. "All the interviews we've conducted in the past twenty-four hours? Those were just in case we got lucky and the bad guy burst into tears and fessed up to shooting BB, soon as we walked in. So much for that. Now we need to start chipping away at their alibis, putting their backgrounds under the microscope. If this idea about everything being connected is right, then the same ripple effect that went from Hank being discovered to BB being killed will still be in motion. Somebody benefitted from BB's death. It might've been emotional, or financial, or something I'm not thinking of. But it's there. You don't plug a guy with three bullets and just go back to the way things were."

He stood up and looked at them all. "Our job now is to find out whose life has just changed and how."

CHAPTER FIFTEEN

The best time to sneak up on a paranoid, Dan believed, was when he thought he was most prepared to meet the enemy. Of course, it was Dan's own obsession that informed this theory, and explained why he was again inside Johnny Lucas's house one week later, in the middle of the night, with Lucas and his wife sleeping upstairs.

Even by Dan's risky standards, this was extreme. His only concession, however, was that this time, he'd left his daughter out of the equation. Otherwise, it was business as usual, based not on hubris, but on the reasonable assumption that since Lucas was in residence, he'd be less inclined to have the internal alarm activated.

Dan's two aces were that by now, he was familiar with the intricacies of the system confronting him, and that last time—as was his habit—he'd left behind a secret key of sorts.

Doing so was a private trademark: With almost every house he entered, Dan made enough subtle alterations to make any later re-entries easier—just in case. Some of these were electronic in nature; others purely mechanical, as in rigging a physical lock. In reality, he only rarely took advantage of his ploy later on, it being more a matter of principle than of need.

The problem here, of course, was that he was no longer confident that he'd defeated the house's entire system the first time. As he stood in the Lucases' home, silent and still, he couldn't be sure he wasn't being scrutinized as thoroughly as a bug under a magnifying lens.

The irony of this—the snooper being snooped upon—was lost on Dan Kravitz, whose sense of humor was sparse, at best. For him, tonight's mission was to right a wrong—one he was fearful he'd committed through sloppiness. Willy's suggestion that Dan's first visit here might have resulted in a reprisal upon Lester Spinney's boy had worked on Dan's conscience like acid. However perverse his sense of propriety, Dan's devotion to family and orderliness couldn't stand that he might have violated them both through carelessness.

The problem was that he was very good at what he did, and had been at it for a long time—a combination leaving him with little room to find what he may have missed. Nevertheless, his senses ratcheted up high, he began his survey of the house, almost inch by inch, looking to rule out that he'd been spotted the first time.

Dan had a second, more permanent base than his residence—an office of sorts, located off Arch Street in Brattleboro, alongside the railroad tracks. There, behind a series of locked doors in a building that looked ripe for a wrecking ball, he had an almost sterile laboratory jammed with computers and reference materials, in which he researched not just his people of interest, but where he also kept abreast of the latest developments in surveillance technology.

He therefore fully understood what he might be up against in Lucas's house—cameras had shrunken to the size of buttons, didn't need to be hardwired, and could be placed almost anywhere. There was essentially no aspect of any room—from its contents to its architecture— that didn't offer itself as potential cover for a device.

On the flip side, most of these instruments, and especially the wireless models, emitted signals of some kind. That, along with his experience, is where Dan had an edge. On his own, he'd constructed a portable wavelength sniffer, calibrated to his needs, which he'd brought along. It hadn't yet picked up anything he didn't already know about, but it offered him the kind of security a handgun might have during a stroll through the jungle at night—a little.

The downstairs analysis having been completed in just over two hours, Dan silently climbed the stairs to the bedrooms above.

He was still at a disadvantage, given his usual methods. For starters, under Willy's initial deadline, Dan hadn't had time to establish the nighttime habits of Mr. and Mrs. Lucas—as in, did either of them have a small bladder?

He got his answer with startling abruptness when, as he stood in the upstairs hallway, the nightgown-shrouded form of Lucas's wife appeared five feet in front of him.

He froze, standing in plain view, the glow of a faint night-light as effective here as a searchlight.

But she didn't glance in his direction. She swung away, walked a few feet to the guest bathroom across the hall—which he knew from before that she'd claimed for herself—and noisily placed herself on the toilet, without closing the door.

The safest but longest route to safety was to retrace his steps. But he didn't know how fast she might finish her ritual. He therefore opted for the bolder course of quickly passing before both bedroom and bathroom doors—timing his move to her turning and reaching for the toilet paper—before she re-entered the corridor without washing her hands, and repeated her near miss of him, in reverse.

It had all occurred within moments. He was still safe—or so it felt—but, along with a rapid heartbeat and suddenly being damp with sweat, he'd also had enough. What he'd been searching for was probably downstairs, where he'd found nothing. Mrs. Lucas's near sleepwalking experience implied that no one was tracking Dan's progress. And, finally, now he knew for a fact that the homeowners were clearly no longer fast asleep.

It was time to go.

Nevertheless, he remained of two minds. While he hated to leave unsatisfied, he also remembered that Kunkle had offered no proof of Dan's earlier entry being recorded—or used to target David Spinney. Indeed, Dan's lack of success tonight reinforced that Willy had merely been responding to his own hyped-up fantasies.

This wasn't a bad thing, Dan thought. If nothing else, he could say as much to Kunkle later, and perhaps help him to pursue an alternative scent.

Feeling better, Dan retreated as carefully as he'd advanced, and found himself in the cool night air some twenty minutes later.

It was only then that he tumbled to what he'd been seeking all along.

Leaving the building, he'd carefully attached his wavelength detector to the harness he wore on these adventures. But he hadn't shut it off, nor had he removed the earpiece he used to eavesdrop on its probings. That turned out to be a piece of good luck.

He froze in place upon hearing the unexpected signal, and carefully unhooked the detector to better interpret the tone's direction, strength, and distance.

All three came as a surprise. Exterior cameras were nothing new. In general, they outnumbered inside units, both because of their practicality and cost—they could be bigger, more obvious, and thus cheaper.

But they were usually attached to the houses they protected. What Dan quickly calculated was that this signal was originating from nowhere near the building, and, in fact, came from across the road and off the property altogether. Had he not been facing the wrong way, Dan never would have heard it.

This was a first for him, and it put him in a quandary. Not only was he being documented by a camera he hadn't known about, but the possibility existed that while it was watching the Lucas residence, it didn't belong to Johnny Lucas.

Kravitz met with Kunkle early the next morning, still dressed in black, as he had been inside the Lucas house—if minus the ski mask he habitually wore.

"You sure about this?" Willy pressed him after hearing his report.

"Yes," Dan confirmed. "I had nothing to lose by then, so I tracked down not just the unit that had triggered my detector, but two more that were placed at different angles. They were all wireless and remote, all equipped with long-lasting batteries and hidden solar panels, and, from what I could determine, all rigged to use the house's own Wi-Fi router for transmission, meaning that whoever was at the receiving end could be anywhere in the country, or outside it, for that matter."

"Damn," Willy said. "I wish to hell we could figure out what that's all about. The make and model didn't tell you anything?"

"I couldn't get that close. I doubt it would have mattered."

Willy nodded thoughtfully and gave his CI a sympathetic look. "What're you gonna do now?"

"Since I may have been caught twice on camera?" Dan asked. "It depends on who's doing the watching. You do realize this still doesn't prove a linkage between my visits and what happened to your colleague's son."

"Prove?" Willy asked. "Yeah. I know that. But come on. Sure as hell something's going on."

"Can't you do something legal?"

"No probable cause, not to mention it's in the wrong state. We don't even know for sure those three cameras *aren't* Lucas's."

Dan didn't argue. He had more pressing concerns. "Mr. Kunkle, do any of your colleagues know about our relationship?"

"My wife—" Willy stopped himself, startled by having used that word to describe Sammie. "One of them does, but she knows not to repeat it. You're worried, aren't you?"

"I'd be an idiot not to be," Dan said plainly.

Willy shared the concern, and was embarrassed by his role in the man's predicament. "You want help?"

Dan was sensitive enough to know what was going on, and irritated enough not to let Kunkle off the hook. "In what way?"

"I don't know. Maybe we could park you someplace."

"As in jail? Where did you have in mind?"

"No. That wouldn't work."

Dan moved in slightly, forcing Willy to look at him. "I wasn't being serious, and nor are you."

Willy didn't respond.

"Mr. Kunkle," Dan stated. "I think we've just officially entered a new arrangement. I do not owe you a thing any longer. Is that agreeable?"

Willy didn't hesitate. "Yeah."

"I won't bring attention to myself, as before, but you leave me alone. Clear?"

Willy nodded. "You could've gotten me in almost as much trouble as I could've gotten you."

"If that helps you in your decision, fine," Dan told him.

"It's not that," Willy came back, surprised by how Dan's tone had stung him. "I just meant I didn't really see you as a CI anyhow. More like an ally."

"Well, now you can consider me a nodding acquaintance."

Willy's eyes narrowed. "You've made your point. I still have a vested interest in your safety. I put you in this mess."

"Nice of you to say," Dan said honestly. "If I need you, I'll reach out. Until then, please leave us alone." He stuck out his hand—an unusual gesture for him, as Kunkle well knew. "Deal?"

"Deal," Willy said quietly, shaking hands mournfully.

Dan walked away. Willy watched him go, hoping it wouldn't be for the last time.

Dressed in worn jeans and a baseball cap, sitting at the wheel of his battered, secondhand pickup truck, David Spinney was parked along a darkened backstreet in Bellows Falls, a village of roughly one square mile, whose problems—social, political, and financial—had always seemed disproportionate to its small size.

The perpetual irony of the place was that aesthetically, it was quite appealing, in part due to a cluster of abandoned mill buildings that had once made of the town a bustling and prosperous community. Sadly, the quaintness was largely skin deep, and it was, in fact, this darker underlayment, stubbornly resistant to improvement, that had drawn David here, late at night, on his mission of self-redemption.

He knew he was on shaky ground, and that the sheriff, his father, Joe Gunther, and probably even his kid sister would be rolling their eyes had they known of his ambitions.

But they didn't—nor would they—if he had anything to say about it, at least not until he'd achieved his goal.

He'd never been one to strut around or put on airs. He harbored no embarrassment about loving his parents and seeing the value of a good education, or being patriotic, or having integrity. He believed in all that. But he'd been unnerved by what happened to him—perhaps more so because it had ended so benignly. The sheriff might have hoodwinked the press, but law enforcement's rumor mill was something else, and Dave knew all too well how that bunch loved to rag on one of their own, especially if he was young, unproved, and the son of a colleague.

For Dave, there was no question that they be delivered a more positive final impression—and that he'd be the one to deliver it.

That wishful thought remained in the future, however. Right now, he was staking out the address of someone he knew nothing about, except for what he'd read on a rap sheet, which wasn't much. If it hadn't been for the tattoo, in fact, Dave would never have stopped at Steve Hobart's name. Hobart appeared as just another aging teenager, hanging out with the wrong people and trying hard to become one of them.

Two hours into his vigil, Dave spotted Hobart leaving his apartment house, highlighted by a nearby streetlamp. Even before he raised his binoculars for a closer look, Dave knew that he'd located his man. Seeing the clear and colorful rendering of the dragon on Hobart's left shoulder, peering out from under the trendily torn shirtsleeve, came only as confirmation.

Along with that recognition, however, came an unexpected problem. Dave was a cop—no longer simply a young man near bursting with outrage. His actions involved greater consequences than those of a civilian who could simply confront an opponent and bash him over the head. Hobart had done more than debase David Spinney—he'd also broken the law and violated the uniform. It was that law and uniform that had to be honored now—Dave's personal restitution would have to follow.

This did not involve a belabored internal debate. Dave had watched his father act within the same constraints for as long as he could recall. More, he'd seen Lester live by an equally strict moral code in his dealings with his wife, and children, and the people he encountered every day.

David therefore knew where the right course lay, but it did make him angry.

"Fine," he conceded, lowering the binoculars and starting up the truck as Hobart climbed into his own car and backed out of the pot-holed driveway.

Dave's dilemma was that he had no proof of Hobart's guilt beyond his own split second's glimpse of a popular tattoo. Also, he couldn't account for Hobart's confederates, had no idea of what alibi he might tender in his own defense, and had no corroboration or witnesses to line up against him.

As a result, now that he had his target identified, Dave needed time to build a case.

Satisfied at last, if missing the gratification of a cleansing outburst of violence, Dave turned on his radio, pulled into the street, and slipped into Hobart's wake.

CHAPTER SIXTEEN

"Full disclosure, boss."

Joe sat back and cupped his cheek in his hand, eyeing Willy from across the office. He'd suspected something amiss when he noticed Sammie's averted glance upon her entrance moments earlier.

Lester stopped typing, anticipating whatever might be coming.

"Do tell," Joe said.

Willy's phrasing was conspicuously precise. "In the best interests of all concerned, I will not go into details, but let's say that if you or any member of the public were to drive down River Road in West Chester-field and pause opposite the Lucas residence, you might be able to pick out three very well hidden surveillance cameras, aimed at that house."

He paused, allowing Joe to ask, with equal care, "By 'opposite,' I'm assuming you mean across the road, and therefore not on land belonging to Mr. Lucas."

"That is correct."

"Are there any visible connections between the Lucas property and those three cameras?"

"None. In fact, if you had the right equipment, and used it standing in the public right-of-way, you'd probably discover that the radio signals from those units are directed right at the house, and use its router to be broadcast wherever."

Joe smiled. Willy smiled back. Sam and Les watched them both.

"I guess, then," Joe finally said, "that I can only express my gratitude for your extraordinary eyesight—honed to a sharp edge during your employment by the United States government—and for bringing this observation to our attention."

Willy sidled around to his chair and sat down. "You're very welcome."

Lester was shaking his head. "Are you two done? I think we can now say, if we're ever deposed or put on the stand, that this discovery fell into the 'plain view' category." He clapped his hands. "Nicely done."

Joe let loose a frown in Willy's direction, silently challenging the truth of his story. "If you say so."

Sammie moved the conversation along. "If it is what it looks like, who has him under surveillance?"

"And why?" Lester added.

Sam was reading her computer screen. "Boss, after BB was found dead and we all split up to check alibis, it says here that you went back to Lucas's, quote-unquote, without effect. I take it that means you got the same treatment as last time?"

"Right."

She took them all in with her next question. "Has anyone ever set eyes on this guy?"

"Presumably his old drinking buddies," Lester said, based on his conversation with Jimmy Stringer and Carlo Fuentes. "Although I don't think I asked them when that last was."

"Stringer's wife," Sammie offered, "told me she hadn't seen Lucas since Ridgeline sold to Vermont Amalgamated and BB and Johnny went their separate ways."

"That was years ago," Joe said.

"She also said Johnny kept to himself."

"What about the fusion report on Lucas?" Joe asked. "What's that say about him?"

Lester read from a printout. "I just ran that off. The fusion center collects everything, as you know—local tax records, driver's license, car registrations, houses sold and bought, criminal offenses, marriages and divorces, family members, even next-door neighbors. Given all that, Lucas looks boring as hell. Married to the same woman for ages, nothing criminal, no kids, owns a boat, stuff like that."

"When's it say he was born?" Joe asked.

"Nineteen forty-seven."

"And when's the first entry on that report?"

"Bingo," Willy said from the sidelines. "Great minds think alike."

"Nineteen sixty-nine," Lester responded after a moment's scrutiny. He glanced up. "You thinking witness protection?"

"Wouldn't be the first time," Joe said.

"Especially back then," Willy contributed, looking contemplative. "Wild and woolly times."

Joe made a sour face. "Great. If that's true, there's no way the marshals're going to tell us about it—not without a warrant, and there's no way we have grounds for one of those."

Willy and Sam remained silent as Lester asked, "Even after all this time? Couldn't we claim exigent circumstances?"

"I'll try," Joe said. "But I already know the answer. They're rigid about that. Always have been. And it's not like we have a smoking gun."

He looked at his other two squad members. "No suggestions?"

"Not for that," Willy said vaguely.

Joe studied him a moment, wondering where Willy's mind had wandered—and what therefore lay in store.

He turned his attention to Les and Sammie. "Well, I do. I think it's time we buddy up with New Hampshire law enforcement and stop being so polite about meeting Johnny Lucas. We need to put an interview into him, sooner the better. That'll also tell us if he's in witness protection, and fast, too, if I know the marshals. By the way, with what Willy has just given us, are any of you still thinking the Hank and BB murders are unrelated?"

No one answered.

"It's not like they both don't need solving. That being said, I think we should really focus on that connection as our primary working theory, especially given some of the other oddball angles that're cropping up."

"Like my son?" Lester proposed.

"For example," Joe agreed. "Any developments there?"

"Not really," Lester told them. "Dave's back on the job. The press seems to have swallowed the sheriff's cover story, and the real scoop hasn't leaked so far. Meanwhile, the cops chasing it down can't find much to chew on, so I don't know if it'll be hitting the fan or not."

"Well, keep in touch with them—with an eye to what we're working on."

"What the hell *are* we working on, exactly?" Willy challenged, back from his reverie. "Is it really an avalanche, starting with Hank being dug up? If it is, it's not moving much. We have no leads on his case, no leads on who shot Barrett, no clue if Dave's adventure is related or not, and now we maybe got some wild card involving Johnny Lucas—whose name may not be Johnny Lucas."

Joe was nodding as Willy finished. "I couldn't agree more. But the avalanche image may be to our advantage. We just need to figure out which part to kick loose to discover how everything is interconnected."

"If it is," Lester said.

"Right," Joe continued. "Right now, the Barrett case is on the hot plate. For sanity's sake, we better assume that whoever shot him is still alive and well, and still in the neighborhood. Also, if we think that BB was killed because of Hank resurfacing as a homicide, then maybe that tells us the triggerman was also around forty years ago."

"Triggerman or -woman," Willy pointed out.

"You mean Sharon?" Joe asked.

"Or Lacey Stringer," Sam threw in, adding, "And don't leave out Bonnie Barrett, the grieving rich widow, in case we're wrong about the two murders being linked."

"All right," Joe picked up. "Start with Sharon. Loved Hank, but tossed him out because of another woman—according to her. She's then wooed by BB, but rejects him with no hard feelings. Everything ends happily ever after, unless she killed Hank because of his philandering. Question is: How and with whom? She couldn't've pulled it off alone. And even if she had help, what happened to him—or her—and why did she now kill BB?"

No one answered, knowing his question to be rhetorical.

"Lacey," he continued. "She loved Hank, too, which as Willy pointed out last time, is one of the four Ls. Following that logic, did she kill him? Same questions as for Sharon, if so. Why? Who with, et cetera?"

He took them in with a glance, waiting for objections or suggestions. Again, there was silence.

"Last but not least, Bonnie. It's true that there are no indications she goes back to the Hank era, but as Sam said, she's sitting pretty now. Did she make that happen?"

"She has an alibi," Lester said. "Complete with witnesses."

"Moving on to the men," Joe spoke without pause, although nodding once in Lester's direction as acknowledgment. "Fuentes, Stringer, Neathawk, Greg Mitchell, and Lucas are the ones we know about. Tom Capsen died."

"Neathawk's dead, too," Lester announced. "I meant to tell you. Just got confirmation. Car crash out west, twenty years ago."

"Fuentes also has an alibi for the BB shooting," Sammie said.

"Why not list Lucas first?" Willy asked. "He's the elephant in the room."

"I don't want to ignore the others in his favor," Joe explained. "But what about Lucas, Willy? You have anything on him we don't?"

Joe saw Sam cut Willy a look, but the latter merely shook his head. "Only what I told you. He is the one with the other *L* in the game, though: loot. He worked under Hank and became BB's number two man after Hank left the picture. Which means this could be a lot easier than we're making it. After Hank was established as a murder victim instead of a disappearing act, it may have thrown BB and Lucas into conflict somehow."

"Winner take all?" Lester said.

"More like loser take his story to the grave," Willy suggested. "It still doesn't explain who's got Lucas under surveillance—unless BB rigged those cameras before he was croaked."

There was a telling pause in the room, prompting Joe to say, his frustration clear, "I'll reach out to New Hampshire—see about getting Lucas out from behind his front door. Somebody's got to know something, for Chrissake. What about the other two on our list—Greg Mitchell and Stringer?"

"I went by the cabins to see Mitchell again," Willy said. "No luck this time, but I'll go back. I got a feeling when we talked first that he was holding back. I'll find him."

"Stringer was mine," Sam reported. "I found him as usual in Carlo's bar, his home away from home, but he told me to drop dead. Wouldn't give me squat about his whereabouts when BB was killed."

"That can be changed," Willy said menacingly.

Sam took it in stride. "No need. He was showing off 'cause he knew he was safe. I rounded up Carlo and Lacey later—individually—and they both accounted for him being at home or at the bar during our time slot. Lacey even said she wished she couldn't cover his ass—her words—but there it was."

Joe looked disappointed. "Okay. Thanks. Let's keep digging, then. But please"—here he looked pointedly at Willy and Sam—"no more dancing around the letter of the law. This is tough enough without opening up another can of worms."

"Yes, boss," Sam said.

Willy, as befit his style, stayed silent.

"God, I felt uncomfortable at that squad meeting," Sammie said later, placing a bag of groceries onto the kitchen counter, next to the fridge. "It was like lying to Joe's face."

"Oh, please," Willy protested. "And that was worse than getting fired? What he doesn't know won't hurt him. I told him about the cameras."

He was sitting at the kitchen table, Emma in her portable playpen nearby, contentedly whacking at a plastic keyboard with a wooden spoon. Outside the window, a neighbor was mowing his lawn, taking advantage of the day's extended light. Sammie had just walked in, having stopped by the store on the way home. Willy had been there several hours already, with proof of his labors scattered across the tabletop.

Sammie cast it a glance. "I take it that's from Dan Kravitz's midnight outing?"

Willy laughed, making Emma look up and smile. "I like that. Right—the inner life of Johnny Lucas."

Sam crossed to the pen and scooped her daughter up into her arms, making the child chortle happily. She buried her face in Emma's neck, blew a raspberry, and twirled her around the room.

"Find anything interesting?" Sam asked, still dancing.

"Yeah. I don't know if he's in witness protection—it's not like they give those guys a special ball cap or anything—but I'll guarantee he wasn't born Johnny Lucas. For one thing, can you lay your hands on your social security card? Right now?"

Sam stopped to stare at him. "I don't know. Maybe. I haven't seen it in years."

"Right," Willy said, holding up a copy of one. "And if you could, it wouldn't look like this—pristine as the day it was printed, which sure wasn't in the 1940s. Just like exhibit number two." He held up another document. "His birth certificate—also fresh off the press, by the looks of it."

Sammie kissed Emma and returned her to the playpen, where she began foraging through her plush animals. Sam pulled a chair alongside Willy's. "Cool. What else?"

"Usual stuff—insurance records, tax receipts, utility bills, bank statements. It's what's missing that's interesting—no photo albums, no old letters, no framed pictures pre-dating the early 1970s. He married Linda Lucas—making her sound like a sitcom character to me—but that was seventeen years ago, after he made most of his dough. So, there's junk in this pile relating to them, but nothing like most people have—keepsakes, pictures of parents, grandparents, shit like that. My gut tells me that if someone went wandering around some small-town cemetery somewhere, they'd eventually find a headstone for a John Lucas who died at the age of three months, or something. That's how people used to steal identities back then—ask the local town clerk for a reissued birth certificate—" Here he held up Lucas's version. "—and then start building from there—social security, eventually a passport. After you finally got something with a photo on it, you were off to the races. The resurrection of Johnny Lucas."

Sammie was looking intrigued but skeptical. "How many of those old documents do any of us have? If you didn't like where you came from, or maybe grew up in an orphanage, you wouldn't have any mementos, either."

Unusually for him, Willy didn't argue. "Maybe. Linda has items going back to her childhood, but there's nothing for him—no high school yearbook, no old favorite toy or baseball or hat, no beaten-up books or knickknacks with a sentimental value. You and I have some of that. Both of us do."

Now it was her turn. "You're right." She reached out and pushed some of the papers around haphazardly. "So what do we do?"

"Well, the boss is right about squeezing Johnny. That's an obvious first step. But if I'm right that there's something wrong about him, he's gonna clam up."

Willy leaned back, staring thoughtfully at Dan Kravitz's stolen treasure trove. "I'd be more inclined to go after the lovely Mrs. Lucas—see what pillow talk she and the hubby might've shared." He let out a sigh and checked his watch. "But that's the boss's turf now. Me, I'm gonna see if ol' Greg's decided to come home."

Tony Tribuno had been Chesterfield's police chief for more years than even he could remember. A mostly picturesque rural patch of New Hampshire, located between the Connecticut River and Keene, and bisected by the heavily traveled Route 9, Chesterfield was also host to a couple of large parks and a popular boating, fishing, and swimming magnet named Spofford Lake. As a result, Tribuno and his officers routinely had their hands full with rowdy tourists, reckless drivers, and a steady diet of thieves and burglars who used Route 9 as a quick getaway after filling their trunks from the seasonal homes dotting the map.

It wasn't New York City, but nor was it some modern version of Mayberry, North Carolina. And Tony Tribuno—an old friend of Joe's—was no rube.

They agreed to meet at one of the gas stations on Route 9, overlooking the twin bridges spanning the river, connecting West Chesterfield to Brattleboro. The two parallel, metal arch bridges—one rusted, closed off, and dating back to the Depression; the other a wider copy, but not fifteen years old—represented the almost farcical end result of years of political wrangling.

Instead of simply tearing the old one down and replacing it with its safer but equally attractive replacement, the powers that be decided to keep the old-timer as a pedestrian span, but not to maintain it. They gave it a new name, dubbed it a historical artifact, and watched benignly while some locals struggled to transform it into a "bridge of flowers." To Joe, the fact remained that a structure once deemed too dangerous to travel had been sanctified in order not to pay for its dismantling. Now, glowing like a postcard in the setting sun, the end result was a bizarre double image, one half of which looked ready to fall into the water.

Joe was reflecting on all this when Tony pulled up in his threatening black Dodge Charger police car, his open and pleasant face at odds with the vehicle's hormonal growl.

"You liking how it feels to be in a non-Socialist state?" Tony asked, rolling down his window.

Joe shook hands. "I'm a happy Vermonter, Tony. Give me taxes and tree huggers over a state motto that reads, 'Live, Freeze, and Die' any day."

Tribuno laughed and waited for a convoy of loud motorcycles to roar past, headed east. "Right. Meantime, all your countrymen come blasting over here, where they can eat cheap, avoid taxes, and not wear helmets."

"Cruel, Tony. Cruel."

Tribuno wrapped it up, the subject as threadbare as the jokes. "But not that off base. So, you want to roust one of our fine citizens without a warrant?"

"You hear about our Concrete Man?" Joe asked him.

"Who hasn't? That's what you get for living in that slum."

"Well, West Chesterfield resident Johnny—or more properly,

John—Lucas used to work with the guy in the old days, before everybody thought he'd headed for California to enjoy the fun and sun."

"Ouch," Tony said sympathetically. "So much for Plan A. And you think Lucas had something to do with his becoming part of a building slab?"

"For starters. Lucas used to work for the guy who got shot a few days ago."

"No kidding? Clearly not a guy to stand next to in a storm."

"Nope. Which is why we wouldn't mind having a chat with him," Joe confirmed. "So far, though, all we've talked to is a speaker by the front door, telling us to disappear. I thought having you and the Batmobile along might make a better impression than my out-of-state badge."

Tony nodded. "Glad I wore a uniform today. Let's go be intimidating."

Ten minutes later, the two cops pulled up alongside the Lucas house in separate vehicles, Joe not willing to leave his back at the gas station. The stark, sharp-edged building remained as silent and still as an abandoned bunker. As Joe got out of his car, he studied the trees across the road—having earlier asked Willy precisely where the mystery cameras were located.

"What're you looking at?" Tony asked him, walking up.

"Nothing," Joe answered. "I'm supposed to be seeing some discreetly placed surveillance cameras. Up there." He pointed.

Tony followed his gaze. "'Discreetly' must be the operative word. I don't see anything."

"They're gone," Joe said.

Tribuno let that sink in. "Huh. Weird. Were they trained on people like us, or your shy pal inside?"

Joe gave him a look. "That's one of our growing list of problems—we think they were there to watch him."

"And now they've disappeared."

"Apparently."

Tribuno pondered that before asking, "What the hell have you dumped on us, Gunther? Being your next-door neighbor used to be a lot more fun."

Joe wasn't so sure that was true. Back when Hank Mitchell was entombed, Brattleboro had been like a western bar town, straight out of the movies.

He turned and indicated the forbidding house. "Shall we?"

"Absolutely." Tony Tribuno shifted his gun belt slightly and marched toward the front door.

"Yes?" a female voice asked over the speaker, moments after he'd pressed the bell. "May I help you?"

Tony's voice was suddenly lower and more authoritative. "This is the Chesterfield Police, ma'am. We'd like to have a word."

"What about?"

"Please open the door, ma'am."

There was a moment when Joe thought they'd hear only a variation of the familiar theme, when the voice responded, "Yes. Okay. I'll be right there."

"Miracles'll never cease," Joe said in an undertone.

Tony smiled and rocked slightly on his heels. "It's the uniform, man."

"Of course it is." On a more serious level, however, Joe did wonder about the change.

The door swung back to reveal a worried-looking woman, her hair tousled and her eyes wide. "Oh, my God. Did you find him? Is he okay?"

Both men hesitated before Joe asked, "Is Johnny missing?"

She opened her mouth, closed it again, and then asked in turn, "You didn't find him?"

"We didn't know he was lost," Tony explained. "Did you call the police?"

She stared at the ground, touching her temple with her fingertips. She shook her head. "He wouldn't like that."

"When did you last see him?" Joe asked.

"When we went to bed. He must've left in the middle of the night." She slumped against the doorframe and began crying. "What's going on?"

Tony looked at Joe, who shrugged and answered, "Fair question."

CHAPTER SEVENTEEN

"Have a seat, Mrs. Lucas."

Joe had found an office down the hall from the VBI, on the Municipal Building's second floor, whose occupant he knew to be out of town for the week.

"Could I get you a cup of coffee or a soda?"

The still distraught Linda Lucas settled nervously onto a padded metal chair and shook her head. "No. I'm fine. Thank you."

Joe sat across from her and laid a small recorder on the table nearby. "With your permission, I'd like to record this, so there are no misunderstandings later on. That okay?"

She barely glanced at it and nodded. "Like I care."

In that context, Joe recited his and her names out loud, along with the day's date, before asking her, "How long have you known Johnny Lucas, Linda?"

"We've been married seventeen years."

"Any kids?"

"No. Johnny didn't want them."

Joe gave her a sympathetic look. "Was that hard to hear?"

Her response was unexpectedly honest. "At first. Do you know where Johnny is, Mr. Gunther?"

"No. I wasn't misleading you, Linda. I have no idea. What did he do for a living?"

"Now? Or what did he used to do?"

"Both, if you don't mind."

"Will this help find him?"

"I hope so. It's like being asked to find a missing child. You have to know what they look like, what their interests are, their friends. All of that. If you want our help, everything and anything might be useful."

She considered that for a moment. "Okay. Is he in trouble, though?"

"Not as far as we know," Joe answered truthfully.

"Why did you want to talk to him?"

He paused, impressed by her asking questions, instead of just following his lead. At this early stage, he wasn't sure if that reflected a native intelligence, or past experience of being too open with law enforcement.

"An old business associate of your husband's died recently—"

"You mean BB?"

"Yes. So we've been trying to interview everyone who knew him. Not surprisingly, Johnny's name came up."

"They were old friends. Helped build a roofing business together. You asked what Johnny used to do—that was it. Ridgeline Roofing. BB owned it, but Johnny played a big role in making it a success."

"Were he and BB friends recently, as well?" Joe asked hopefully.

But she disappointed him. "Not in years. BB created a new company, or merged with somebody. I forget which. Anyhow, he kept with the business, where Johnny had had enough."

"What did Johnny do next?"

"Investments," she answered simply.

"Like, stocks?"

She shrugged. "I guess so. I know nothing about business. That's what he called them—investments."

Joe suffered a moment of envy. In TV shows, this was where one detective turned to the other with instructions to "get a warrant for his bank records." In reality, that wasn't so easy.

"How's he been seeming lately? Different at all? At the house, you showed us a note from him saying something came up and he'd be gone for a while. That sounds unusual. Is that why you're worried?"

Her expression returned to its look of concern. "He's been nervous as a cat. I kept asking him what was wrong, but he wouldn't tell me. He said it was a big business deal and he had a lot riding on it. That scared me a little, so I asked if we were in trouble, but he said absolutely not—that he never messed with our savings, and he hadn't this time, either. He was just excited, is all."

"Did you believe him?"

She hesitated. "Not really," she then conceded. "This couldn't've been the first big deal he'd ever done, and he's never acted like he did this time, disappearing and leaving a note. Before, I figured he just didn't want to tell me, and I respected that. That was our deal. But now, I don't know."

"Your deal?"

"When we got married. He said he had a complicated financial life—that he liked it that way—and that, number one, he'd never risk our own funds, and two, that I wasn't to bug him about it. It was separate from us."

"Was it?" Joe wanted to know. "Truly?"

She seemed to consider that. "Yes."

"But there must've been meetings," Joe pressed her. "Phone calls. Maybe even business trips, now and then?"

"Of course. All the time. I just didn't ask about them, and he didn't say."

"And he was never upset or unhappy after one of those trips, or one of those phone calls?"

She shook her head. "No. He was very good about that."

"Were you close?"

She didn't take offense, although Joe wouldn't have minded if she had. Her answer was ready and apparently open. "We were best friends. Maybe that was helped by not having kids, and lots of money. We could travel where we wanted, and take vacations whenever. Neither one of us really had a job—not a nine-to-five one, anyhow. So, if the impulse grabbed us, and we both thought it'd be fun, we'd just go."

"What kind of places?"

"Hawaii, Paris, the Grand Canyon. It didn't matter. How's this going to help find him, Mr. Gunther?"

"Let's talk about his friends," Joe suggested. "Not so much those you'd have dinner or go to the movies with. More like business types. You meet any of them?"

"No. That was the dividing line I was talking about. He kept that away from me."

"Did he have an office somewhere, outside the house?" Joe asked.

"Not that I know of," was the answer.

"All right," Joe redirected the conversation. "Maybe we *should* discuss the social friends. Were any of them particularly close to your husband, in a best-buddy kind of way?"

Linda thought again. "Not really," she said. "Johnny's not too outgoing. I mean, he's friendly, and he never said no when I suggested having dinner with someone. But it's not something he did on his own. He likes to keep to himself—doing business or watching sports on TV, or going out on the river in the boat. And," she added with a sad smile, "our trips together. He does enjoy those. Or did."

Joe was touched by her awkward use of present and past tense when referring to him. "Mrs. Lucas. Linda. What do you think might have happened here?"

Her eyes teared up. "I don't know. He seemed so on edge lately—even looking out the windows at traffic. And he was fussing with the security system just yesterday, complaining that it wasn't acting right. I can't get it out of my mind that something terrible has happened."

She scrounged around in her purse and produced a small pack of tissues, with which she dabbed her eyes, trying to keep her makeup in place.

"Where did Johnny come from, originally?" Joe asked.

"New York, I think," she said, studying the tissue for mascara.

"Where, exactly?"

She looked up. "Oh, I don't know. He never said."

"Really? That's unusual, isn't it? You probably told him all about where you grew up."

She laughed without much enthusiasm. "Yeah. I never shut up. That's what some people say."

"I didn't mean it that way," Joe said quickly.

But she waved that off. "It doesn't matter. Johnny said nothing good happened where he came from, so he didn't want to talk about it."

"No family, either?"

"He said the less he thought about them, the better. It was incredibly sad. I have two sisters, and we're on the phone all the time, or on Facebook. They mean the world to me. But Johnny didn't have anybody. It was like he was an orphan."

"But he wasn't?"

"Not really, no. I think he just had such a terrible time as a kid that he didn't want to think back. I always figured that had something to do with his not wanting children. But he might've been an orphan. I just don't know. He never said."

Her tears welled up again as she added, "He's such a nice man—especially after some I've known. He's private and a little reserved sometimes, but he's always been good to me. I want to know what's happened."

"Let's roll back the clock a little, Linda," Joe suggested. "When Johnny spoke about his early years with BB, building up the business with Hank Mitchell and the others, how did he refer to all that? Did he have good memories of those days?"

That diverted her from a new bout of crying. She blinked several times while she reflected. "I suppose. It was more like he mentioned it in passing—you know what I mean? You have to understand that my husband has a careful way of speaking sometimes. He doesn't babble like me. He's quiet a lot, and he thinks before he says stuff. Some people think he's cold, or insincere, because they don't understand. But he's just being thoughtful."

Or careful, Joe reflected.

"So you never got an impression of how he felt about any of those people?"

"Not really. Apart from BB, of course, but even there, like I said, that friendship cooled."

"I want to ask you about something more recent, Linda," Joe began. "And it's important that you understand that I've asked the same thing of everyone I've talked to recently, so it's not a loaded question in any way. Okay?"

She looked confused. "Okay."

"On the day of BB's death," he continued. "What was Johnny up to? I just want to account for his whereabouts, for the record."

Her reaction caught him off guard. Her face brightened as she said, "Oh—that's easy. We were at Stratton, overnight. They had a wine-tasting event, with localvore cheeses and cured meats and music. It was wonderful. It was a Welcome to Spring theme. Really festive. We had a great time."

"You said overnight?" Joe asked.

"Yes. It started in the afternoon and ran till late. We spent the night and had brunch the next morning. That's when we heard about BB, on the news."

"Lot of people there with you?" Joe asked.

"It was jammed. Johnny wasn't crazy about that part, but he still had fun. It was a pain getting our car the next morning because of the crowd. It was really popular. I guess everybody was a little stir-crazy after the winter we had."

"What do you mean, getting your car was a pain?"

"Well, we'd arrived early enough the day before that they buried it in the back row, so when we wanted to leave the next morning, it was a whole ordeal getting it out. There was something about another car that they couldn't get started. Anyhow, it took a while. Johnny wasn't too thrilled."

"How did he take the news about BB?"

Her mood sombered as she considered the question. "It was funny, now that you mention it. He was quiet for a long time, as if he couldn't really make up his mind. I'd always wondered why they'd drifted apart, not that you don't hear of that happening between old business partners, but still . . ."

"Did he say anything later on?"

"No," she answered thoughtfully. "That was it. He just seemed to process it, and then left it at that. But it was afterwards that he started acting weird."

"What about several days before BB died? When I came by and knocked on your door, just looking for a conversation about old times at Ridgeline Roofing?" Joe asked. "Did Johnny act oddly after that? Or make any comments you recall?"

She gave him a blank look. "You came by? I didn't know that."

"I rang the bell. He answered over the intercom."

She smiled slightly. "Oh, right. He did that a lot. It's not like a regular bell, and he doesn't want me answering the door anyhow—at least not when he's there. He was pretty concerned about security, so I let him do all that. He'd talk to people who rang, and I didn't pay attention. Our friends all knew to call ahead, so anyone who just dropped by was pretty sure to be a stranger." She paused again. "I'm sorry he didn't let you in. I don't know why he didn't."

"He didn't say the police had come by?"

"No."

"Today was actually the third time."

She frowned, her expression darkening. "What's going on, Mr. Gunther? Where's Johnny?" she repeated.

"I wish I knew," Joe said, rising and inviting her to stand. "More than you can imagine." He paused to ask further, "Does your husband have a cell phone? We could possibly use that to trace his whereabouts."

She shook her head. "He left it behind."

As they reached the door to the borrowed office, he tried a different tack: "In light of all this, Mrs. Lucas, to help us locate Johnny as quickly as we can, would you allow me or one of my officers access to his papers? It might be extraordinarily useful."

She stopped dead in her tracks. "I don't know about that," she said nervously. "I told you how private he is. I think he'd hate that."

"It's up to you, of course," he said soothingly. "But you are the one who thinks something bad may have happened."

She was stuck. "I don't know. . . ."

Her reaction caught him off guard. Her face brightened as she said, "Oh—that's easy. We were at Stratton, overnight. They had a wine-tasting event, with localvore cheeses and cured meats and music. It was wonderful. It was a Welcome to Spring theme. Really festive. We had a great time."

"You said overnight?" Joe asked.

"Yes. It started in the afternoon and ran till late. We spent the night and had brunch the next morning. That's when we heard about BB, on the news."

"Lot of people there with you?" Joe asked.

"It was jammed. Johnny wasn't crazy about that part, but he still had fun. It was a pain getting our car the next morning because of the crowd. It was really popular. I guess everybody was a little stir-crazy after the winter we had."

"What do you mean, getting your car was a pain?"

"Well, we'd arrived early enough the day before that they buried it in the back row, so when we wanted to leave the next morning, it was a whole ordeal getting it out. There was something about another car that they couldn't get started. Anyhow, it took a while. Johnny wasn't too thrilled."

"How did he take the news about BB?"

Her mood sombered as she considered the question. "It was funny, now that you mention it. He was quiet for a long time, as if he couldn't really make up his mind. I'd always wondered why they'd drifted apart, not that you don't hear of that happening between old business partners, but still . . ."

"Did he say anything later on?"

"No," she answered thoughtfully. "That was it. He just seemed to process it, and then left it at that. But it was afterwards that he started acting weird."

CHAPTER EIGHTEEN

It was after sunset when Willy drove up the dirt road above Brattleboro, his windows open to the night air. Ahead of him, unfolding in the headlights like the twin tread marks of a Caterpillar tractor, the rutted, gluey, twisting narrow road came at him in bold relief, making the surface's gleaming texture look worse than it was. In fact, many of Vermont's roads were slippery washboards like this—especially after winter—and served the state well enough, if perhaps not to the tastes of many transplants from farther south.

And, as familiar and comfortable as he'd become with such terrain—and this particular address—Willy almost missed the poorly marked entrance to Greg Mitchell's cluster of remote cottages.

He racked the wheel harshly, slithered into the driveway, and ground up the curving slope, seeing the ghostly row of small and isolated homes rise up before him, one by one—four-walled cells of people self-banished from the rest of the world.

At the end, separate from the others, as seemingly abandoned as the severed caboose of a forgotten train, Willy again found Greg's tiny cabin, its one window spilling light onto the surrounding grass.

He sensed how that might force her to go, and tried for a compromise. "Tell you what: If you accompany whoever comes by, you could control whatever they examine. How would that be? We just want to help."

"Nothing tricky?" she asked.

"You call the shots," he reassured her.

She nodded reluctantly. "Okay."

Excellent, he thought, betraying nothing.

True to his nature, he parked at a distance and got out of the car without a sound, drifting over to the window to ascertain what he might find upon knocking on the door. Inside the one-room house, Greg sat in the single chair, an open newspaper on his lap, but staring at the floor before him.

Willy waited a couple of minutes, watching to see if this posture was temporary or a reflection of something more—a body-language glimpse into a man at sea within himself.

Greg never moved. Willy sidestepped to his right and knocked.

Mitchell opened the door and stood staring at him—tall, heavy, bearded, and silent.

Willy brushed by him, establishing control. "We need to talk," he said.

His impromptu host turned, the door still open.

"Close it," Willy told him. "You'll let in the bugs." He gestured to the bed as he repositioned the chair. "Sit."

Greg's shoulders slumped as he reluctantly sat on the edge of the bed. "What do you want?"

"You didn't think I'd be back?" Willy asked him, slipping completely into his comfortable bad-cop role. "Really? Right after the same guy we'd been talking about is found dead with three bullets in him? I thought you were off dope."

"I am."

"Doesn't sound like it. The same man who was putting moves on your mom, Greg. I wouldn't want to ask you about that?"

Greg was shaking his head. "Ancient history, man."

"Ancient when you thought Dad had stepped out on the whole family, maybe. But after you found out he'd really been bumped off? That changed things, didn't it?"

Mitchell didn't respond.

Willy leaned forward suddenly and smacked him on the knee, making him jump. "*Didn't it, Gregory?*" Willy yelled.

"Fine," Greg shouted back, his face flushed.

Willy sat back just as abruptly. "Struck a nerve?" he asked in a normal voice.

Greg struggled for composure. "What do you think I've done, anyhow? Why're you here?"

"Isn't that obvious? BB was killed right after it was revealed your father was murdered. Either Barrett killed himself out of remorse—pretty unlikely, considering how many times he was shot—or somebody offed him because they thought he'd killed Hank. It is what it is, Greg—straight up and down. Where were you? Sitting in the bushes, waiting for BB to present the right target?"

Mitchell stared at him, openmouthed. "What?"

"Where were you when BB was killed, Greg? Not that complicated." Willy half rose and pulled his chair closer, still speaking. "And you know what? When we hear somebody dance around a direct question like that, it's a dead giveaway they're cookin' up a lie."

"I didn't kill anybody."

"Too late. I don't believe it." Willy shifted gears, smiling and crossing his legs. "Don't get me wrong. I totally sympathize. The son of a bitch fucked up your life—and everybody else's. Am I wrong? Your mom never remarried, your sister's a shadow of what she should be, and you . . . Well, look at you." Willy gestured with his hand. "One guy, one selfish act, and everybody gets screwed. You think I don't get that?"

In a sudden, well-practiced move, Willy reached across his body and pulled his withered hand free of his pants pocket, flopping his arm like a dead animal between them. "It happened to me, Greg. I'm reminded of it every . . . single . . . goddamned . . . day."

He released the arm, it thudded into his lap, its palm landing face-up and looking like a sun-bleached starfish. Greg's eyes darted to find something else to stare at.

"I know what it's like, having someone ruin your life. BB Barrett destroyed everyone you loved."

"It's not the same." Greg was barely audible.

"Where were you?" Willy asked again.

"I was at a meeting."

"What meeting?"

"AA."

"Where?"

"The Unitarian church."

"Who saw you?"

Greg's eyes flashed with anger, very briefly. "It's AA. It's anonymous."

"It's Vermont, stupid. There're twelve people in the whole state. Everybody knows everybody else. Who else was there?"

"I don't know," Greg said slowly. "The usual."

"How'd you know that?" Willy asked out of the blue. "I don't know where I was when Barrett got popped. It's not like the Twin Towers going down, when everyone remembers where they were. The news didn't cover the shooting till way later."

"But they said when it happened, and I thought it was lucky, 'cause I knew I'd be asked," Greg countered reasonably.

Willy stopped abruptly and fixed him with an analytical look. "That's very calculating," he said slowly, sounding impressed. "You've given this some thought, after all."

"Go away, Detective," Greg said at last. "I didn't do anything, and you can't prove I did."

Willy knew he was right, and stood up as a result, saying neverthe-less, "Not right now, but I gotta tell you, Mitchell: You left me with a bad feeling last time we met, and it's worse now. You're up to your neck in this, somehow or other, and I will figure it out. I promise you."

Greg let out a long breath, his face slack. "Do what you gotta do."

* * *

David Spinney was back at his post, watching Steve Hobart's house. This was his third night in a row, and despite his lack of success, he was still convinced he'd eventually get to prove that he was no man to cross.

The problem was that he'd also begun to doubt his methods, his reasoning, and even his self-confidence. He'd been able to reflect—following Hobart to the convenience store for beer, or the Laundromat, or even, last night, to nowhere at all—about the value of all this hormonal posturing. He'd received nothing but courtesy and support from the sheriff, his father, and the few other senior officers who knew the details of his mishap. On the flip side, he'd sensed some snickering from a couple of peers who'd added two and two, even though he knew to discount such criticism. So, did his supporters deserve his possibly making things worse?

By keeping on this course, he was withholding evidence in an on-going investigation—a detail that would no doubt reduce any success to less than Pyrrhic, to the point of costing him his career.

He let out a sigh, wrestling with this niggling bit of maturity, when he was abruptly slapped out of his reverie by the truck's passenger door flying open, the dome light coming on, and the dark figure of a man sliding onto the seat next to him.

"*Fuck*," he yelled in alarm, his hands flying up to no purpose.

His father laughed good-naturedly. "You oughta kill the dome light when you're on stakeout. Really gives you away."

"Dad. For Chrissake. What're you doing?"

Lester raised his eyebrows. "Shouldn't that be my line?"

David passed his hand across his face. "Jesus. You knew?"

Lester smiled. "I get the big bucks for this stuff, Dave. Be pretty embarrassing if I didn't notice it inside my own house. Your mom got concerned, I made a few quiet phone calls about your whereabouts, and then I went looking for your distinguished mode of transportation." He reached out and patted the truck's dashboard. "That's the short version, anyway. It only took a couple of nights." He pointed ahead with his chin. "Anything yet?"

Recovering somewhat, Dave managed to say, "Nope," while his brain groped for what might be coming next. This was only a variation on his earlier fears. His father had become a hero to him, only in part because he'd once risked his job to extract Dave from the fringes of a drug investigation. Disappointing him once more—again through poor judgment—made him queasy.

But Lester seemed to be on a completely different plane.

"I take it something dawned on you once everybody stopped asking questions," his father said pointedly. "Like maybe the name of one of the guys who grabbed you?"

"No," David answered bluntly. "It was his tattoo."

"Ah," Lester said, his wording almost theatrically pointed. "So, again, with the passage of some time and reflection, you remembered enough about it to want to confirm that it belonged to whoever's living over there?"

Dave hesitated, perceiving what the old man was up to. "Right," he said slowly. "I wanted to bring a name to the investigators, and not just a description of some cartoon figure."

"Right," his father agreed happily, watching him closely.

Dave flushed, embarrassed and grateful. "Probably a little dumb, huh?"

"A little enthusiastic," Lester agreed. "But not over the top, especially since this just came to you tonight, before you were planning to share your sudden recall tomorrow morning."

This time, David smiled slightly. "How did you know?"

Lester pointed ahead of them. "That him?"

While Dave had been following Lester's line of thinking, he'd forgotten to keep an eye on Hobart's address, where his quarry was now getting into his car.

"Yeah," he said. "Steve Hobart. When I remembered about the dragon tattoo, I ran it through the computer, and out came this guy." He patted the binoculars, resting on the console between them. "I confirmed it using these, three nights ago."

"You mean tonight," Lester corrected him. "With me."

Dave nodded. "Yes. Thanks, Dad."

Hobart's backup lights came on as he eased into the street.

"Wanna keep him company?" Lester asked.

His son fired up the truck's engine.

Hobart didn't go far. He drove to the south end of Bellows Falls, headed west on Route 121 into neighboring Westminster, and pulled into the gouged-up, dirt dooryard of a dilapidated rooming house a few minutes later. Dave killed his headlights, drifted over to the side of the road a hundred yards away, and stopped under the cover of a large and scraggly bush, allowing just enough room for his father to train the binoculars through the windshield on the building. As luck would have it, the nearest streetlamp cast enough light on the scene to throw everything into sharp relief.

"Huh," Lester grunted, adjusting the glasses. "He's not getting out. Good for us, maybe."

The rooming house's front door opened and three men stepped into the light. Both Spinneys watched as Hobart emerged to greet them, exchanging complicated and formulaic handshakes—imitations from urban neighborhoods that would have eaten these four alive in minutes.

"I recognize the older one," Lester stated. "Who woulda thunk it? The some'bitch got outta jail without telling me." He turned to his son. "Any of them ring a bell besides Hobart?"

Dave nodded. "Kind of. The one with the thick leather wrist thing, with spikes on it? I remember something scratching my ankle when they picked me up and tossed me in the trunk. I couldn't figure out what it could be, but that would fit."

Lester handed over the binoculars and reached for his phone as the group by the car began filing into the building. "I'm calling for a warrant and a backup team, with high hopes these guys'll be in there for a while."

"Who caught your eye, Dad?"

"William 'Bullfrog' Kruse," his father answered, dialing. "I arrested him seven or eight years ago, for Internet porn. He swore he'd get back at me when he got out. I'm calling his parole officer, too. That'll make disturbing their party in there all the easier."

He paused before adding, "You may have just figured out how and why you were grabbed by these jackasses, Dave. Nice work."

It took them over two hours to get everything organized—so much for the oft-televised version of law enforcement's speediness, and the reality of rural cops getting the right people in the right place with the right paperwork in short order. Nevertheless, as Lester had hoped, time was on their side—Steve Hobart and Bullfrog Kruse were no doubt happy to spend the evening indoors sampling drugs rather than roaming the neighborhood making pests of themselves.

Whatever the truth, Dave Spinney accepted that he'd been relegated to a spectator seat. As both the victim of this case and the one who'd stretched protocol to crack it open, he knew it behooved him to play no active role in corralling these suspects.

But it didn't mean he couldn't watch.

As a result, he was still in his pickup truck, sitting alone, still under the shaggy bush by the road, when the signal was given and the night lit up with blue strobes, bright lights, and shouted commands issued by a heavily armed entry team.

Of course, not everything went as planned, which was almost the rule in such operations. As Dave sat watching people running about, he saw a second-floor window suddenly explode, blown out by a catapulting body tucked into a ball. It curved through the air like a discarded bag of trash before crashing onto the roof of Steve Hobart's already battered car and bouncing onto the ground.

Dave let out a short laugh of astonishment before realizing not only that the person was still moving—even getting up and struggling to open the car door—but that it was Steve Hobart himself.

"Shit," Dave said, seeing the distance the nearest cop had to cover in order to stop Hobart from driving off. "I bet they forgot to take his keys out."

Sure enough. An oily plume of smoke spewed from the car's exhaust, seconds before Dave started his own engine and threw his truck into gear as Hobart spun his tires and began squealing toward the street.

His heart sinking with the knowledge of what he had to do, Dave launched himself at a tangent toward the quickly approaching rust-stained beater, slamming into Hobart's vehicle, forcing it across the dooryard, and folding it around the light pole by the edge of the road.

Dave leaped out, pulled out his off-duty weapon, jumped onto his own hood, and jammed the gun into the neck of the semiconscious Hobart.

"*You are such a dick,*" Dave screamed at him. "You made me fuck up my truck."

"I don't care if Bullfrog copped to grabbing Dave to scare Lester," Willy complained to Sammie at home later, after hearing of the Westminster raid's outcome. "There still may be something else goin' on, and I am goddamned if I'm gonna expose our kid to danger just because we're all singing 'la-di-dah, it's just a bunch of loser woodchucks beating off as usual.' No fucking way."

Sammie was nodding patiently. "You got it," she said soothingly. "We'll keep Louise on the job and make sure she's still packing. Emma doesn't care, and it's fine with me."

Willy, however, wasn't finished. He chose his next words carefully, and voiced them calmly, to better make his point. "Sam, you don't have to tell me I'm the wacko paranoid around here. I got that. But high-tech cameras coming and going? Guys who get born at twenty years old? And a jailbird so dumb his nickname is Bullfrog putting together the only kidnapping of a cop in Vermont history? Along with two homicides we can't figure out? Grant me there's more goin' on than meets the eye."

Sam considered the point, knowing him well enough to distinguish a rant from his uncanny insight.

She reached out to interlace her fingers with his. "I'll not only grant you that," she told him, "I'll trust you to figure it out. And along those lines, you'll be happy to hear that Joe's asked me to meet with Linda Lucas. She gave him permission for a limited search of Johnny's stuff at home, to help in locating him."

"Limited, how?"

She smiled and glanced at the documents spread before them. "She gets to stand by and choose what we see and what we don't. It occurred to me that I might be able to lean on the tiller a little, now and then, based on what we already got—it'll help us later, when we're explaining how we learned what we know."

He smiled and kissed her. "Attagirl."

PART TWO

CHAPTER NINETEEN

Tina Panik slipped her hands into the pockets of her tailored slacks and stared out at the waters of Great South Bay. Her fifty-foot motor yacht, temporarily attached to the seawall beyond the Olympic-sized swimming pool, bobbed gently up and down, reminiscent of a cradle rocking its occupant to sleep. It was a manicured scene of lazy luxury, as offhand, casual, and lacking in subtlety as a peach pit diamond worn by a weekend gardener in designer jeans—not atypical of the Hamptons.

Sleep, however, wasn't something Tina had enjoyed much recently, not since that first completely off-the-wall phone call from Vermont.

"BB" the man had called himself, sounding like a car mechanic and copping a 'tude to boot. Lucky Tina hadn't been the one answering the phone, or she would've told the guy to fuck off. But it had been made to the New York City office Tina's father had once called the HQ, as if he were Douglas Goddamned MacArthur, which—in his own mind—he probably had been.

It was recorded, of course, as Tina had made sure they all were nowadays, so she received the benefit of BB's outrage by proxy. That had been the start of it all.

Now, Christ only knew where and how it was going to end.

She sighed and turned at the quiet knock on the all-white living room's open doorway. "What now?" she asked.

An older man stood on the threshold—slightly built, cheaply dressed, with a small potbelly and a thin, white comb-over. In this glaringly bright, modernist setting, he looked almost comically out of place. Walter, one of her father's antique retinue, and someone she hadn't seen in years before this mess. He had brought the phone call to her attention, because—as he'd explained—she was the boss now, and the boss needed to know what was goin' on. Sometimes the old ways had value. If he hadn't acted on instinct, God only knows where this might have led.

"Sorry to bother you, Miss Panik," he said, bobbing his head respectfully. "But Johnny Lucas has disappeared. The cops pulled in his wife for questioning."

"She going to know anything?" Tina asked.

Walter shrugged tentatively, as if fearful Tina would lash out at him. The small gesture made her reflect once more on how her father must have handled his subordinates. She'd never seen any of that, being the boss's cloistered daughter. But she'd always imagined Jack Panik to have been a hard man. Her mother down to the entry-level kitchen help had all certainly behaved as if he were someone to displease at high risk.

"I don't know what he told her about himself," Walter said. "Or if she even knows about the old days. They met after he moved up there. He was never supposed to tell nobody, but you don't know about people."

"You know, though, don't you, Walter?" Tina asked. "Isn't that what you said?"

"Yes, ma'am. When we were starting out for your father, Pauli was like a little brother. That was his name back then."

She held up her hand. "I don't need details. I just need to know what's going to happen next—based on your knowledge."

Walter looked awkward, and spread out his hands feebly. "It's kinda up in the air."

Tina pursed her lips and motioned to one of the two ten-foot Roche Bobois sofas bracketing a large coffee table in the middle of the enormous room. "Sit down, Walter. Make yourself comfortable. Would you like a drink?"

Walter perched on the edge of the couch, as comfortable as a cat on a highway. "No, Miss Panik. I'm fine, thanks."

Tina chose an armchair, sitting back and crossing her legs. "Worst-case scenario," she proposed. "If Johnny Lucas—let's just call him that—gets caught by the police, how much crap can come back to hit us?"

Walter appeared slightly pained by her harsh language, looking down at the white wool rug before answering. "It could hurt. He's not all the way out, like most of the old-timers, but he ain't in, either, like me. That makes him kind of a bridge, connecting the past with nowadays—but out in the world, if you get me."

"I get you. And not that it matters, but how many others like him are there, drifting around like bad smells?"

Walter grimaced. "Good one. Right. I guess only a couple by now—guys we had to make invisible 'cause of the hot water they got in, but too loyal to make disappear. Pauli—Johnny—was a good boy. A stand-up guy. Wasn't nuthin' he wouldn't do for Jack Panik. We were like Army Rangers back then—hot to trot and tough as hell."

Again, Tina held up a hand. "Stay on track, Walter."

"Sorry, miss. Anyhow, a few of us got carried away, and when your father decided to change the operation slightly, and distance ourselves from the bad old days, we had to figure out what to do with 'em—the ones that weren't dead or in jail already. This was when you were still in school—long time ago."

Tina's gaze drifted over to the cold fireplace. Despite keeping the past at arm's length, she wasn't such an idiot as to have been ignorant of its existence. The Kennedys had cut their teeth running booze across the border, and John D. Rockefeller's father was a snake oil salesman, after all. On a lesser scale, Jack Panik had merely copied from such ruthless examples of American enterprise—and then concluded his career with an equally adept display of soothing public relations. Tina had only continued the trend, posing as a venture capitalist and entrepreneur, while in fact generating most of her income through insider trading, fraudulent stock deals, and an assortment of white-collar schemes. Nevertheless, she'd known little of her father's earlier machinations.

She took a breath and asked Walter, "I know I told you to handle this when it started, and not to involve me directly. But I need to know if it's getting messy. For example, when this BB character called and started screaming about . . . whoever it was."

"Hank Mitchell," Walter said softly.

"He said we weren't supposed to have killed him. What did he mean by that? Who was Mitchell?"

"A nobody, miss. Just somebody in the way."

"In the way of what?"

Walter shifted in his seat, getting slightly more comfortable without actually sitting back. "Your father was changing the old ways, like I said. Pau . . . Johnny was in a jam; Jack needed to clean the money he was taking in. At the time, it seemed like a no-brainer. Give Johnny a new identity and have him set up a money-laundering operation, someplace in the boondocks."

"Vermont," Tina filled in.

"Right. Jack already had others like it, around New York. This wasn't such a leap. And Johnny, who was a go-getter, said that part of Vermont was ripe just then 'cause of a major construction project—a nuclear power plant. He said there had to be a bunch of businesses who'd be good for washing money. And he was right."

"So our cash went through a nuke plant?" Tina asked skeptically.

"No. A roofing business. That was Johnny's point. The plant was tapping labor and resources like nobody's business. Which meant that outfits around the edges were looking for capital to take advantage. It was real smart."

Tina carefully scratched her forehead with one perfect fingernail. "Right. So Johnny Lucas got into bed with BB . . . What's his last name?"

"Barrett."

"BB Barrett. Okay. Where's Hank fit in?"

"He was BB's right-hand man," Walter explained. "But not as broadminded as BB."

Tina tilted her head back to look at the ceiling. "Jesus Christ. So Johnny reverted to old habits and took care of the problem."

"Which was fine," Walter followed up, "till Hank's body was discovered in concrete a couple of weeks ago. That's what got BB fired up—he'd been told by Johnny that Hank had just conveniently dumped his family and taken off to 'find himself,' or something."

Tina stared at him. "Concrete? Really?"

Walter lifted one shoulder haplessly, as if apologizing. "I know, right? Still, it worked. The deal was done, Johnny moved into the number two spot after a while—so nothing would look too suspicious—and everybody was off to the races. Johnny had a new life, and your dad another way to launder cash."

Tina studied his hopeful expression glumly. When she spoke, her voice was hard. "I put you in charge. This is our third meeting, Walter. The first time, you broke the news and gave me the bare bones about Barrett—which, by the way, was a real CliffsNotes version of what you said just now. The second time, you told me Barrett had been found dead, and made it sound like our problems were over. But if I got it right this time, you're telling me that Johnny Lucas whacked BB Barrett à la

Al Capone, and has now taken off, with every hayseed cop who knows how to tie his shoes hot on his trail. Am I getting this right?"

"Except for the whacking part, yeah," was the mumbled reply.

"What?" she asked loudly.

"Except for the whacking part," he repeated. "Johnny didn't kill Barrett."

"Why not? That's his style."

"Maybe, miss. But BB was killed before Johnny could get to him."

Walter stopped abruptly, realizing what he'd just let slip.

It was too late. Tina slid forward in her seat. "Walter," she said slowly, her tone menacing, making him think of her father—dead these many years. "Did I in any way, shape, or form *ever* tell you to have BB Barrett killed?"

"No, ma'am."

"Then why, unless it was under your direction, was Johnny even contemplating 'getting to him'—to quote you exactly?"

Walter sat with his hands between his knees, wondering how he'd ended up in such a mess, so many years after he thought he'd left this life behind him.

"Use your words, Walter," Tina coaxed him, her voice suspiciously gentle.

"I told him to take care of it," Walter said quietly.

"And—given Johnny's background—how did you think he'd interpret that?"

Walter looked at her sadly. "They used to be friends, BB and him. I didn't mean what you think."

She matched his emotion, not one to bemoan spilled milk. "It's not what I would have thought that matters, though, is it?"

"No, ma'am. I messed up."

She stood up, prompting him to clumsily do the same. She took his elbow and steered him toward the door. "I messed up, too. You've been a loyal friend for a long time—to my father, and to me. I should have given you more direction. I didn't give it enough attention."

They paused on the threshold and she placed her hand on his shoulder. "I will now. Use whatever resources to do what you need to do. Go where you need to go. Clean this up." She leaned forward slightly, so their eyes were inches apart. "I mean it, Walter. Do you understand? Make it go away. No muss, no fuss, and no interest by the police. This mosquito must disappear."

Walter nodded once. "It will, Miss Panik. I promise."

Walter crossed the peastone drive to where he'd parked under a tree near the courtyard's gate. Tina Panik's house was only about ten years old, but built to look like some downscale appendage to Versailles. Back at the office downtown, rumor had it that the ambition had been to rip off Marie Antoinette's pseudo farmhouse, where she'd pretended to be a happy peasant shortly before they'd lopped off her head.

It was a dangerous comparison, as Walter was well placed to know. He'd witnessed Jack Panik's ascendancy, and was therefore appreciative of the daughter's inherited ruthlessness. She had become a poster child of respectability lately—complete with this mansion in the Hamptons and a season's pass at the New York City Ballet—but she was no dingbat queen, soft and suffering from self-delusion. Born to the business, she was a chip off the old block, and Walter could attest to the fate of those who'd sold her short in the past.

And now, he'd just lied to her face.

He got into his car and aimed it out into the street, but only to drive a quarter mile before pulling over to consider his options.

He was in a pickle. In the vernacular of politicians, he hadn't been entirely forthcoming with the facts, which meant that if he stumbled from here on, and Tina caught wind of it, all his decades of currying favor, keeping his head down, and building a fat nest egg would be for naught. Tina Panik didn't have screwups killed—that dated back to her father. But Walter had seen her reduce people's prospects to the level of an unskilled migrant worker.

He rolled down the window and killed the engine, letting the salty breeze drift in from the beach, one block over.

When that call came in from BB Barrett, demanding to know why he'd been lied to about Hank Mitchell's fate, Walter hadn't hesitated to contact his pal Pauli—or Johnny, as he'd been known a lot longer.

That had been a mistake. Lucas had heard about the body at the nuke plant, but he'd had no idea about BB's reaction. He hadn't thought about BB Barrett in years. Walter's phone call had come like an electric jolt and—sadly, only in retrospect—set a screw loose in the man, apparently.

Walter stared straight ahead sourly. Damn. After that, it had been like a snowball rolling downhill, getting bigger and bigger. Barrett turned up dead, Lucas denied having anything to do with it, and Walter—despite what he'd just told his irate boss—didn't believe a word of it. As a result, now worried and scrambling—Walter had sent a team north to set up cameras at Lucas's place and tap his phone. And here was the icing on the cake: Those cameras had now captured some mysterious intruders creeping around and stealing stuff.

Walter had warned Johnny—even sending him a copy of the footage. What choice did he have? He had to make sure Lucas hadn't been keeping anything that might blow up in their faces. Instead, the police showed up, and Johnny evaporated.

Goddamned disaster. Walter's only break was that he'd had the cameras taken down almost as fast as he'd ordered them up.

Frustration making him antsy, Walter left his car and walked down a sandy alleyway to where the view opened up to a distant panorama of Fire Island.

Walter hated the ocean, hated Long Island, hated the rich and their attraction to glitzy crap, and—as he glanced down at his wing tips— hated getting sand in his shoes.

"Shit," he swore.

He knew what was getting to him. A company man from puberty, he'd always done what he was told, never asked questions, toed the party line, and had been handsomely rewarded.

Now he was dangling over the edge, between an impatient boss standing on his fingers and some country cops raising their heads like dogs on a scent. Not to mention having to find an old triggerman on the lam and being haunted by a couple of black-clad Ninjas whose origins and intentions were anyone's guess.

And it was all his to sort out. If he didn't placate the employer who didn't want to know, locate the paranoid who didn't want to listen, and identify the comic book couple and their reasons for being, his only remaining decision was going to be whether to accept the blindfold when he was placed before a firing squad, or not.

Assuming his ending was that neat.

CHAPTER TWENTY

Joe stepped into the dry cleaners, making an old-fashioned tiny metal bell above the door jangle. The air inside smelled faintly of sunbaked cotton, although he knew from what he'd read that, far in the back, there were toxic chemicals at work.

But they were nowhere in evidence. Instead, there was a cheerful woman at the cash register, straight ahead, and another woman—tall, razor-thin, dark-haired, and ghostly silent—operating an ironing press off to one side, located behind a different counter.

"Hey, Joe," said the cheerful one. "Haven't seen you in a while. Not getting your clothes dirty anymore?"

Joe nodded to the thin one, who ignored him, and approached the speaker. "Hi, Holly. They're getting dirty, all right. I just stopped caring, I guess. I probably ought to bring in a few jackets, now that you mention it."

"Always happy to oblige," Holly said, eyeing his empty hands. "If it's not laundry, how can we help you?"

Joe partially shifted toward the other woman as he answered, "Actually, I'm here to have a chat with Patrice Celli, if she's amenable."

The thin woman looked up, a partially pressed shirt suspended in midmotion. "Me? Why?"

"I'm looking into a bit of history," Joe said cheerfully. "Dating back almost forty years. That be okay with you?"

Holly spoke up quickly, knowing her colleague's natural reticence. "It's okay, Patty. Joe's a regular—or used to be. And take your time—we've got a light load today." She laughed and turned back to Joe in explanation. "The yuppies have brought back pure cotton shirts, but do they like us to press 'em and throw in a little starch? No, they do not." She winked and added, "Whaddya gonna do? Wrinkles are in."

Joe faced Celli fully and gestured toward the front door. "It's a nice day, and I noticed a bench outside. How would that be?"

She nodded without speaking or changing expression, making Joe wonder just how long the conversation might last. He'd met women who reminded him of Patty—shy to the point of muteness, silenced by abuse, loss, heartbreak, or all three and more.

He ushered her outside and led the way to the spot he'd referenced, which was set back from the business's driveway, and thus somewhat isolated and quiet. Nevertheless, it faced the road, and allowed for a view of continually passing traffic. Joe imagined that it was probably the store's designated smoking perch.

"Have a seat," he offered.

She settled down stiffly. She was quite beautiful in her way, reminiscent of a Dorothea Lange photograph—lean and weathered, with intense, thoughtful, somewhat soul-dead eyes.

He sat beside her and asked, "I heard Holly refer to you as Patty. Is that what you prefer?"

"Patrice," she said quietly but clearly.

"Patrice it is, then," he said, grateful for any sound at all. "The reason I'm bugging you is because of a job I think you had a very long time ago—according to what I heard."

She remained silent.

"Did you once work for Ridgeline Roofing?" he kept going.

After a pause, she murmured, "Yes."

"In what capacity?"

Her gaze had been fixed on the traffic, and it didn't move when she asked, "Why?"

"You're not in any trouble, Patrice. I promise. I'm just trying to put together the pieces of an old puzzle. Did you hear that BB Barrett had died?"

This time, she did look at him—her eyes an almost liquid brown. "I had nothing to do with that."

The words were flat and without inflection, but the nature of her reaction surprised him. He responded in an equally level tone. "I know that, Patrice. But you asked why I wanted to know about your past employment. That's the reason."

"Who told you about me?"

"There are a few Ridgeline graduates still living in town," he answered indirectly. "It was one of them."

In fact, it had been Lacey Stringer, whom Sammie had revisited with some follow-up questions, one of which had been whether Ridgeline had ever had a bookkeeper.

Despite Joe's vagueness, Celli didn't press him for more. She simply nodded once and resumed her appreciation of the scenery.

"What was your job with them?" Joe asked.

"I did the books."

"For how long?"

"From '67 to '71."

"You worked directly with Barrett?"

"There wasn't anybody else."

"There was Hank Mitchell."

Again, the single nod. "Right."

"Was he a problem? Bad to work with?"

She frowned as she took him in again. "Hank? No. Is that what they told you?"

"Not at all. I was just trying to read between the lines when you said there was no one beyond Barrett."

"Hank wasn't in the office much."

"What kind of guy was he?"

He expected something noncommittal, given her responses so far, but she surprised him by saying, "He was a good man—nice to work with, friendly, considerate. He always asked how I was doing, and if he didn't like the answer, he'd stop to find out more. Not like BB at all."

"Describe BB."

Like a rusty hinge in need of a few swings, Patrice Celli began loosening up, perhaps encouraged by Joe's tone or style, or perhaps simply because someone was asking something involving her. "He was decent enough. More like a typical boss—acted like you weren't in the room. He was the one with the big dreams. Hank was the nuts-and-bolts man."

"But they got along?"

"Mostly, especially in the early days."

"What happened then?"

"What do they say? Either money or sex."

He gave her an appraising glance, startled by her unexpected frankness. "And this one?"

"Money."

"Okay. Tell me about the money."

"There wasn't much at the start. We were just a small outfit, the two guys and me, and I was straight out of high school, wide-eyed and mostly innocent. Like I said, BB was full of plans, and for a while, it looked like he was right. Hank would go out and place the bids, BB would put together the deals for the workers, subcontractors, and materials, and we began making money. It wasn't as fast as BB wanted, but it was steady."

She lapsed into silence, seemingly lost in her thoughts, where Joe imagined she spent most of her time.

"And then?" he prompted.

Her face resumed its former mask. "Johnny Lucas," she said without inflection.

"I heard about him," Joe said, trying to sound vaguely chatty. "What was his story?"

"The man from nowhere," she said slowly.

"How did he first show up?"

"Just did. One day, he walked in with BB, all smiles, and he never went away. I did, though, pretty soon, and Hank did, too—forever."

"But Hank left before you, is that right?"

She nodded. "It took a few months for Johnny to do his razzle-dazzle."

Joe shifted in his seat, facing her more directly, struck by her contempt. "Patrice, you probably know by now that both Hank and BB were murdered."

"I do. That's why I'm talking to you. As soon as I read about the buried body at the nuclear plant, I wondered if it might be him."

"And you think Lucas played a part in that?"

"Yes. I don't know anything about BB dying. I lost touch with all of them a lifetime ago. But when I heard he'd been shot, I figured it was connected to what happened to Hank."

Joe urged her on. "Okay. And what was that? I'm asking about what you know, of course, although I don't mind hearing what you suspect, too."

"It's not what you're thinking," she cautioned him. "I can't tell you Johnny Lucas killed Hank—or that anybody did. As far as I knew, Hank just disappeared. That's what we all thought—that Hank and Sharon

"Was he a problem? Bad to work with?"

She frowned as she took him in again. "Hank? No. Is that what they told you?"

"Not at all. I was just trying to read between the lines when you said there was no one beyond Barrett."

"Hank wasn't in the office much."

"What kind of guy was he?"

He expected something noncommittal, given her responses so far, but she surprised him by saying, "He was a good man—nice to work with, friendly, considerate. He always asked how I was doing, and if he didn't like the answer, he'd stop to find out more. Not like BB at all."

"Describe BB."

Like a rusty hinge in need of a few swings, Patrice Celli began loosening up, perhaps encouraged by Joe's tone or style, or perhaps simply because someone was asking something involving her. "He was decent enough. More like a typical boss—acted like you weren't in the room. He was the one with the big dreams. Hank was the nuts-and-bolts man."

"But they got along?"

"Mostly, especially in the early days."

"What happened then?"

"What do they say? Either money or sex."

He gave her an appraising glance, startled by her unexpected frankness. "And this one?"

"Money."

"Okay. Tell me about the money."

"There wasn't much at the start. We were just a small outfit, the two guys and me, and I was straight out of high school, wide-eyed and mostly innocent. Like I said, BB was full of plans, and for a while, it looked like he was right. Hank would go out and place the bids, BB would put together the deals for the workers, subcontractors, and materials, and weren't getting along, and that he finally lit out. But I'd seen Lucas at work, and I knew it wasn't that simple."

"What was he doing?"

"Conniving," she said simply. "Almost as soon as he showed up, I saw him figuring out who was who and what made them tick. He tried to get me into bed. Lots of luck there. He was so sleazy. That's what made him the exact opposite of Hank, and why Hank ended up in his sights."

"In what way?"

"If you ask me, he started the whole thing between Hank and Sharon. I don't know what was happening there before Johnny, but from then on? Suspicions began flying. BB was knee-deep in it, too, of course. He had a soft spot for Sharon, anyhow, so it was in his best interest to fan the flames. But Johnny was the one who got it going—rumors of girlfriends, stories about fights at home. Wasn't long before Hank had to leave home."

She finally faced Joe directly, her eyes intense. "Hank would come to me—a teenage girl—to get me to understand that he loved his wife and kids. I didn't need convincing, but nobody else cared. All those other jerks—Stringer, Carlo, the rest—they all thought it was funny. Johnny had an office pool going, on who was the most likely girlfriend Hank had on the side. It was disgusting."

"And then Hank was gone," Joe prompted her after she fell silent.

"Yup," she said. "Just like that. That's when BB really moved in on Sharon, not that it worked. I'll give her that much. After Hank disappeared, that was it for her—as far as I know. It's not like we kept in touch. I barely knew the lady. I heard a lot later that she'd done well financially, so maybe BB did the right thing by her there."

"Speaking of finances," Joe picked up. "You, being the bookkeeper, must've had an idea of what they were like."

"I thought so, but I wasn't so sure toward the end. That was Johnny's doing, too, if you ask me."

"How so?"

"I could tell he and BB were cooking something up. When Hank would be out checking on jobs, Johnny and BB would hole up in BB's office. And even there—" She suddenly interrupted herself. "How could BB afford to hire Johnny? We didn't have that kind of money. And Johnny didn't *do* anything. He wasn't a roofer. Hank and BB were partners; they shared the business. Johnny had nothing to do with that. And yet, there he was."

"He didn't draw a paycheck?"

She scowled. "He did, which didn't make sense, either. All of a sudden, I began seeing that we were making more money than expected. I couldn't figure it out. But I was a kid. I took it at face value when BB told me that customers were paying bonuses for work done ahead of schedule, or whatever. Now I can't believe what an idiot I was, but he made it sound so convincing. And things were good. I got a new typewriter and copying machine. BB got a bigger desk."

"Hank wasn't suspicious?"

"He was, but that's what I meant: Johnny had given him other things to worry about. Plus, he was gone before all this really got going."

Joe thought back over what their research had yielded so far. "What was Lucas's job description during all this?"

"He didn't have one. That's what I was saying. BB made him a partner later, after Hank had been gone awhile. That was right after I left—or was forced to leave."

"They fired you?"

"Not in so many words. I was happy to leave, and they were happy not to have me asking questions."

"You were getting curious?"

"You would've been, too," she said. "I don't know what was going on by then, but it sure as hell had nothing to do with roofing."

"What kind of money are we talking about?" Joe asked.

She shrugged. "I would've been the last to know. At the end, all I did was payroll. But just the way they were living, you could tell they were raking it in—new trucks, fancy watches, throwing cash around. I always thought I'd read about them getting arrested one day. But it never happened. Instead, a long time after, there was a huge merger announced. That's when BB Barrett became a really big deal around here." She paused before adding, predictably, "Made me sick to my stomach."

There was a moment's silence as they both studied the distant traffic.

"I better get back to work," she said then.

They both rose. Joe hesitated before asking, "Patrice, I know you already touched on this, and I'm not looking for you to go beyond your comfort zone, but what did you think was motivating Johnny Lucas? What kind of man was he, beyond being conniving and sleazy, like you said?"

She looked at the ground a moment, a small passing breeze shifting her dark hair. "Dangerous," she answered. "He scared me."

Johnny Lucas studied his reflection in the bathroom mirror, appraising the speed with which his beard was coming in. It made for a major change, he thought—that and the newly bald head. He passed his hand again across the unfamiliar smooth pate. He had been a remarkably hairy man from puberty onward, shaving twice a day to keep the girls from complaining about whisker burn. Who knew it would turn into an unexpected advantage? He'd always colored the hair to maintain its original near-black hue; now, it was gone, and the beard below it was almost white. Once the process was complete, he imagined his own mother would've had a tough time picking him out, were she still alive.

So far, so good. He left the mirror and entered the living room to admire the view of the mountains across the valley. He was in Vermont—Dummerston, above Brattleboro—tucked away in a small, converted hunting cabin, surrounded by wilderness. He'd bought the place for cash years ago, unbeknownst to Linda or anyone else, and under an assumed name, just in case.

In case of what? Well, that was the point, wasn't it? In case of a mess like this one, he mused. He pulled out the disposable cell phone he'd just purchased for emergencies. But who was he supposed to call?

All these years, he mused regretfully, basically without a hiccup. Good-looking wife, nice home on the river, pile of cash, facing a life of retirement and travel while still in the pink of health—until some sorry asshole bureaucrat decides to tear down a perfectly good warehouse.

He reached out and squashed a lethargic fly against the window-pane. What were they gonna do? Remodel? Everybody knew that once you built a nuclear power plant, it was there till the next Ice Age. Perfect place for a burial site.

He replaced the phone and removed the gun from his holster. It had been a while since he'd fired it, and chances were he'd have to soon. Time for a little practice, with it and the other weapons he'd stockpiled here over the years.

At the time, even he'd thought himself a little paranoid. Now he was wondering if his resources were deep enough. He had two hundred thousand dollars in a duffel bag, a passport under another name, and several overseas banking accounts, not to mention the guns. It was a start.

But he didn't want to just take off. He was getting too old for that kind of stunt. Plus, he didn't know everything he was running from. The Paniks, he understood, and he figured their envoy would be Walter, since he'd reached out when Barrett got whacked. But what about the others? The people who'd broken into his place? Who the fuck were they? Had they killed Barrett? Were they after him now? And who did they work for?

Johnny had first been sure that Walter was just jerking him around, pretending to be clueless when in fact he'd sent out a team to take out both BB and him as soon as Hank resurfaced. That's what Johnny would've done—tied up all the loose ends.

Now he was less sure. Why rig those cameras and then give Johnny a heads-up? Had they gotten so weird under new management that they gave you a warning before they killed you?

So, maybe it was something else.

Lucas reholstered the gun, opened the sliding door, and stepped out onto the cabin's small deck. Leaning on the railing, staring at the scenery, he considered his more immediate options.

Running is what they'd expect him to do—maybe even encourage. So, his best response would be to turn the tables. Make them the target instead of the hunters. It shouldn't be all that hard. He had the stills Walter had sent him, and unbeknownst to anyone, he'd had his own cameras rigged a quarter mile down River Road in both directions— just as he did here—to log anyone trying to park supposedly "out of sight." They were high-end, traceless, without detectable radio waves, designed to slip by the tracking equipment of anyone snooping.

He'd done this kind of surveillance before, after all. He was no beginner. And once Walter's footage had revealed those black-clad nocturnal visitors, it hadn't been any trick to review his own archival footage and find a similar twosome getting into a discreetly tucked-away car.

That would take care of them—probably locally hired help. The next hurdle would be Walter himself, since Johnny had no doubt that a veteran like Walter would be heading north to check things out— especially if the local talent turned up dead.

Walter might be trickier. He was Tina Panik's direct link, after all, and the only connection that Johnny had maintained from his past life—the one to whom he'd funneled all that laundered money during the Ridgeline Roofing years, and the equivalent of a career counselor after Johnny had bid BB Barrett good luck with his Vermont Amalgamated merger.

Johnny frowned. Keeping in touch had been a mistake, he realized. He should've just told Walter and the Paniks "*Sayonara*" instead of being sentimental about old times. Once the money laundering had stopped, after all, nobody had owed anybody else a thing.

But Johnny hadn't opted for a clean break, and Walter sure as hell hadn't encouraged it.

Too bad, Johnny thought. From now on, that's all it was going to be about—clean breaks, forever.

CHAPTER TWENTY-ONE

Sally Kravitz watched her father as he sat by the window, observing the street below. They were in their apartment above the restaurant—a room that had been a social hall a hundred years ago. All the lights were off except for the small one beside her bed, which now seemed like a single star in a dark galaxy, given the space's vast gloominess.

Of the various places Dan had called home, this was Sally's favorite. Part of that fondness, she knew, had to do with her age. As a kid, she'd paid little attention to location, focusing instead on playmates, which her father had made sure were in ready supply. After that, she'd gone off to boarding school, thanks to a combination of scholarships and money that Dan always seemed to have available, and whose source she now better understood. During those years, she'd often not lived with him, copying his example by camping out with families of her own choosing, albeit ones that he'd vetted.

But now, things were different. She was older, as was he. They understood, even if it had never been discussed, that she'd be going off to college after her so-called gap year. And that might be it—she could use college as a springboard to head out into the world; probably would, in fact, leaving him behind to his own strange devices. She imagined that had been the basis of his finally confessing to her about his alternate life. He had wanted, in a single gesture, to give her access to his inner workings, his hidden abilities, and to explain, however indirectly, how hard he'd worked to give her some extraordinary advantages through extremely unusual means.

In many ways, his latest effort had been matched by her own. Her choice to pause a year between high school and college, she thought, had been born of a subconscious hunger for such an explanation. And he had risen to the request naturally and without prompting, as always with her.

But he was worried now, and she knew why. The role of a gatekeeper, after all, went beyond simply monitoring who came and went. Dan Kravitz was his daughter's defender, as well. By taking her into his confidence, and involving her in his activities, he'd compromised his protectiveness by exposing her to danger.

It had turned out to be a high price for additional bonding, and she knew the guilt was wearing at him.

She left her reading and joined him in his vigil of the street, sitting in a beanbag across from him, now in the shadows herself. "You okay, Dad?"

He kept his eyes on the outdoors. Brattleboro was rarely completely void of activity, especially downtown, and the coming spring had made people more restless than usual. "Not really."

"I know that being cautious is smart," she said. "But nothing you told me about what Kunkle said seems all that conclusive."

He gave her a thin smile. "Meaning my fears are outdistancing reality?"

"Meaning maybe your fears have become your reality," she offered. "Given they're all we have."

"Sometimes that's the difference between getting away and being eaten," he said, his smile broadening at her sparring.

She laughed. "Okay, Obi-Wan. So what do we do now?"

"That's what I've been pondering," he said. "I don't actually like acting on fear alone, especially when it's based on ignorance. But," and here he looked at her, "my overriding concern is your safety."

He shifted in his seat. "Sweetheart. I have reached where I am in this life through any number of crazy deals with the Devil, most of which I've spared you. Those choices have resulted in two absolutes: a happy and stable—if unconventional—mental state, and you, the center of my universe. All of a sudden, maintaining the first has put the second at risk. It is no contest what matters more to me. Without you being safe and sound—as best I can control such things—my world ends. I hope that makes the point without being too melodramatic."

She leaned forward and held his knee between her hands. "I love you. You're the weirdest, most wonderful dad I know. Whatever you decide to do—regardless of whether it's based on fear or fact—is fine with me."

He gave her a slightly sheepish expression, wrinkling his nose, and said, "Okay, then I think we ought to pull up stakes and lie low for a while, just to be on the safe side."

"Leave Brattleboro?" she asked, keeping her voice neutral while inwardly cringing. Unlike her father, she was a social creature, and had lifelong friends spread all across this town, of every stripe and background.

His response surprised and pleased her. "Not for starters. I don't want to lose access to my eyes and ears, in case I can find out what's truly going on." He cast an encompassing gaze around them. "But we ought to leave here. If you don't mind being a little isolated for a while, I think I can find us a spot you'll find pretty nice."

She slid from her beanbag chair awkwardly and leaned forward to kiss his cheek. "I can't wait, Dad."

"Assuming Lucas was Mobbed-up when he was cutting his teeth," Willy argued, "then all the more reason to think what happened to Lester's kid wasn't just some hormonal woodchucks acting out. I say everything stays connected till somebody proves otherwise."

"His name's David," Lester said wearily, having made the same comment an irritating number of times.

"Despite that Bullfrog's copped to organizing the whole thing and is currently cutting a deal with the SA," Sam added.

"Or," Joe couldn't resist, "that we had the inside of Hobart's trunk compared to what we collected from under Dave's fingernails, and it was a perfect match."

Willy was not receptive. "The Mob can't buy testimony all of a sudden?"

"Patrice Celli never invoked the Mob, or organized crime, or anything else," Joe said, hoping to get the squad meeting back on track.

"That's what *we're* supposed to do," Willy continued. "It's *our* job to connect the dots."

"I think we got it," Sam cautioned him.

Willy heard the warning in her voice and backed off. "Just sayin'."

"And we hear you," Joe told him. "I agree that Lucas may've pulled a fast one forty years ago, and maybe killed Hank Mitchell in the process. We've had more convoluted cases before. The catch is—whether it's true or not—how does it tie into BB's death? If we are being paid to connect those dots, we're not doing a great job of it."

Lester indicated the phone by his elbow. "I double-checked the alibi Linda Lucas gave Johnny," he said, mostly to Willy. "The wine tasting and doo-wa-diddy weekend at Stratton. I talked to several people who remembered him, including the guy he yelled at for burying his car at the back of the lot. I even built a time line, to see if he might've rented a car or something and snuck out, but given Barrett's estimated time of death, I couldn't make it work. Course, I suppose anything's possible."

Sammie was shaking her head. "I don't see it. According to Joe's notes, Linda said Johnny was sweating bullets from then on. That's not what I'd look for in a killer playing a cool game of 'Who, me?' Not only that," she added, casting a conspiratorial glance at Willy, "but when I was looking through Lucas's papers earlier, with Linda breathing down my neck—as arranged by Joe—I chatted her up, and she confirmed that everything was hunky-dory up to when they heard of BB's killing, right after that weekend."

"You find anything when you were there?" Lester asked.

"No more than what we knew. He might as well have been born at the age of twenty-two. Every scrap of paperwork identifying him looked like it had just been printed in the basement."

Sammie looked around, feeling like a kid who couldn't believe her tall tale had gone over. Not that she'd actually lied, except about what documentation she'd seen where, and how she'd come upon it.

Willy helped her out by moving the conversation along. "I know I said Mob before. But the Marshals Service was mentioned, too—not that one precludes the other. But the marshals usually set up their people with new jobs, homes, the works. Lucas sounds like he made it up as he went. That's sort of what got me going. According to what Celli told you, boss, Lucas just walked into the office with Barrett one day and went right to work."

"Agreed," Joe said. "She also said it seemed like he was being paid with money she couldn't account for."

"Right," Willy supported him. "Bonuses from happy customers. Bullshit, more likely."

"The interesting thing to me," Joe continued, "isn't that Lucas worked to drive Hank out of the business, or that he took the bookkeeping away from Patrice. It's that nothing could've happened without BB's cooperation."

"Right," Lester joined in. "Celli said Lucas and he would hole up in the office for hours, presumably cooking things up."

"The AG's office assigned a bunch of number-crunchers to BB's finances, didn't they?" Willy asked. "We hear anything from them?"

Joe shook his head. "Not yet. I called late yesterday to find out how they were doing. No smoking guns so far. I think we better be prepared for little to nothing, given the time gone by. My bet is either Lucas or somebody else made an offer to BB he found attractive, and that no threats were ever made."

"Old-fashioned greed," Willy filled in.

"Okay," Joe resumed. "Let's say Lucas walked up to BB forty years ago and promised to make him a millionaire by laundering money Lucas would supply. Who stood to benefit from that original cast of characters?" He counted them off. "The dead Hank Mitchell, whom Lucas had to dispatch because he was too high-minded to play along, and the people who needed the money cleaned in the first place—along with Lucas, the facilitator, and BB, the compliant business owner. That about right?"

No one disagreed.

"If that's so, then Hank resurfacing as a homicide is the ripple that got BB killed and put Lucas into the wind, both probably as a result of the original financiers wanting to keep the past in the past. How does everyone feel about that?"

Again, the squad reserved its collective judgment, pending what more he had to say.

"Then I think we have a problem," Joe accommodated them. He eyed Kunkle as he explained. "I'm not getting on board with Dave's kidnapping being anything other than an unrelated distraction, but

I am concerned that if we're right about this, and Lucas did make a deal with BB back when, then the logical final act is that the financiers—call them the Mob or whatever—are alive and active, and taking things into their own hands. How else do you make sense of Lucas getting all sweaty and bothered upon hearing of BB's death? It must be because his old cronies got madder 'n hell when they heard Hank wasn't past history anymore, and took it in their heads to wipe the slate clean."

"Meaning," Sammie concluded, "that Lucas isn't running from us, but from the same people who made sure BB wouldn't tell us some interesting stories, either."

"It's what I would do if I was Don Corleone," Willy agreed.

"Which is exactly where I would caution you," Joe told him. "To invoke the Mob is very dramatic, but it clouds our vision. My instincts tell me we're talking something less glamorous. Think about it: Between the average street mugger and the legendary Mafia, there's a huge population of . . . call them middle-class crooks, or even upper-middle-class. They have the same needs as the big boys—people to pay, operations to fund, money to move around, burned gangsters to hide under new identities—but they aren't restricted by the bells and whistles of full-fledged organized crime. They're more like entrepreneurs, and if they stay out of the neighborhoods and/or businesses that're favored by the real Mafia, then it's live and let live."

"Why not make it the Mob?" Willy asked. Being from New York, he was more naturally predisposed to seeing that model as the norm.

"Because I don't see them taking the time and effort to travel to Vermont, find a down-at-its-heels roofing business, and turn it into a money Laundromat. It's too provincial, too far away, too unlikely, and, finally, too pissant for them to consider. They're city types. That's where they make their money, and—more important—where they wash their money. It's neither practical nor realistic for them to come to Brattleboro, Vermont. It is *very* possible, on the other hand, for a smaller outfit to do so, based on the simple fact that the Mafia won't. Again, it's the art of staying out of the way of the major players."

"It's also the difference," Lester picked up, "between running a multibillion-dollar illegal enterprise, and one that generates a couple of hundred million a year, if that. In today's terms, that's almost chump change."

"Especially," Joe threw in, "if your plan from the start was to run funneling operations like Ridgeline Roofing all over the Northeast—small companies where a steady and healthy profit, however bogus, wouldn't stand out."

"On top of that," Sam said, "it would help explain why it was then allowed to quietly die on the vine. I'm guessing this laundering wasn't still taking place when Ridgeline got bought out by Vermont Amalgamated."

"I doubt it," Joe agreed. "Vermont Amalgamated was scrutinized just a few years ago as a result of a civil lawsuit, and its books were thoroughly examined. Nothing was found like what we're talking about."

Willy appeared to have been won over. "It does have a nice feel to it, I'll give you that. But if you're right, there's another problem: That ripple you talked about—that made BB a dead man and sent Lucas running for safety—implies that your minor-league mobsters have a hit man in our backyard, looking to permanently close the history books."

Joe dropped his chin onto his chest and considered that a moment, hoping to find a flaw in it.

"Correct," he said instead. "And speaking of closing books, when BB turned up dead, we reinterviewed some of the same people we'd talked to about Hank—among them Greg Mitchell. Willy, I never heard what you got from him."

"He's covered," Willy said shortly. "AA meeting."

Lester couldn't resist. "That's where nobody knows nobody, right? Perfect."

Willy gave him a dark look, being a regular at such meetings him-self. "Very funny. I called in a favor. When Greg said that's where he was, I didn't believe it, either. From the second I met him, I thought he was holding something back, and I still do. But he was front and center there the whole time. He's clean—at least for doin' BB."

Lester was on a roll, however. "Unless he hired a triggerman," he proposed, only half in jest.

Willy paused from playing with Emma on the living room floor when Sam came home that night, and looked up as she laid her case on the coffee table. "I told Louise we're going back to the usual schedule," he said. "And starting up day care again."

Sammie stretched out beside them so that their daughter could stagger over and happily throw herself into her mother's arms. In all her life until now, Sam had never imagined the sheer warmth that such simple displays of love could generate.

"Why the change of heart?" she asked, tickling Emma's ribs.

Willy straightened his legs and propped his head on his hand to gaze at them both. "The squad meeting today. Finally got me past the idea that Bullfrog's stunt with Dave Spinney was connected to anything else. Most likely, nobody's got the rest of us in the cross-hairs."

"Yeah," she agreed. "Probably right."

He read between the lines of her diplomatic brevity. "You just thought I was being paranoid, anyhow."

She surprised him by laughing outright. "Of course you were. *Duh*. But for all the right reasons." She grabbed hold of Emma and half rolled, half crawled across the carpet to where she could kiss him with Emma squeezed between them.

"You love your daughter," she said. "And God forbid, you love me, too. What you did is called being protective. I thought it was sweet." She tweaked his cheek. "Just like you."

He pretended to look grim. "Don't push your luck."

Walter parked the car in the motel lot and got out slowly, letting his stiff body adjust. Despite the boredom of a long drive, he was actually enjoying himself. Being back in the field after so many years of running odd jobs in the city was not only invigorating but also brought him back to his roots, when he and Pauli and a bunch of others had worked the streets under Jack Panik's iron rule. Those had been tricky years, unlike the sanitized present. Not only had they needed to stay beyond the long arm of the law, as it used to be called, but they'd needed to mind their manners around the Mafia, which they'd all called "the Outfit." Jack himself had once told them they were like the wild dogs of the savanna—fast, tough, and vicious—and wily enough to keep clear of the lions. There was plenty of food out there, he'd told them, so don't attract people who could add you to their lunch.

Those had been good times, Walter thought, pulling his bag out of the backseat and crossing to the lobby entrance.

The young woman at the counter spotted him as he stepped inside— the sole other person within sight.

"Hi," she said. "Long drive?"

He nodded. "Long enough."

"Well," she said, smiling. "Then, welcome to Brattleboro."

CHAPTER TWENTY-TWO

Her father hadn't been kidding, Sally thought. This was a big improve-ment. He'd relocated them to a borrowed penthouse, complete with a sheltered deck, overlooking Brattleboro's Main Street on one side, and the open air Harmony parking lot on the other. From where she was sitting on a chaise in the sun, she could see the mountain across the Connecticut River and a lesser range of rooftops all around. But when-ever she rose to stand at the low privacy railing, she felt she was hover-ing above the whole town like a bird.

The owner of this aerie was out of the country, which meant that she and Dan had the run of the place for a period of time only he knew. Sally hadn't asked if he was even acquainted with the owner, much less if they were here by invitation, but Dan didn't seem at all concerned, as he came and went at will, and so she had ceased to worry.

Despite the amenities—the apartment was fully furnished with art on the walls and a large assortment of books—restrictions had been imposed. Dan had made it clear that Sally wasn't to wander about as she was used to, commingling with her many pals. Her friends were an extended and socially variegated family, and she'd spent her life drifting among them freely and spontaneously. To be denied that access was understandable, she knew, but onerous. With Dan gone more often than not, hell-bent on discovering who might be on their trail—if anyone—Sally was getting lonely.

This was one area where life with Dad became a little stressful. His obsessions, born long before her time and never discussed, offered insights and amusements to a forgiving kindhearted observer like her. But when it ricocheted in the form of restrictions and/or illusions of persecution, her free-spiritedness felt the pinch.

She adjusted herself more comfortably on the chaise, struggling to contain her mounting frustration, and studied the address book on her smartphone.

At least she still had texting.

Johnny Lucas was feeling the old familiar adrenaline. He had always imagined it was what cops felt upon closing in on a case—the stakeouts, surveillance, eavesdropping, and, finally, the arrest. But where they had the burden of statutes, probable cause, warrants, bench orders, judges, prosecutors, and public opinion to deal with, Johnny Lucas and his ilk only had not getting themselves killed, and not jacking up the boss. Everything else was pretty much live and let live, or screw up and die.

Like Hank Mitchell. All Hank had needed to do was keep his mouth shut when Lucas made his play. Barrett was on board; the money was guaranteed. It had just been a matter of going along. But, oh, no—screw up and die. So Mitchell had died.

Now it was Sally Kravitz and her dad's turn. Lucas sat at the wheel of the bland, secondhand car he'd purchased three days ago and again studied the enlargement of one of the surveillance-camera stills showing two people getting into a vehicle on River Road. An older man and a young woman, both of whom had removed the ski masks they'd worn earlier, with the female glancing up the road, revealing her face to the distant streetlight. Might as well have been a studio portrait.

It had certainly functioned as such when Johnny had shown it around. He'd already pinned down an identity for the man—Daniel Kravitz—which he got from cross-referencing the car's license plate. Sally's name hadn't taken more than an hour or two at the town clerk's office.

The hitch had been an address. There were just under a dozen that he'd found in one reference or another, some of which served for only a few months. But the challenge had simply invigorated him. Lucas had calculated that any twosome so transient must be known in the community; and not just that, they were probably better acquainted with the down-and-out crowd than with the mainstream.

He'd been right again, as usual. Another few hours spent in the parts of town most moneyed people avoided had yielded confirmation of the names, and the fact that the girl was as sociable as the father was withdrawn.

That had then led him to his penultimate step. If finding an address was going to be problematic, then the solution was to lure one or both Kravitzes out of their current bolt-hole.

From what Johnny had learned, that part of the operation hinged on Sally. Use a friend of hers as a cat's-paw, and then the daughter to snag the father.

He returned the photograph to his pocket. Just like a cop closing in, but without the legal constraints.

And he was pretty sure he'd found the right friend: the young woman a hundred feet up the street—Sally's current BF, according to his new-found sources—who was chatting with friends on the stoop of the building where she rented an apartment.

*   *   *

Dan Kravitz worked his shift in the hospital basement, mopping the hallway floor. As with all his jobs, it was menial work, befitting his druthers to never plug into the system for more than basic sustenance. He kept to himself, as usual, was never aloof or hostile to others, but engaged in conversation only when addressed. The point almost always became apparent—here was a nice man, but a private one, and certainly not one to pester with idle chitchat.

Some of the people with whom he worked, however, were slower to get the message. One of them was a heavyset kitchen helper named Keith, who during time off from his duties would wander the basement corridors, either looking to talk or traveling to and from the designated smoking area outside.

Dan did his best to avoid Keith, a tactic made easier by the latter's tendency to hum loudly as he walked. Today, however, Dan was too lost in his thoughts, calculating some way to avoid a threat he couldn't even identify. In this, he was at a disadvantage—a man skilled at invading the privacy of others, he was less adapted to receiving such treatment.

"Hey, man," Keith said loudly from behind, making him whirl around in surprise.

"Got ya, didn't I?" The big man smiled broadly. "You're a hard guy to pin down, the way you drift around like a ghost."

"Just doin' my job," Dan said quietly.

"Hell, I do my job," Keith argued less convincingly. "But people see me doing it, too." He laid a heavy paw on Dan's shoulder, making Dan shift away gently. "You're like—I don't know—invisible. Don't get me wrong. I don't mean no offense. Everybody says how neat and tidy you are—and a hard worker. I'm not sayin' that."

"I understand," Dan tried helping him to the finish line.

"It's just that most people make a big deal about what they do, you know? Not me, of course. I'm no show-off. Some people, you can't shut them up. It's all about them all the time, and before you know it, it's quittin' time and they haven't done a damn thing. You know what I mean?"

"I do."

"I can't stand people like that—don't have no respect for 'em. People oughta put up and shut up, right? Do your job and don't make people pick up after you. I hate that, worst of all."

Dan had returned to his mopping, allowing the flow of words to become more of a jumble than something to interpret, until Keith asked, after a pause, "You have a daughter, don't you?"

Dan straightened, the mop forgotten. "Why?"

"I was on Elliot Street, before coming to work. A guy walked up— real nice—and said he was trying to find this girl. He had some good news for her but no address, 'cause she moved. Called her Sally Kravitz, which is why I ask."

"What did he look like?" Dan asked.

"I don't know—bald, white beard. New to me."

"What did you tell him?"

"Nuthin' to tell. I said I'd seen her around—that she was a local. I didn't tell him I knew you, Dan. I know when to keep my mouth shut. He just said thanks and left, anyhow . . ."

Keith finally stopped speaking, given that Dan was already halfway down the hallway, moving at a run.

Sally paused before the store window on Elliot, as she'd seen it done in the movies, and pretended to study the display, while actually studying the reflections of pedestrians behind her. She'd had no training in this, admittedly, but she still didn't see anyone who had an obvious interest in her. And this was the third time she'd checked since leaving their nearby hideaway, which added to her self-confidence.

With the passage of time, she'd begun to minimize her father's concerns, in any case. He was perpetually on the alert, after all—wary and compulsive, and she knew that she was his constant source of concern. She'd long ago come to see most of his worrying as baseless.

Plus, she was now on a mission. Occupying herself on the penthouse deck, she'd received a text from Kelly Doane, a friend from years ago, asking for help. Kelly had a propensity for getting jammed up, ever since Sally and she had hung out in junior high. This time, however, the tone of the message had an edge to it that caught even Sally's jaded attention. Stating, "I'm in real trouble and I don't know what to do. Please come," it both invoked dire need and inspired immediate action—especially when there was no response to Sally's further inquiries.

She'd considered contacting Dan, of course, but ruled it out for several reasons, not the least of which were his own teachings about rendering aid to others, if possible. Also—more petulantly—she was feeling cooped up, however comfortably, and in need of some independence. Besides, Dan's worry that they might have been observed while lurking inside someone's house was hardly the end of the world. They'd worn masks, hadn't they?

She reached Kelly's apartment building, quickly entered the front door, next to a furniture store, and paused in the lobby to watch through the door's glass panel, as a final homage to her father's instructions. As before, no one passing seemed even vaguely curious.

Unburdened, she bounded up the narrow staircase to the third floor.

Dan pulled out his cell phone as he reached the hospital's parking lot.

"Good luck with that, buddy," a man told him, entering the lobby.

Kravitz stared at him blankly.

"No coverage near the hospital," the man finished, the sliding doors closing behind him.

Dan stood where he was, staring at the phone. He knew that. Here, as in so many small pockets across Vermont, coverage was thin to non-existent.

He dropped his hands to his sides and stared out into space. This was probably okay, he thought. Keith could hardly be considered reliable, and even if he was, Dan knew his daughter was popular. Why shouldn't someone be asking after her?

But a man in a white beard? Pitching the oldest line in existence—good news but no address? Such a crock. They are after her, probably to get to me. And they have our names.

Dan ran to his car to drive downtown, keeping his phone out for when he'd get reception. Sally always had her cell—he only prayed that she was available to answer him.

Sally traveled the dark and fetid corridor. The building was old and neglected, pockmarked with tiny, cheap apartments. Brattleboro was forever making strides to comb out such beehives of substandard housing, but it was an expensive and cumbersome process, and for the residents of such dives, the allure of price and invisibility overrode the obvious drawbacks. Kelly Doane, with her history of poor choices and worse luck, was a perfect inhabitant.

Sally reached her door and knocked. "Kelly? It's Sally."

No answer.

She tried again.

This time, she heard a scraping, as from a chair being shifted. "Yes?"

"It's Sally," she said, speaking louder, slightly irritated. "You said you needed help."

"Come in."

Sally raised her eyebrows. Well, by all means, don't open the door or anything.

She twisted the doorknob and stepped inside. Kelly was sitting at a table facing the far wall, her back to the door. "Hey," Sally said. "What's up?"

Kelly's shoulders flinched slightly, but she didn't turn around.

Sally took two more steps. "Kelly, are you—?"

That's all she managed. In the same instant that she sensed a movement behind her, a large hand clapped across her mouth as a man told her softly, "Move and I slice your stomach open. Understand?"

She froze, feeling him pressed against her back, and something sharp poking her abdomen. Not a submissive person by instinct, she'd heard a self-confidence in that voice that scared her, and made her believe in the threat.

"I asked if you understood."

She nodded.

"Good. Then let's get started."

Linda Lucas entered her kitchen carrying a bag of groceries, mostly filled with canned soups and microwavable items. Recent events had ruined her appetite almost completely.

A man was sitting at her breakfast table, a steaming cup of coffee before him. He was about Johnny's age, but rougher in appearance— a little paunchy, and balding with a comb-over.

She stopped dead in her tracks.

"Hope you don't mind," he said, indicating the cup.

She opened her mouth to no effect, and quickly looked around the room, like a bird searching for an open window.

The man stood up, took the bag, and placed it on the counter beside the sink. "Walter's my name. Johnny ever talk about me? From the old days?"

"What're you doing in my house?" she finally asked in a higher-than-usual voice.

"C'mon, Linda," he said pleasantly. "I'm lookin' for Johnny."

"He's not here."

Walter smiled. "Yeah. I got that."

"I don't know where he is. The police want to find him, too."

"I bet." Walter glanced around the kitchen. "You got a living room? Let's go there and talk."

Linda tucked her chin in a little. "No. You need to leave."

Walter approached her, standing too close for comfort. His voice remained at a soothing pitch. "What I need is to talk. In the living room. Now."

She blinked. "All right, but then you should leave."

He gestured politely for her to precede him through the door. "That I will."

They entered the living room, where Walter directed her toward an armchair, into which she settled uneasily. He sat on the coffee table directly opposite her, his knees almost touching hers.

"Linda," he began. "Listen carefully. Johnny's been up to things that could get him into hot water. I think you know that."

He waited for her to nod, which she did after a slight hesitation.

"Good. Then your options are simple. You tell me how to find him, and I move him off the hot seat, or you keep playing dumb and he ends up dead. In the latter instance, by the way, you don't turn out that good, either. Just so you know."

"You don't scare me."

He smiled again. "Of course I do. And I should. Johnny really never told you about me?"

"No," she said, sounding forlorn.

"That's okay," he said softly. "You should be the one talking any-how."

Dan had taken a personal pledge long ago, which he'd thought he'd never break. When it came down to it, however, he barely gave its violation a second's thought. When he'd purchased Sally's smartphone, he'd created a clone of it for himself. He'd never accessed it—out of a paradoxical respect for her privacy—but his peculiarly driven psychosis had demanded that he keep such a back door available into his daughter's life and activities.

Now, standing in their empty borrowed penthouse, her cell not answering his repeated efforts to reach her, he didn't hesitate to open up his copy of her phone in order to read any messages received or sent that might tell him of her whereabouts.

Within moments, he was taking two steps at a time, running back downstairs, headed for Kelly Doane's apartment, two blocks over.

"What do you want?" Sally asked the man behind her.

"That's *my* question," Johnny Lucas said, placing one hand on her throat and angling his knife so that she could see it aimed at her face. "You and your old man were in my house a few nights ago. I want to know why."

Sally's heart tripped a beat as she tried to calculate what might be coming. "We're thieves," she said. "We steal stuff."

The hand on her throat tightened a bit. "Nice try. You were after information."

"If you already know the answer, why ask the question?" she challenged him, her fear mixing with anger.

His hand slipped a little lower on her torso, pushing her closer to losing self-control. She opened her mouth slightly in an effort to pace her breathing and heartbeat. Keep cool, she repeated to herself. Keep cool.

"Feisty, aren't ya?" he said in her ear. "I can deal with that, too. It's your choice. Now . . . tell me why you broke into my house."

"We work with the police," she tried hopefully. "They need a reason to get into people's homes. We don't. If we find a smoking gun and they don't explain how they got it, it's a win–win situation."

She wasn't sure how her mention of the police would go over, but she hoped that he'd find it intimidating enough to back off.

Of course, he didn't. "Did you find this smoking gun?"

At that moment, Sally sensed more than felt a minute change in the atmosphere around them, causing Lucas to swing her around in an awkward dance step so that the now silently opened door was to their left, while the still-frozen Kelly Doane remained seated on the right.

In the doorway, as still as the dim light behind him, stood her father.

"Let her go," he said quietly.

Sally didn't wait for more. She'd been fighting her rising fear by inventorying every detail about Lucas—how he was pressed against her, the placement of his hands, his flat-footed stance—and contrasting those with her own array of escape options.

Her missing ingredient had been any element of surprise, possibly combined with a weapon, or even an ally. With Dan's arrival, she suddenly had two out of three. She wasn't about to hesitate now.

Trusting to her father's perpetual readiness—as exhibited by the care and stealth with which he'd opened Kelly's door—Sally enacted the moves she'd been rehearsing since Lucas seized her. She went limp at the knees, slipped from Lucas's distracted grip like a burst balloon, and turned her collapse at his feet to her advantage by twisting around in one powerful movement and catching both his knees in her outstretched arms like a linebacker.

The surprise of her attack combined with its abrupt low center of gravity caught Lucas off guard and brought him down to the floor with the force of a dropped tree.

His knife skittered across the floor, and Dan was beside them inside of a second.

But no more action was needed.

Lucas was out cold.

CHAPTER TWENTY-THREE

Ron Klesczewski was head of the Brattleboro Police Department's detective squad, which had recently begun calling itself the Criminal Investigation Division, perhaps to keep up with lofty titles like the VBI's, which hadn't been around all that long, either. Ron had risen through the ranks, been mentored by Joe Gunther when he was chief of the unit, and still occasionally wandered upstairs from his office on the ground floor to compare notes with his old colleagues, who included Sam and Willy.

This time, however, the call wasn't social. He merely stuck his head through the doorway, said, "Got a homicide on Elliot, if you want it fresh off the boat," and left just as abruptly.

Willy laughed. "Small-town policing. Gotta love it."

He and Joe, the only ones then in the office, swung in behind Ron, who was already moving rapidly toward the stairs.

"Any details?" Joe asked his back.

Ron glanced over his shoulder. "Not much. A male in an apartment not his own, which is listed to Kelly Doane. She's a known player to us."

"Doane," Willy repeated—he of the elephant's memory. "That rings a bell. Prostitution and drug use?"

"That's her," Ron told him. "Although we have no clue of her whereabouts right now."

"The dead guy have an ID?" Joe asked.

"Maybe. We just got the call. Patrol's there, and the scene's sealed."

Well sealed, too, as they discovered minutes later, Elliot Street being only a couple of blocks south of the municipal center. There were two cruisers in the street, and four patrol officers positioned along the way to the apartment, three flights up. The last cop was at the open door, holding a clipboard.

"Anyone inside?" Klesczewski asked, struggling into his white Tyvek suit, as were his two companions—including Willy, with his own well-practiced, one-arm technique.

"Only the dead guy," the officer said, registering their names. "And you're the first ones I've logged in."

"Any word on the girl who lives here? Doane?"

The man merely shook his head.

"The medical examiner been called?"

"ETA's about ten minutes. He happened to be in town when we paged him."

The three of them entered the sparsely furnished room and stood silently, looking around. The daylight barely eked through a pair of small, filthy windows. A single overhead light provided a harsh and graceless glare to the place, all the better to bounce off the flat pool of dark blood that held the body in its midst like a large blob of sealing wax. The dead man, bald and nicely dressed from what they could see, was facing the distant wall.

"Jesus," Willy observed. "That looks like every drop he had in him."

There was some talking at the door, and the trio turned to see Jerry Senturia again, the local ME, already half dressed in white, being entered into the log. He looked up at them as he finished pulling on a pair of latex gloves.

"Hey, guys. We meet again. Another homicide? I get like one of these a year."

He stepped inside, carrying a small silver case, which Joe had once heard him refer to as his "corpse kit."

"We need to point out your customer?" Willy asked.

Senturia whistled instead. "You boys don't fool around."

"We were wondering if that puddle represented a complete bleed-out," Ron said.

Senturia gave an appraising grunt, followed by, "Close, I'd say. It's arterial, too, by the color of it. Wherever he was hit, it bled out like a garden hose." He hesitated at the edge of the pool, somewhat at a loss on how to proceed.

"Hang on," Ron told him, crossing to the door and asking, "You guys bring those little stools we bought for scenes like this?"

He was almost immediately handed a stack of shiny metal blocks designed to create a non-contaminating path through any field of potential evidence. In the meantime, Senturia had begun taking general scene photographs.

In short order, they arranged a staggered row of the metal blocks like stepping stones across a pond, leading up to the body's edge. Awkwardly, working to not lose his balance, Senturia juggled his camera, his clipboard, and a small flashlight, all while kneeling atop the carefully placed pedestals.

"Crime techs coming?" he asked as he examined the body.

"You want to make it easy?" Willy asked from the edge.

"They're on their way," Ron told him. "Won't be long. What've you got?"

Senturia glanced at him. "I'll show you in a sec. I've updated some of my toys. You'll love it."

He finished doing the best he could, poking about and taking photographs without disrobing the body as he usually did, and then retraced his steps back to dry land.

"Okay," he said triumphantly. He took his camera, cabled it to a tablet computer he removed from his kit, and entered a few commands.

"There," he said, sitting back on his haunches, having set it all up in the middle of the bare wooden floor. His three companions clustered around him like shuffling ghosts.

The first images showed the body's neck. "See that line?" Senturia asked them, tapping the screen with his gloved finger.

"What the hell is it?" Ron asked. "A knife wound?"

"I don't think so," Senturia said. "You can't see it in this shot, but it goes about ninety percent round."

"A garrote," Joe spoke softly. "I saw those in combat—used to take out sentries."

"Right," Willy agreed. "A piano wire with wooden handles at both ends. I've only seen a couple of those, in New York." He glanced meaningfully at Joe before adding, "Almost like a signature Mob hit."

"It certainly explains the blood," Senturia told them. "I poked my finger into the wound to see how deep it is. Basically, the only thing keeping the head attached is the spinal column. All the major vessels have been transected."

He forwarded through several more photos as he spoke, until he reached a shot of the body's face.

"Damn," Joe muttered, straightening. "That's not good."

Senturia looked up at him. "You know him?"

"Yeah," Willy said. "That's Johnny Lucas."

* * *

"I'd normally say that we ought to stop meeting like this," Beverly told him. "But that would be completely disingenuous."

She glanced around the autopsy room, saw that Todd, her diener, had stepped out briefly, and pulled down her surgical mask for a kiss, which Joe happily supplied. He had never seen her so spontaneous and playful as he had since they announced they were a couple. It didn't make him regret the months they'd been circumspect, but it certainly pleased him that he no longer had to tiptoe around the issue.

They were gazing down at Johnny Lucas, who'd been opened up from neck to groin and had his innards removed. Beverly had also made the incision across the top of his head and peeled down his face in preparation for the removal of the skullcap, when Todd realized that his saw blade needed replacement.

"I didn't ask you before," Joe said, putting his own mask back in place. "But a garrote was the weapon, wasn't it?"

She glanced at the traumatized neck. "It's consistent with that," she said. "Interesting thing to use, though."

"Why?" he asked. "It clearly worked."

"Oh, it did that, all right," she agreed. "But this is the first such case I've had on this table. Garroting is an ancient form of execution, and as you've discovered, impressively messy."

"Fast, though," Joe said. "And subtle, in its way."

"In what fashion?"

"Well, it's just a wire, isn't it? If the handles are kept elsewhere, you could say you got it off a picture frame, or from around a bundle. And it's fast, assuming you have the element of surprise and know what you're doing."

She nodded at the body. "Indications are that his attacker was behind him, but that his head was turned to the left—the way it was when he was found, facedown and with his right cheek in contact with the floor."

Todd reentered with the saw, and efficiently went about removing Lucas's skullcap. After he'd stepped away, Beverly approached the glistening brain itself, gingerly removed it, weighed it on a scale, and moved it to a small cutting board near one of the sinks.

"This may be useful," she announced after a minute's careful examination.

Joe moved beside her, seeing little more than a slightly bloody, lumpy blob, the size of a deflated half-soccer-ball. "What?"

"He suffered a cerebral bleed before he died."

Joe shrugged. "That would've made it easier. Whack him on the noggin and then garrote him on the floor. Probably explains the positioning you just described."

But she was shaking her head. "True, but that's not exactly what's being suggested here." She tapped the brain with a fingertip. "This was given a longer interval to hemorrhage than that."

Joe paused, staring. "How long an interval?" he asked.

"Hard to say without knowing the circumstances," she predictably answered. "But he definitely was not struck and then immediately killed. From the scene photographs of the body's placement and the subsequent pooling of blood inside the cranium—which I can see here—I'd say it was beyond a half hour between events."

"Huh," he grunted thoughtfully. "That opens up the possibilities." He brushed her waist surreptitiously with his hand and stepped back. "Guess I better head back and start poking into a few of them."

She turned toward him, a carving knife still in her hand. "By the way?"

He removed his mask and smiled. "What's up?"

"I've seen this kind of head injury often enough to venture a guess on what caused it."

"Really? You're kidding. You almost never do that."

She looked embarrassed. "Well, as I said—familiarity. And I did stress it's going to be a guess."

"Fire away."

"It's consistent with a fall," she said. "Combining the findings on the brain with the markings on the scalp suggests that Mr. Lucas landed with some force."

"Like from a roof?" Joe asked, incredulous.

"No, no, no. Nothing that grand. More likely from a standing height, but forcefully. I've seen it in children, adults—multiple times. It's similar to a skiing injury."

"As if he'd been tackled," Joe revised his scenario.

"Yes," she said. "That would fit. And it would nicely correspond with a bruise that I found on his right hand, consistent with someone reaching out to break a fall—and which I couldn't explain until I saw the brain injury."

He shook his head in wonder. "I know I'm prejudiced, but I think you're terrific."

"What is this? *The Godfather*?" Willy groused. "Next we'll be falling over packages of dead fish."

Joe ignored him. "We have a location on Kelly Doane?"

"Not yet," Lester told him.

"You think there might be an organized crime element, after all?" Sam asked from her desk.

Joe swiveled his chair around to take in the falling rain outside. He'd just returned from Burlington and Lucas's autopsy, and delivered his report about both the garroting and the brain injury. "I've never ruled it out, given what we learned about the funding of Ridgeline Roofing, complete with a requisite burial in concrete. But extending that out so

She turned on him, her eyes wide. "What?"

He patted her shoulder, never great with soothing gestures. "You didn't do it, sweetie. He was unconscious when we left with Kelly."

"But maybe he had a concussion or something."

"No, I promise," her father stressed. "He was killed. Murdered."

"How? By who? I don't get it."

"I don't know the who, but it sounds as if his throat was cut."

She shuddered involuntarily. "Dad. What's going on?"

"It has nothing to do with you, Sally. It started with those documents I was asked to take."

She stared at him, her expression angry. "What do you mean, it has nothing to do with me? He had a knife at my throat."

"And you handled him like a pro," he reassured her. "It was amazing. You were terrific."

"But he's dead."

"I know, I know. That's why we have to lie low, so I can sort that part out."

She rolled her eyes. "This is a little more out of control than one of your B and Es, Dad. I don't think you can organize it quite so neat and tidy. Do you get that he was going to kill me?"

Dan's eyes darted around, betraying his eagerness to move things along. She'd seen it often enough, whenever he felt his space was being invaded. "He was just trying to get to me, honey. It wasn't that bad."

"Swell," she flared, her anger revived. "And how did you know where to find me, anyhow? Were you following me? You said you were going to work."

"I asked you to stay here," he argued, looking away, his voice trailing off.

"You *did* follow me," she railed at him.

"No, I didn't."

"Then what?" she demanded.

He looked pained. "You know all those electronics I use to monitor people."

He stopped there, as if further explanation was unnecessary. Sally stared at him furiously until he added, "Well, I was terrified. I was at work. A colleague told me that some man had been asking about you earlier, showing people your photograph, trying to locate you." He spread his hands in supplication. "I tried to phone you. There's no coverage at the hospital. I drove home as fast as I could."

Her eyes narrowed. "You cloned my phone."

He opened his mouth to correct her phrasing, to bring some of the order he cherished to this free-falling moment, but he realized the spot he was in. "Yes," he said instead.

"How many other times have you invaded my privacy?" she asked, stepping away.

"I was in fear for your life," he cried out.

"How many times?"

"Never," he said emphatically. "I have never done that. I would never do that. You are everything to me."

"But you were able to do it in no time, right? How long have you had it pre-programmed?"

He was anguished by the bitterness in her voice. "Sweetie, if you ever got hurt, my whole world would end. It was like putting you in a life jacket before going out in a canoe. It was a precaution."

"It was a violation."

He looked at her, dumbstruck. "I came to save you from being killed. Surely that's an allowable exception."

Her response was grim. "You didn't know if I'd ever be threatened. You did that to my phone because that's what you do, Dad. You protect your own turf while you trespass onto everyone else's, including mine. And, by the way, you didn't save me. I took that asshole out on my own, thank you very much."

He couldn't respond. He wasn't even sure his heart was beating anymore.

Sally stared out at the falling rain, composing herself.

"I'm sorry," she heard him finally say, his voice barely audible.

She fought with her own inner turmoil, balancing her options. She could forgive him, leave him, or meet him on some undetermined middle ground. Above all, she couldn't forget what he'd done for her, over her entire life, or that they'd reached this impasse because some homicidal maniac was still unaccounted for—and possibly still interested in them.

She reached out and touched his cheek. "We'll sort it out. I love you, even if you drive me crazy sometimes. Let's just drop it for now, since we've got bigger fish to fry. A wild guess is you've come up with a plan?"

He looked abashed, but her comment drew a slight smile. "I think I have."

"Let's do it, then," she encouraged him.

CHAPTER TWENTY-FOUR

"What is that?" Linda Lucas asked.

Walter was wiping a length of wire between a cotton ball soaked in alcohol, which he'd found in Johnny Lucas's well-stocked remote cabin.

"Something I got dirty. Your husband keeps a tight ship here. Impressive. He ever bring you for an overnight?"

"Wouldn't you like to know," she said bitterly.

He laughed dismissively. "I actually don't give a shit. You flew your real colors when you helped me find Johnny, telling me about his favorite hangouts around town, like that coffee shop where I picked up his tail. Lost his touch, giving in to habits like that." He finished, placed the wire in his pocket, and turned in his chair to face her. She was sitting on the sofa with her ankles and wrists duct-taped.

"Did you meet him?" she asked. "Is he all right?"

Walter gave her a comforting smile. "He's all set. You were a big help, and I'll get you two back together soon."

"Where is he?"

"Out of trouble. I told you I'd make sure of that, and I did. But I'm not quite done—coupla loose ends, still."

"If you don't need us anymore, then let me go. We won't bother you."

Walter's expression hardened. "You're not in our league, Mrs. Lucas—Johnny's or mine. That ain't a bad thing. Trust me. I don't know or care what he told you about his past, but I'll guarantee it wasn't the whole truth, or you wouldn't've hooked up with him. You're a civilian. You'll always end up like this—doing what you're told. If I tell you I'm gonna fuck you, for instance, you'll go along, 'cause people like you—civilians—always think that'll save your life. People like Johnny and me know different. That's why we go down fighting, and why other people kill us instead of trying to take us alive."

"What do you want?"

"Johnny tell you about the visitors you two had a few nights ago? They came over twice."

She looked baffled. "We didn't have people over. Johnny doesn't like it."

Walter gave a small grunt. "Didn't think so. Don't worry about it. Anyhow, they represent a small cleanup job I have to do. Then I'm outta here, and you get your life back—what's left of it."

"What do you mean?"

Walter crossed his arms and studied her appraisingly. "You'll find out soon enough. You know what? Johnny did pretty good choosing you. You're a fine-looking woman. He ever tell you that?"

She didn't answer, her fears compounding by the second.

"I may have to take advantage of that," he mused, as if considering the purchase of a kitchen appliance. He waved his hand in the air. "Be a shame to waste this little love nest, after all."

"What're we doing, Dad?" Sally asked in a near whisper.

Dan patted her back. "I'm sorry. You asked if I had a plan. Well, this is it. We wait here. It won't be too much longer, and we are safe. That I promise."

She had once found such statements comforting. Lately, not so much. As gap years went, this had been a lulu—fun and thrilling and unexpectedly revealing at first; now a lot more disheartening. In her eagerness to better understand her enigmatic father, she had found herself—not unlike Icarus—imperiled by the proximity she'd been yearning for. He had become more human and frail in her eyes, despite his proven talents. And certainly his manipulation of her phone—while understandable—had shaken her badly.

"I wouldn't promise too much," a clear and quiet voice said from the pitch-black depths of the parking garage. "You're not the invisible man anymore."

Sally shivered at the message, straining to see its source and alarmed at how it echoed her very thoughts. The setting helped the frightening impression. The municipal garage—a multilayered, low-ceilinged stack of concrete slabs—had the same appeal late at night as a dead-end urban alley in a bad neighborhood. Add to that the steady beat of a heavy rainstorm outside, the mist of which permeated the air through the structure's open sides, and the place took on the feel of a film noir thriller.

Slowly, without a sound, a shadow separated itself from the surrounding gloom, and Willy Kunkle stepped into view—the only man she knew who could move more quietly than her father.

"That's why I called you," Dan said calmly. "That and the fact that this all started because I did you a favor."

"Do tell," said another voice.

Joe Gunther joined them as Dan looked from him to his subordinate guiltily. Kunkle was unperturbed, having invited his boss, for once.

"Sorry," Dan said softly. "I thought we were alone."

"Don't be sorry," Gunther said, glancing at Willy. "He just thinks

I'm a complete idiot." He stuck out a hand to Sally. "You may not re-call meeting me a few years ago, but I'm Joe Gunther. I'm supposed to be this one's commanding officer."

"I remember," she said. "A pleasure."

"Glad somebody thinks it is." Joe eyed all three of them like a disap-pointed father, removing a hat dusted with raindrops, dimly sparkling in the red light from the exit sign at the top of the garage's ramp. "I'm here because at least two of you have colluded in carrying stupidity to new heights, and breaking several laws in the process."

Dan opened his mouth to respond, when Joe interrupted him with a raised palm.

"Not yet. Unlike some law enforcement representatives here, I take my oath of office seriously. With that in mind, I urge you to phrase what you're about to say very carefully. To clarify: What I'm dealing with right now—within the confines of Vermont only—is the homicidal death of a man named Johnny Lucas. Focus on what I need to know."

"I didn't do it?" Sally phrased it as a question.

"You're on the right track," Joe told her. "Now, give me the slightly more elongated version and we'll see where we stand."

The three men remained silent as Sally began speaking slowly. "I got a text from my friend Kelly, saying she was in trouble and would I come over. I did, and was ambushed by this guy."

"You know him?" Joe asked.

She paused thoughtfully before saying, "No. A bald man with a short beard."

"Okay. Keep going."

"Anyhow, he grabbed me from behind. Had a knife at my neck. Then my dad showed up, and I took advantage of the distraction to take the guy's legs out from under him. He hit his head, lost consciousness, and Kelly and we took off. That's it."

"What did he want?" Joe asked.

Sally didn't answer, glancing at her father. Dan spoke smoothly, "We'd made inquiries into Mr. Lucas's background, on behalf of Mr. Kunkle. Lucas apparently took exception."

Joe smiled slightly, not as used to Kravitz's syntax as the other two. "Nicely put. You can no doubt figure out my next question."

"As Sally just stated," Kravitz continued, "he was alive when we left him."

"You saw nobody else nearby, who might've played a role in his death?"

"No, but my guess is that he was watching the apartment building. I have no idea if it was Sally or I who stimulated him to enter the place. It had to have been one or the other, since Lucas was already in the apartment with the young woman, waiting to spring his trap."

"And where is the aforementioned young woman?" Joe asked. "You said her name was Kelly?"

"Kelly Doane," Dan confirmed. "We took her to our place to recover. You should be able to find her there to confirm all this." He recited the penthouse's address.

The conversation trailed off after that, the awkwardness emphasized by the steady drum and hiss of the rain, which swelled inside the resonant hard-walled garage.

Joe spoke to Dan directly. "Mr. Kravitz, I am not unaware of your extracurricular activities. I also know that Willy has found your services helpful in the past. But I gotta tell you: While I'm too busy right now to go after you, I think I've reached my limit in turning a blind eye. You pull any of this shit again, I will do everything I can to throw your butt in jail. Is that clear?"

"Yes, sir," Dan said subserviently.

Joe looked at Sally, adding, "I don't know what your role is here, but I doubt I'd like it. So the same goes for you. It's all very romantic to be acting out some *Father Knows Best* fantasy with your old man—assuming you even know what that means—but trust me, sooner or later, somebody like me's bound to mess it up, if you're lucky. Having Johnny Lucas hold a knife to your throat should give you a hint of the darker alternatives."

He stopped and took all three of them in before ending with Willy. "I'll leave it to you. I'm glad everyone's okay, but I never want to refer to this, or"—he glanced at the Kravitzes—"see you two in this context again." He said to Willy before walking away, "Make sure they go by the PD tomorrow morning to make sworn statements about all this. Tell Dispatch to expect them, and Kelly Doane."

They waited until he'd faded into the night before Willy said to Dan, "I guess this is good-bye."

Sally watched her father as he pondered a response. For herself, Gunther's words and what had led to them marked a watershed, along with a confirmation that a future involving college and a life apart from her attractive but obviously troubled father was the only one viable.

He had been her foundation from infancy—thoughtful, loving, supportive, and generous. Now her own maturity allowed her to see the perils he'd be facing in her absence. In that funny way, their roles had flipped with what had befallen them recently—Dan was now at an impasse, while she was facing a distinctly well-marked road ahead.

She was concerned about his odds, especially with what Joe Gunther had just said. Sally knew her father was an addict, as driven in his lifestyle as any drinker by his craving. Coming to a crossroads as he had at the hands of Willy Kunkle and Johnny Lucas might have struck Sally as an obvious sign, but she was unsure of its impact on Dan. For that matter, she was all but convinced that, especially after her departure, he'd rationalize what had happened, and try to resume where he'd left off.

That realization made her sad and a little lonely.

She barely heard him as he said to Willy, "I guess so. Try not to take too many chances, Mr. Kunkle," and shook his hand.

The following morning, Joe made no mention of his meeting with Willy and the Kravitzes as he stood before his desk and addressed the squad.

"Yesterday afternoon," he said instead, "I contacted the U.S. Marshals and informed them of the death of Johnny Lucas, asking if the name rang any bells. They are feds, of course, so the fact that one of their own witnesses is dead may not stop them from not answering, but I thought it couldn't hurt to ask. So far, I haven't heard back."

"Will they at least tell you if he *wasn't* one of theirs?" Sam asked.

"I put my request in exactly those terms, but—like I said—we'll have to see," Joe answered her. "In the meantime, we've also circulated his fingerprints, hoping that something in his past—which I expect was full of law enforcement involvements—will come drifting up to give us a hand."

He looked at Lester. "Any luck on the Elliot Street canvass for around the time Lucas was killed?"

In response, Spinney turned his laptop around to face most of the small room. "Not with the canvass. I'm coordinating that with the PD, so something may still pop up. But in the meantime, I went after every camera I could find on that block, which turns out to be quite a few."

"Look at how many times they've come up in this case already," Sam commented.

"The interesting thing," Lester went on, "is that my best footage came from the PD itself. A few years ago, they hung a couple of high-end cameras downtown, including one on Elliot. They've had maintenance problems with 'em, off and on." He manipulated the computer to bring up what looked like a static street view, familiar to them all. "But, as you can see, everything was working fine when Lucas met his end."

He pointed at the image with a pencil. "Here's Lucas, pulling up before the Kravitzes appear. He gets out, locks his door, and heads for Kelly Doane's. But check this out," he added, clearly pleased. "A second car, registration in clear view, with one man at the wheel. He parks and waits. Keep an eye on him and the time stamp. Here come the Kravitzes, first daughter, then dad, a few minutes apart. But our second driver stays put. Then, who leaves Kelly Doane's building, moving fast and looking a little freaked?"

"Presto," Willy grunted.

"Kravitz, father and daughter, half carrying Kelly between them," Joe said.

"Implying that Lucas's killer was tailing him, and maybe had no clue about either the Kravitzes or Kelly."

"Maybe, maybe not," Joe said. "But it does make it look like Lucas and his killer knew each other."

"Last but not least." Lester tapped the screen. "So far, you haven't been able to make out the guy in the car. But here, right after those three take off down the street, he gets out, feeds the meter, like a good citizen, and walks up the sidewalk, where—" He paused to make the image a little larger. "—he enters Kelly's building."

"Hold it," Willy suddenly ordered. "Freeze it there. Look. Just before he goes inside. He's signaling somebody."

"You sure?" Lester asked, embarrassed at having missed it. "Looks like he's tossing something into the gutter."

"Trust me," Willy said, smiling confidently. They did, of course. Surveillance was something he knew about.

This time, he was the one pointing at the screen. "Right here. Watch the little dude. Mr. Hit Man goes inside, and Little Dude chucks his butt into the street and falls in behind the Kravitzes and Doane. Perfect tail setup."

"Shit," Joe said, straightening. "If we're right, the bastard's gonna have it both ways. He can focus on taking out Lucas, and with his hired hand on their tail, also chase down Dan and Sally at leisure. Assuming that's what he's here to do."

"Sure he is," Willy stressed. "That's gotta be what's behind those mystery cameras across from Lucas's house. Hit Man was keeping an eye on Johnny, saw Kravitz do his thing, and added him to his to-do list."

"What thing?" Lester asked.

"I'll tell you later," Willy told him. "Anyway, it must be tied to the distant past—Hank, Ridgeline Roofing, money laundering, where Lucas came from before all that."

"What's past is prologue," Joe quoted, almost to himself.

"Whatever that means," Willy shot back. "The good news is that I know who's working for the man with the garrote."

"The tail?" Joe asked, pleased but not completely surprised.

"Darren Leroy," Willy stated. "And we haven't chatted in way too long."

CHAPTER TWENTY-FIVE

As irony would have it, Darren Leroy and Dan Kravitz shared the same social orbit. But here, as among the rich, the middle class, or any other lumped-together group, their contrasting outlooks put them a universe apart. Where Kravitz was an intellectual loner, whose pathology combined a need to pry with a craving to be invisible, Leroy was a rodent whose aversion to work was offset by an inclination to steal. Both were crooks, legally speaking, but where Dan was unconventional and thus oddly appealing, Darren was predictably mundane.

When Willy located him, after tracing his whereabouts through a network of like-minded layabouts, Darren was supposedly volunteering at a local senior center, serving up lunch and washing dishes, while actually keeping track of any momentarily abandoned purses or unlocked cars in the parking lot.

Willy knew his man. Instead of entering the center openly for a straightforward conversation—as logic might have suggested—he borrowed a patrolman from the Brattleboro Police to walk through the front door and make a display of asking for Darren's whereabouts. The result, as predicted, was that within a minute, Leroy came bursting through the service entrance, only to trip headlong over Willy's out-stretched leg.

"Got him," Willy said dourly into his radio to the patrolman, watching Darren trying to gather his wits, spread-eagled on the parking lot. "Thanks for the help."

"Ten-Four. Anytime."

Willy crouched beside the fallen man, incidentally placing one knee into the small of his back. "Hey, Darren. Long time."

Leroy squirmed. "Ow, man. That hurts. Get off me."

"Why'd you run?" Willy asked, ignoring him.

"I forgot I had to be somewhere. I'm late."

Kunkle laughed. "It wasn't that uniformed gorilla at the front door?"

"No, man. I told you."

Willy increased his weight, making Leroy cry out, "I want to change topics, Darren. Tell me how much you got paid to follow those three people on Elliot yesterday."

His victim's momentary stillness gave him away, not to mention his transparent stall: "What three people?"

Willy shifted position, seized Leroy's scrawny shoulder, and flipped him onto his back. He then patted the man down, removed two wallets from his baggy cargo pants pockets, and laid them side by side on Darren's chest.

Leroy stared down the length of his body, seemingly transfixed as Willy opened both wallets.

"You don't look like Gertrude Williams," Willy said, reading off the first wallet's license.

"I found that on the floor," Darren said. "I was about to turn it in to Lost and Found when you rousted me."

"Thought you were late for an appointment, Darren," Willy reminded him, sounding bored as he opened the second wallet. "Or should I call you William . . . how do you pronounce this? Benajic? Benochick?"

He let the wallet drop, along with the subject matter. Instead, he grabbed Leroy's T-shirt in one massive fist, pulled him upright, and propped him against the wheel of a nearby truck like a rag doll.

"Okay—enough. You know what I want. You know what I can throw at you for charges. Let's cut the crap and treat each other like professionals. Give me what you know about the old guy who hired you to tail the threesome."

Leroy visibly wrestled with his options—to the point where Willy half expected him to start counting odds on his fingers—when he finally gave up with a sigh, perhaps defeated by the math.

"I don't know the guy. Never saw him before."

"How'd he know to reach out to you?"

"He said a mutual friend. Didn't give me no name."

"And you didn't ask."

"He paid me a hundred bucks," Leroy protested.

"Okay," Willy agreed. "Point taken. Was there anything about him you remember—accent, reference to some city or state, maybe another local, like you?"

Darren shook his head.

"How 'bout his own name?" Willy continued. "What'd he call himself."

"Walter."

"Walter Who?" Willy asked, struck by the name actually sounding real, unlike something like Bob or Bill. Had that been carelessness? Or hubris, from a man thinking himself above the need for anonymity?

"Nuthin'. That was it."

"Fair 'nough. Did he describe the people? Give 'em names? What?"

"No names, and he only told me about the geeky guy in black with glasses, and the good-looking teenage blonde. The skanky girl was just with 'em. Didn't matter—there weren't gonna be too many like the two he described coming outta that rathole."

"And what was your assignment?"

"Like you said: Follow 'em. That's it."

"Where'd you meet Walter? Motel room?"

"Nah. His car. A rental. I could tell from the sticker."

"Same one he had parked on the street when he signaled you?"

"Yeah."

"You notice anything in the car that told you anything about him?"

For the first time, Darren looked thoughtful. "Just the opposite. They coulda turned that thing around for a new customer in five minutes. The floor mats weren't even dirty. There was nuthin' except the dude himself."

"When was this?"

"Maybe fifteen minutes before the job."

Good planner, Willy thought. Walter probably had several contacts like Darren, available for instant service if needed.

"All right," he said. "Last question about Walter: He give you any way to reach out to him? Cell number, location, signal, anything?"

There was—to Willy—the telling hesitation of a fraction of a second before Darren replied, "Nope."

Willy smacked him across the temple, hard, and leaned in so their noses were almost touching. "Don't you even *think* about fucking me around right now. How the hell was he supposed to find out where you followed them to? You may think I'm an asshole, but don't you *ever* treat me like one." He cuffed him again. "Do you understand?"

"*Ow.* Yeah, man. I'm sorry, all right? It's a habit. I didn't mean to."

"I bet. Answer the question. How were you supposed to tell him where they'd ended up?"

"He gave me a cell phone with a number already in it."

"You still got it?"

He couldn't help himself. Darren gave Willy a pitying look, which earned him a third whack.

"*Damn*. Cut it out. I gave it back. You're not supposed to hit me."

"You're not supposed to dick me around," Willy countered. "What about the three you followed? Where did they go?"

This time, Leroy's expression showed pure bafflement. "It didn't make no sense. First they went to a fancy penthouse downtown—that's where they ditched the skanky girl. Then, later at night, they hooked up with a couple of guys in the municipal garage. I didn't get a good look at them. After that came the crazy part: they left the two guys pretty quick and went to that busted-up old falling-down green-house at the edge of town, with all the broken windows. I hung around after they got there, but they never came out. That's what I told Walter when we met. He didn't seem to care. Paid me my money, took back the phone, and told me he'd already cancelled the number on it—as if I hadn't guessed—and that was it. We were done."

"You talking about Grissom's Greenhouse?"

The other man raised his eyebrows. "That's what I said. The big abandoned one."

Willy rose from his crouch, thinking how that made sense.

Darren stared up at him. "We good? Can I go?"

Despite his better instincts, Willy stepped back. "I catch you jay-walking, you're going to jail. Go away."

Leroy needed no more encouragement. He scrambled to his feet and trotted off, leaving the wallets on the ground, where Willy picked them up to be delivered to the center's management—along with a warning about the quality of their volunteers.

* * *

Joe and Lester waited patiently for the clerk at the car rental agency to read the court's paperwork—word by word—before he looked up at them and blinked.

"So, you'd like to know who rented this car?"

Joe considered his choice of responses, tempted to give Kunkle some competition in his absence, before settling on, "That's the gist of it."

"I'm sorry?"

"Yes," Lester answered shortly, less generous of spirit.

The clerk nodded before turning to his computer, where he engaged in a sequence of eloquent facial expressions, as if responding to an interesting bit of dialogue only he could overhear.

"Okay," he finally said. "Looks like we have a Charles Kuralt, from Bayonne, New Jersey."

Lester laughed quietly as Joe commented, "Clever—using a man with a double life. Our boy has a sense of humor."

The clerk again paused wonderingly.

"Never mind," Joe soothed him. "Did you take care of Mr. Kuralt?"

"I did," he said brightly.

"Tell me about that."

The man stared at him. "He was nice."

Both cops waited for more. In vain.

"Nifty," Joe finally said. "Good to know. Did he say how long he wanted the car for? Take out insurance? Mention anything about why he was here or where he was from? Look funny? Smell funny? Stand out in any detail?"

The clerk's mouth half opened, and Joe knew he'd overstepped again.

"Smell funny?"

Lester leaned on the counter, bringing his face close enough to their quarry's to make the latter step back. "What's your name?"

"Dick."

"Of course it is. So—Dick—if somebody walked in right after we left and asked you what it was like dealing with us, you might have something to say, no? I was the tall one, he was the older one. He was polite, I got visibly more irritated as the conversation went on. Stuff like that. Get the idea?"

Dick nodded.

"That's what we want concerning Mr. Kuralt. Give us your impressions of the man."

Gathering his thoughts, Dick nodded, swallowed, and said, "I get it. Well, he was about average height, pretty skinny but with a gut, and a white comb-over across a mostly bald head. He wore reading glasses when he filled out the form, and they were on a cord around his neck. He had a fancy gold watch and what looked like an organization ring on his left hand. On his right, he had one of those bad-looking blue thumbnails, like when you hit yourself with a hammer, and he had an old scar across his knuckles. He was wearing a white shirt and black tie, partly loosened, and an older dark blue suit that didn't fit him too well, and could've done with a cleaning. He had two pens in the outer handkerchief pocket—cheap clicker models. His shoes were brown and scuffed."

Joe and Lester exchanged startled glances.

Dick took no notice, lost in some mental middle space. "He wasn't happy or sad," he continued, "but something in between, like somebody you interrupt when they're watching TV. He had to think about how to sign his name, 'cause he paused for a second at the bottom of the form, and he was super vague when I asked him why he was in the area."

Lester was laughing enough by now that Joe had to ask, "Very nice. Excellent job. These folks required to give you a driver's license? Which you're supposed to keep on file?"

"Yup," Dick replied. "That's it."

Joe looked at him without comment, hoping the man's earlier burst of insight would continue. But apparently it had gone missing again, forcing Joe to add, "You think we could see it?"

"Oh, sure."

He moved to a filing cabinet adjacent to the counter and smoothly removed a file from one of the drawers. He flipped it open and handed them a single, full-color, Xerox copy of a New York State license, which showed neither the real Charles Kuralt or the thin-haired man they were after.

Lester eyed Dick suspiciously and asked, "Did you look at this when you copied it?"

"Sure."

"And you didn't notice that the address was different than what he wrote on the rental form—New York versus New Jersey?"

Dick didn't appear troubled. "Lots of people have that. They moved or something. Doesn't mean anything."

Lester then indicated the photograph. "How 'bout this? This look even vaguely like the man you just described to us?"

Dick leaned forward and studied the image. He shook his head. "Sure—a few years ago, maybe."

He appeared completely unrepentant.

Joe displayed his frustration by placing his business card on the counter and stating shortly, "If you could copy the whole file for us, we'd appreciate it. Someone'll be by later to pick it up. If this guy ever comes back with the car, don't tell him about our dropping by, but give us a call, okay? We'd like to talk to him."

"He like a crook?" Dick asked, his eyes bright.

"He's a source of information," Lester said. "Like you."

Both cops were at the open door when Dick followed up with, "'Cause, if he is, his car has a GPS."

Joe straightened without turning, rolled his eyes, and sighed at having overlooked something so obvious.

Lester merely asked, "Is it on?"

"Sure—company policy. The guy signed the agreement, so it's legal. He could've checked the box saying he wanted it turned off."

Joe said in an undertone, "Except it probably never crossed his mind. Like somebody else I know."

They returned to the counter. Lester asked the agent, "Do you have the data we'd need to track this customer's movements? I just want to make sure."

"Yeah," Dick said happily. "It's a map, with time stamps and everything. I have to download it, but I'll add it to the other stuff you want. There's also a printout that goes with it. It's pretty cool."

Joe started walking back toward the door. "Can't wait to find out," he said.

Lester's cell phone began ringing as they reached their car.

"It's Willy," he told Joe, answering, "Go ahead—you're on speaker," and placing the phone on the console between the two seats.

"Chased down Darren Leroy," Willy reported. "He had diddly on Mr. Hit Man—who called himself Walter—but he told me he did a roundabout tail on Dan and Sally, all the way to Grissom's Greenhouse."

"I thought they went out of business," Lester said.

"What better place to hide out?"

Joe couldn't argue. "Where're you now?"

"Downtown."

"Get Klesczewski to order up the PD's rapid response team. Tell him we think the same guy who killed Lucas is after both Kravitzes at the greenhouse. But," he added, "also tell him to wait for us before he goes in, so we all stay on the same page."

"Boss," Willy said despairingly, "you know that ain't gonna happen. They gotta put on their fancy black outfits first. We'll be there long before they are."

CHAPTER TWENTY-SIX

It was raining hard by the time everyone convened a short distance away from what had been Grissom's Greenhouse ten years earlier. And while Willy was right about VBI's people getting there first, it wasn't fifteen minutes before Ron Klesczewski showed up with his entire SRT unit, including a much appreciated mobile command center—actually, a secondhand converted ambulance.

It was a tight fit in the back of the truck, where they gathered to discuss how best to proceed. Counting Ron, Joe, Sammie, the head of the SRT—a sharp-eyed young woman named Barb Zonay—and the communications guy who would be their air traffic controller once they got under way, there was barely room enough to display the oversized aerial photograph of the site that Ron had brought along.

"To be clear," Joe began once they'd settled down, bulky in their ballistic gear, "we're not sure what we got here. We know Walter hired someone who followed the two Kravitzes to Grissom's, presumably so Walter could do unto them what he did to Johnny Lucas, and we know from preliminary surveillance that a car matching Walter's rental is sitting right now in the greenhouse parking lot."

He stopped abruptly and looked at Zonay. "Barb, I'm sorry. Have you been filled in on who all these people are and what they've been up to?"

She smiled broadly. "You kidding? It's been better than watching a soap opera. I was hoping we'd be asked to join in."

He liked her attitude—so much for the external grimness of so many other special weapons people.

"Outstanding," he said.

He consulted Ron's photo and began tapping on aspects of the greenhouse as he continued. "That being said, we don't know for a fact anyone's in here. If they are, for sure Walter's a bad guy, and while we have it on good authority that the Kravitzes are targets only, that doesn't mean they don't have weapons for self-defense."

"It is Vermont, after all," Barb threw in.

"Precisely. Anybody else ever been inside Grissom's?" Joe asked.

No one responded. "Years ago," he explained, "it was the Crystal Palace of greenhouses—high ceilinged, all glass, a bit of a maze, and it went on for acres. With the passage of time and the economy going sour, they shut down parts of it, put up cheaper, plastic greenhouse extensions, tried to make it a community farmers' market kind of thing, and then finally just gave up. It's been abandoned ever since."

"Except for the occasional squatter or drug party," Ron added.

"I drove by there, not long ago," Joe said. "It's a mess—lots of wildlife, totally overgrown, broken glass everywhere. The beds have mostly rotted out and collapsed, the concrete is heaved up. In short, it's a confined combat zone." He looked up above them at a burst of extra-loud rain on the truck's roof. "And that's not counting the weather."

"No option to wait out the rain?" Barb asked.

"Not if we're sworn to protect and serve like we say we are," Joe replied. "Plus, the Kravitzes are our only bait for catching this guy. For all I know, we'll get in there and find he's already come and gone, leaving their bodies and his car behind. Speaking of which, your team's already disabled the car, correct?"

Serious and focused, she merely nodded in acknowledgment.

"Okay," he said. "This picture tells you what we got. Buildings radiating out in all directions, all of them big, dark, and cluttered. Field-of-fire concerns are paramount. We don't want anyone getting shot who's not looking for it. By the same token, we don't want to leave any back doors unguarded." He eyed Zonay directly. "Barb, tell us where you want us and how to proceed. We'll all be on the same radio channel and monitored through this command center." He looked at the communications man. "You good with that?"

"Ten-Four."

Minutes later, the rain unrelenting, they had all spread out to their assigned entry points. Barb Zonay and her SRT had taken the lead positions, choosing the old greenhouse complex's several primary entrances, but Joe and others had been distributed as well, the layout being too spread out to be properly contained otherwise.

The decision had been made to announce their approach. As a result, Joe heard Zonay's voice being broadcast over a megaphone, telling anyone within earshot to drop their weapons and come out with their hands in plain sight.

Over his earpiece, however, he also heard that they'd received no takers to that invitation.

Despite his knowledge of the building's interior, Joe was taken aback by the reality. As he cautiously entered toward the rear, he was struck by both the overall jumble and the unanticipated roar of rainfall on thousands of glass panels overhead.

Those that were still intact, of course. Predictably, people had made it their business to apply rocks, bullets, and odd pieces of rubble to everything breakable within reach. Over time, they'd apparently become bored or exhausted, however, leaving half their targets standing, with the effect that, as Joe picked his way ever farther into the gloomy interior, he was beset simultaneously by pouring water and the clamor of its hitting the brittle panes above.

Also, looking around amid the human destruction and nature's ongoing and ironic efforts to reclaim the place, he was hard-put to use any of his old memories of the layout. He and—as he could hear over the radio—everyone else were pretty much reduced to forging ahead as they might have through a long-forgotten, bombed-out warehouse.

The combined muck and tangle eventually begged the question: Why had Dan Kravitz—a meticulous, neat, and careful man—come here to hide out?

"Joe to Barb," he said, avoiding the usual radio handles, as they'd agreed.

"Go ahead," she replied quickly.

"Sudden thought," he said. "Look out for any underground entrances. I'm thinking there might be a basement somewhere."

"Got it. Thanks. Everybody copy?"

There was a chorus of affirmative responses.

Joe was in a narrow, high gallery, dating back to the greenhouse's origins, which meant that it had a brick foundation, a rusting steel skeleton supporting all the glass, and was among the first of the enterprise's extensions to have been closed up and abandoned to hard times. It also had an uneven floor of indeterminate soundness, so covered with debris, dirt, and invading vegetation that he might as well have been back outdoors. One of the reasons he'd been assigned here by Zonay—who got to call the shots as the entry team chief—was the low likelihood that anyone would use it as a hiding place.

When he came upon a four-by-four-foot square hole in the floor, therefore, not five minutes later, he didn't know if he'd discovered a cellar, or merely an earthen excavation. In the dim light, it appeared weighted toward the latter.

He got down on his hands and knees, readied his flashlight, and gingerly approached the hole's edge. Just as he was concluding that the void below reached beyond a shovel's capabilities, he felt the ground beneath him begin to sag.

"Shit," he said between clenched teeth as he dropped the light and began flailing for a handhold.

It was too late. With a groan and a sigh, the flooring took him down like a collapsing playground slide, and dumped him into the darkness ten feet below.

The good news was that he landed in a soft pile, showered by wet dirt, but otherwise undamaged, and within sight of his still-functioning flashlight. The bad news was that his radio had been torn from his belt and mangled by an accompanying floor beam.

He tried it nevertheless, standing up uncertainly and blinking the mud from his eyes. "Joe to Barb. Come in."

He didn't bother repeating the attempt. He knew what he'd done from the unit's complete lack of life, including the usually flickering LED. He dropped it back onto the ground, reached into his pocket, and halfheartedly pulled out his cell phone. He wasn't optimistic. From long experience, he'd found the things generally disappointing, despite how his younger colleagues sang their praises.

Sure enough, there was no signal to be had. He repocketed the phone, brushed off his light, and looked around for an exit.

The easiest would have been a set of stairs or a door, neither of which was apparent. The next hope was for something he could drag under the hole, in order to climb back out. But again, there were no such offerings. Rather, he found himself in a brick-lined room, paralleling the one he'd dropped from, running off into the gloom and equipped with an assortment of rusted, broken, long-forgotten pipes lining its walls, no doubt once designed to deliver water, electrical wiring, heating, or all three.

He quickly checked to make sure that his other equipment was still attached, and that his adrenaline wasn't masking an injury he hadn't yet registered. Aside from a cut on his hand and a couple of bruised knuckles, however, he was whole, if dirty and wet. He set out in the direction he'd been following upstairs, hoping to discover something more encouraging than a blank wall.

At least progress was easier. Confusion and clutter were in spades, coming mostly from abandoned and broken tools, hundreds of rotten baskets, and assorted other piles so lost to disintegration as to defy description. But overall, the middle of the corridor was clear, if soaked, allowing for quick and wary passage.

Even with his mishap, Joe hadn't overlooked that—planned or not— he was now closer to where he'd just warned Zonay their quarry might be hiding—although without any way to summon help.

There was a door at the far end, as he'd hoped, locked, of course. Peering closely, and using his Leatherman as a probe, Joe looked for a way to break through as quietly as possible.

The door was wooden, soft with rot in places, and thankfully, slightly loose in its jamb. Also, both its hinge pins were available. Concentrating there, he seized the top of the lower pin in the teeth of the Leatherman pliers and gently thumped the underside of his right hand with his left fist, hoping to work the pin loose of the hinge's embrace.

It worked. He repeated the maneuver on the upper hinge, which of course proved more reluctant.

"God damn it," he swore under his breath, looking around for some kind of prying tool. He located a sodden chunk of two-by-four in a corner and rigged a crude fulcrum of sorts, against which he could lever the Leatherman's purchase on the stubborn pin.

Finally, the pin slid up just enough for him to draw it out. He then drove the point of the small pliers between the jamb and the door's edge, and slowly worked it free of its seating. When he could get enough of a handhold, he resheathed the Leatherman, grabbed the door with his fingertips, and pulled it toward him.

The hinges came free of their insets, the bottom of the door oozed against the mud at Joe's feet, and slowly but gradually, the whole thing swung open, opposite from the way it was designed to.

When the gap was wide enough, he carefully stuck his head out, along with one hand holding the extinguished flashlight.

He listened, holding his breath, hoping the slight noise he'd made hadn't drawn attention. Hearing nothing, he eased the door back a few more inches, until he could slip through entirely, and stepped into the blackness.

Only then, breathing silently through his open mouth, did he pull his gun from its holster, brace himself, and turn on his flashlight.

Perhaps not surprisingly, the revelation proved a letdown. He was in a square, bland, brick-lined room, with open doorways on each wall.

He quickly checked the openings, conscious of how much time had elapsed since his tumble from above. He still felt he was on the right track—thinking Dan Kravitz went underground for sanctuary—but he had no choice of strategy, and no proof that he was right. For all he knew, his colleagues had already wrapped up operations and were wondering where in hell he'd disappeared.

His survey revealed one tool closet, one dead-end room with more equipment, and a long, dark hallway with a bend in it, far ahead.

He took the latter, still using his light, and moving faster than he'd dared before. As he went, the floor dried out, until he came to where the mud was replaced by dust, and the mold by cobwebs. By the time he reached the hallway elbow, he found himself tiptoeing, the earth underfoot no longer absorbing the sounds of his approach.

Around the corner, he found another door—this time modern, metal, and betraying a thin line of light around its borders.

He paused. The presence of light gave weight to his conviction. The greenhouse had been unplugged for years, its owners long gone, its security nonexistent. There were no known electrical lines still servicing the building. Whatever lay beyond the door, therefore, perfectly suited what Joe knew of Dan Kravitz through Willy—that the man was a human mole of sorts, secretive and ingenious enough to find a way to wire just one part of an abandoned, huge hulk of a building.

But the light presented a dilemma. Given that Joe's suspicions were firming up, where did that put him—alone, in the dark, without communications, heavy weapons, or backup? He was no action hero cowboy, and this was no movie. It had been one thing to pursue a hunch and wander by mischance through a silent, possibly empty building, but what were his options now?

His own words to Barb Zonay about the need to act quickly, if they hoped to save the Kravitzes, rose back up with extra urgency—effectively overriding any thought of retreat in order to somehow rally the troops.

It was an odd and disquieting moment. Joe thought of his family, Beverly, and his extended tribe of colleagues. The results of his actions, if they turned out poorly, would ripple outward to all of them.

With an apologetic shake of the head, Joe pocketed the flashlight, gently placed his left hand on the doorknob, readied his handgun, and stepped ahead.

He entered fast, low, and immediately cut left, his back against the wall and his gun covering the room. From his low-target crouch, he saw—as in the burst of a light strobe—three people before him: two seated and one standing, the last holding a gun, pointed directly at him.

That was all he needed to shoot first.

Except that the balding man beat him to it.

The muzzle flash was more surprising to Joe than the bullet punching into his vest. That hurt, and threw him off balance, but the image of this huge, hot, bright flower of flame—directed straight at him—caught him completely off guard and caused him to blink before he could respond.

It was just enough time for the other man to cross the room, smack him across the head with his gun, and remove Joe's weapon with his other hand.

With the temporary blindness, the searing pain to his temple, and the knowledge that he'd just been shot, Joe was overwhelmed by his own failure and stupidity. After the life he'd been through, he was to end up in a pile on the floor, being killed by someone he didn't even know.

But not now—maybe. The man—whom he assumed to be Walter—retreated two feet, still aiming at Joe, and asked, "You have other weapons?"

Joe winced, trying to clear his mind. He noticed that Dan and Sally had been zip-tied to their chairs, reducing them to targets only. "Of course I do," he replied. "So do the people crawling all over this place."

Walter smiled. "Yeah. Well, you three'll be more than I need to get by them. Especially you. Always nice to have a cop as a shield."

Those were his last words. With no warning, the door facing Joe flew open, and a black-clad Barb Zonay stepped in and shot Walter in the head with a single round. As if he'd been yanked offstage by a steel cable snapping tight, he landed in a heap against the wall.

Zonay, followed by a herd of gun-toting, shouting colleagues, crossed the room in three paces, crouched beside Walter to move his gun beyond reach, and quickly checked his pulse.

Then, her familiar easy smile replacing the grim expression of moments earlier, she turned to Joe.

"Hey," she said. "How're ya doin'?"

"Been better," he answered truthfully. "But I'm alive, thanks to you."

"You kidding?" she said. "You not only told us to go underground; you gave us the perfect distraction, coming through the door like Rambo. Saved me trying to figure out how to nail this yo-yo without getting the hostages killed."

"Great," he said, laughing tiredly, as she slipped a pair of handcuffs onto the lifeless body, per protocol. "I'll give myself the duck decoy award after I check out of the hospital."

CHAPTER TWENTY-SEVEN

Joe looked up as Beverly entered the hospital room. "My God. You must've driven here at two hundred miles per hour."

She crossed over to him, her expression clinical, taking in the bandage covering half his head, and his blackened left eye, and kissed him long and hard without comment. He could feel her lips trembling slightly against his own as he reached up to hold her face in his hands.

"You are a sweetheart to come down," he told her.

"Like I was going to send you flowers and a card," she said sourly, propping one hip on the edge of his bed. "You are such a turkey."

"Doctor," he said, feigning shock, "I'm an injured man."

She allowed a small smile. "I have no experience with that. My patients never complain."

He reached up to kiss her in turn, but winced in the process.

She straightened. "What?"

He shook his head and patted his chest. "My vest caught a bullet—left a wicked bruise. One of the reasons they're keeping me for a few hours."

She absorbed that before saying, "They didn't mention that part."

"I asked them not to," he confessed. "I thought the phone call would be bad enough, and they wouldn't let me do it myself."

Her response surprised him. She took his hand in hers and said, "That's all right. I appreciated being called at all."

Despite the pain, he sat up. "Are you kidding? I had them phone you before my family. Of course," he added with a smile, settling against the pillow, "they're more used to being contacted by hospitals."

"It is a habit with you," she observed, one eyebrow arched. "That much I know."

"You okay with that?"

She smiled again. "I'm not okay with the reasons, but I'm delighted by your phone tree."

There was a knock at the door. He expected her to rise and assume a more professional pose, as was her default. Instead, he was touched and pleased when she stayed as she was, still holding his hand.

It was Willy.

"Hey, Doc," he said in greeting, ignoring the unwritten rule that forbade addressing Beverly as anything other than Doctor Hillstrom.

"Willy," she said pleasantly, with a nod of the head. Joe wondered if he'd ever heard her speak Kunkle's first name, and doubted he had. Miracles were occurring right before him.

"Got some updates, boss," Willy said.

That got Beverly to stand. "Which gives me a chance to find the facilities," she said.

"Don't leave on my account," Willy told her.

"That'll be the day," she said, passing by him.

He laughed as she closed the door behind her. He was in a transparently good mood. "You did good, boss. I always liked her."

"Can't say she thinks the same about you," Joe retorted.

Willy waved his large hand dismissively. "She would if she knew me. I'm a really likeable guy."

"You are many things—," Joe began, before Willy cut him off.

"Yeah, yeah, yeah. My kid thinks I'm the bee's knees. The rest of you people? Who cares?"

Joe smiled. "Whatcha got?"

"Linda Lucas in one piece, for one thing. Backtracked the rental car's GPS readings to some woodsy cabin where he stashed her."

Joe furrowed his brows. Willy cut off his next obvious question. "It was Lucas's *Bourne Identity* hideaway," he explained. "Guns, food, get-outta-town bags. He went there after you spooked him, and it's where Walter set up shop after he grabbed Linda and got her to spill her guts—including where to find Lucas, and through Lucas, the Kravitzes. We even found the cameras that were probably used to watch the Lucas house from across the street, tucked into a duffel bag."

Joe let out a sigh. "Very efficient, our friend Walter. What kind of shape was Linda in? Sounds like he worked her over."

"Safe to say," Willy agreed seriously. "She's not giving any details. She's a tough bird. Just reading the scene when we got there, I'd say he raped her, at least, and maybe pulled a few other stunts. But she's a sphinx."

"Why?"

"Maybe worried Walter isn't the only dog off his leash, maybe about the past catching up if she gets too chatty. Don't know. We collected DNA, fingerprints, mug shots, and got a warrant to search her house through New Hampshire authorities, but I wouldn't hold my breath. We already know Dan scoped out the home-sweet-home. I doubt we'll find much more than he did. We'll try, though. We got a last name for Walter, by the way: Nesbit. His fingerprints came back via AFIS, no problem."

"What's his story?"

"That's where it ends, pretty much. Old-time crook out of New York, according to NCIC, associated with the so-called Jack Panik family."

"Mob?" Joe reacted with surprise.

But Willy was shaking his head. "Nonaffiliated. Also old news. I called a pal down there, to see what they might have. Jack died years ago. His daughter, Tina, took over. She's a spitting image of the old man, according to my source, but more clever and subtle. They got nuthin' on her that'll stick. Walter Nesbit may or may not have worked for her, but in what capacity, nobody knows who'll talk to us. According to NYPD, Walter's kept his nose clean for decades."

"What about before?"

Willy snorted. "Suspected of having knocked off a couple of guys, using a garrote."

"Did you fly this by Linda? To see if she'd open up?" Joe asked, suspecting the answer.

"My guess?" Willy answered indirectly. "Her refusing to cooperate is a dead giveaway she knew what was up. Good luck proving it, though."

"And the Kravitzes?" Joe asked, admitting to himself that Willy was probably right.

"Walter hadn't started on them, if that's what you're asking. Our arrival was, to use your kind of word, timely."

"Did he tell them what he wanted?"

Willy gave him an equivocal expression, not willing to admit that he knew the answer. "He asked who they were working for."

"When they broke into Lucas's?"

"Yeah."

"Huh," Joe grunted. "So, there's an unknown party besides Walter and the Paniks."

"Or Walter thought there was a double-cross goin' on," Willy pretended to muse before moving to another topic. "Maybe it was whoever whacked BB Barrett. That's still the missing piece of all this."

"True," Joe said thoughtfully.

His colleague studied him. "You're sittin' on something, boss. I can tell. My money's on Greg—the son of a bitch's been buggin' me since I met him."

After a pause, Joe said, "Could be. I been chewing on that since I got here."

"You feel like sharing? It's only a class A, top-of-the-list felony."

"Well, for one thing, unless Greg's some sort of *Mission: Impossible* mastermind, you said he had an ironclad alibi."

Kunkle couldn't dispute it. "Lester was the one who joked that Greg hired a shooter, but I get what you're saying. Okay—granted," he allowed. "Who else, then?"

Joe went on, "Lucas was at Stratton sipping wine and abusing parking attendants. The rest of the old crowd—Carlo, Jimmy, Lacey, and the others, including Sharon Mitchell—have all been checked out by us."

Willy remained silent, letting his boss lay out the options.

"It started me wondering about the 'why' part of BB's killing," Joe said. "It could've been mechanical, like we were saying at one of the squad meetings—the Paniks cleaning up old garbage."

"That's what *you* were saying," Willy reminded him. "Basically, that BB was a loose end for a bunch of yuppie crooks who didn't want the past to bite 'em in the ass. I didn't argue the point, since—if we're right about the money laundering—BB still could've named names and caused trouble."

"Which made me suspect that a Walter-type was already in the area," Joe agreed. "Especially after you ruled out Greg."

Willy smiled, enjoying this process, despite his reputation—among those who didn't know him well—as an action-driven, impulsive maverick. "'Cept we're now pretty sure Walter hadn't hit town yet—we backtracked his movements using the timing of Linda Lucas's kidnapping and the motel and rental registrations, not to mention when those cameras magically came and went outside Lucas's house. And it's not likely that the Paniks sent *two* triggermen, and then recalled the first one for no reason."

"Yeah." Joe stretched out the word. "Therein lies the dilemma. That's what got me thinking BB wasn't the purely mechanical problem we thought he was."

"Something more personal," Willy mused. "I can work with that. But again, who?"

Joe gave him a sad and tired smile. "I keep going back in time, trying to connect the Hank and BB killings somehow. We're trained to see a homicide as an act of impulse—you piss me off; I shoot you. Cause and effect."

"That's the way it usually goes."

"As it probably did this time. Except that the two events were separated by decades because Hank was so well disposed of. Where I'm going is that, instead of BB being knocked off as part of all this recent activity, his sins—as seen by his killer—were born when Hank was thought to have simply disappeared."

"Which brings us back to Greg," Willy argued.

"Maybe," Joe hesitated. "I think you're on the right track, but not with Greg. He's the one who—for better or worse—has been wrestling with his demons."

"Sharon?" Willy asked, surprised. "Little Miss Uptight? Lashing out at BB once Hank's vanishing act was explained?" He shook his head. "Why? If she'd thought BB had anything to do with Hank leaving her, she wouldn't've stood for Barrett putting the moves on her."

"Unless she'd always thought Hank was coming back. Remember: We never did nail down if Hank left her or if she threw him out. If it was the second, her guilt might've gone through the roof after he resurfaced as a murder victim. People can get pretty tangled in their thinking."

Willy laughed, rose from the guest chair, and crossed to the door. "Golly gee, boss, I wouldn't know anything about that. I'm as simple as they come. You wanna give Sharon another go with the rubber hose, though, you know who to call for company. I wouldn't wanna miss out on *that* conversation."

Joe gave him a thumbs-up. "You got it."

"Don't strain yourself in the meantime," Willy continued. "And I'm glad you didn't get killed, by the way."

Joe smiled. "Nice of you to say."

Willy scowled. "It was, wasn't it? Sorry 'bout that."

Kunkle stepped into the hospital's newly updated lobby and saw Sally Kravitz sitting along one wall, her hands dangling between her knees.

He sat a couple of feet away from her, staring into the same vague middle distance she was. "You okay?"

"I guess."

"Tough day."

"No kidding."

He reached into his coat pocket, took out a roll of Life Savers, expertly pried one partly loose with his thumbnail, and offered it to her, expecting her to pass.

Instead, she plucked it free and slipped it between her lips. "Thanks."

He worked another one free for himself. "Sure."

The conversation lapsed. He let it hang there for a while before asking, "You waiting for somebody?"

"You, I guess."

"Yeah?"

"Maybe," she said. "Or the other guy. The older one. Joe?"

Willy nodded. "They're keeping him a little longer."

He considered what she'd just been through—and thought of his own daughter, who, though just a toddler, had so distracted him when he'd thought she might be under threat.

"This have to do with your dad?" he asked.

"Yeah," she admitted tiredly.

"You two're pretty tight."

"We were. I don't know now."

Willy twisted around to face her. "He'll always be there for you," he said with conviction. "My bet is you're the one going through changes—maybe rethinking what you had, or thought you had."

She seemed to absorb that.

In the silence, he asked, "If you were waiting for me or Joe, what did you want to know?"

She glanced at him. "For one thing, is my dad in any trouble?"

"The short answer is: No," Willy assured her. "But Dan and I—and Joe—have had this conversation before. There used to be a don't-ask, don't-tell thing goin' on. Your father and I had an agreement, but you know that's over. That puts him out on his own from now on. Just another citizen. And in case you thought what he was doing was cool, I don't need to tell you it was illegal as hell."

"I know. I know."

"So, to answer your question, that's official. No more wink and nod. Your old man gets caught creeping around—or you get caught with him—you're done."

"I won't be with him," she said quietly.

He heard the loss in her voice. "The bloom off the rose?" he asked gently.

She gave him a sad smile. "I was being a kid. I thought it would be fun, hanging out with him. And it was exciting, doing that stuff."

"Sure it is," Willy agreed. "And dangerous, and maybe a little creepy. But no way it wasn't an invasion of privacy, right?"

"Yeah," she replied. "Turns out privacy is a little selective with my dad. I didn't know that before."

Willy guessed there was more to that statement than he knew, but he didn't press her for details. She'd come to him, after all, which was a novelty in his life. Most people worked to avoid him. He was liking this.

"What're your plans?" he asked.

"Get a summer job," she said. "Maybe away from here. Then college. Normal things."

"Ah," he responded. "That kind of a letdown?"

"Kind of. It'll probably be good for me."

She stood up on that, checking her watch without real purpose—more as an excuse to leave.

Willy remained seated. "Probably," he agreed with her. "Do me a favor?"

"What?"

"You just graduated from the knife-and-gun club. You've been tied up, threatened, scared half to death, and God knows what else. Give it time to sink in. And get to know your father. He's screwy, and I guess he hurt your feelings. Kids put their parents on a pedestal sometimes, which they don't ask for. And when that changes, everything collapses, and the parent is left wondering what the hell happened. I'm the first one to call Dan an oddball, but he's solid people. I just don't want you to lose out on finding that out for yourself—especially fresh from a string of super traumatic experiences."

Sally looked at him, her expression soft and accepting. When he'd finished, she stooped and gave him an awkward hug.

"Thank you," she said, and walked away.

It was dark when Joe pulled to the curb opposite Sharon Mitchell's house. The day had been warm, his window was down, and he paused to appreciate the novelty of spring's tentatively announcing itself—along with the otherworldly white noise that came from the unseen interstate running atop the massive berm in the distance.

He'd brought along Willy, less for backup, and more as a show of thanks for his not challenging Joe's thinking earlier, in the hospital.

There was symmetry here, being back where this case had begun, that Joe appreciated. It had even played a part in his current theory. As Willy had said at his bedside, there was maybe something personal beneath the money laundering so long ago, Lucas's early elimination of pesky obstacles, and the subsequent accumulation of cash for a lucky few.

Lost in all the machinations, the passage of time, and the bloody fallout following a chance act of jackhammering was the decades-old tale of a love affair shattered and a family destroyed—a blip on a crowded radar scope that only now had caught Joe's attention.

"You ready?" he asked Willy.

Kunkle hitched a shoulder. "For what, I'm not sure, but yeah."

Joe opened his door and got out slowly, nursing his aching body and whispering to himself, "That makes two of us."

They approached the house, noticing an extra car parked in the driveway. Joe rang the doorbell.

Sharon didn't appear surprised to see them. "Ah."

"Mrs. Mitchell," Joe said as a greeting.

She stepped back slightly. "You want to come in?"

"If you don't mind."

She pursed her lips briefly. "I don't think that's up to me anymore."

She opened the door wide and moved aside, revealing a tired-looking, limp-haired blond woman sitting on the living room couch facing them.

"Julie Washburn?" Joe asked, entering the room, working to hide his surprise.

The woman stared at him listlessly, her eyes red-rimmed and moist. Her expression didn't change, but Joe saw her swallow once, and blink resignedly.

"Yes."

"I'm Joe Gunther, with the Vermont Bureau of Investigation," he said, displaying his credentials. "I think you know Agent Kunkle."

She ignored Willy. "Are you here to arrest me?"

He hesitated, glancing at Sharon, who stood with her hands slack and her head bowed. He'd homed in on this house by instinct, seeking enlightenment as much as confirmation. In his mind, the answer to BB's death had to have come from here—not logically from Sharon, necessarily, but somehow from the emotional tsunami that had engulfed her entire family.

Julie's stark question hit him like the revelation of a much-anticipated, long-secreted solution to a puzzle.

"I am," he answered. "For the murder of Robert Barrett."

She nodded, and then seemed a little confused, glancing around. "What happens now?"

A small moan escaped Sharon's lips as he said, "I read you your rights and place you under arrest."

Her eyes darted for a split second to her mother, perhaps checking that she wouldn't collapse, before she responded, "Okay."

He proceeded without hesitation with the *Miranda* warning, and followed with the unofficial but forever hopeful inquiry: "Will you talk with me now, or would you like a lawyer?"

To his relief, she replied, "What's the point? I did it."

"Those're your rights, Julie."

She pressed her lips together briefly. "No," she then said. "I'll talk to you. Here?"

The inquiry somehow cut free the stillness in the room, releasing

Sharon to move to her daughter's side and embrace her, and prompting Willy to close the front door behind them.

Normally, his answer was routinely, "the office," and certainly without her mother sitting beside her. But Julie was where he wanted her, and he didn't want to lose that advantage. He therefore gave her a supportive half smile, and indicated the living room with a wave of his hand. "Here'll be fine, unless there's someplace else you'd like."

Sharon looked from Julie to them. "You need me to leave?"

Joe sat on an armchair opposite the couch, while Willy chose a ladderback chair near the wall.

Joe addressed Julie, "With the understanding that, if she stays, your mother is to remain absolutely silent during this conversation, what would you prefer, Julie?"

Simultaneously, Julie answered, "I'd like her to stay," as her mother pledged, "I won't say a word. I promise."

Joe reached into his pocket and produced a digital recorder, which he turned on and placed on his knee. In short order, he intoned his name and rank, the date and time, Julie's name and date of birth, and repeated her *Miranda* rights. "Julie," he concluded, "did you understand your rights as I've explained them to you?"

She nodded. "Yes."

"And do you still agree to speak with me without a lawyer present?"

"I do."

There was a standard interviewing template that guided the course of such conversations, designed by experts so that cops could steer clear of trouble once their cases entered the legal system.

But Joe had already muddied that perfection, and wasn't about to miss an opportunity to keep things short and direct.

"Did you kill Robert Barrett, Julie, as you're accused of doing?" he therefore asked.

"Yes."

"How?"

"With my husband's .22 pistol," she said in the same monotone.

"Do you still have this weapon?"

"I put it back in the gun cabinet." She gestured vaguely. "At home."

"We'll collect it later," he said. "Can you tell me how you did this?"

Her voice remained strong, her expression unchanged, her gaze fixed on some middle distance between them. "I drove up near to his house, hid the car behind a row of trees, and walked the rest of the way, cross-country, till I reached his swimming pool. I didn't have a plan; I just figured I'd look around until I found him. But he was already there, reading the newspaper. So I waited. When he got up and started cleaning the pool, I shot him."

"How many times?"

"Three—once in the side and twice in the chest. He fell in the water. I picked up my brass and left."

Despite her best efforts, Sharon let escape a thin, high-pitched note, as feeble as a distant keening almost lost to a breeze.

Joe frowned at her. "You were alone?"

Julie paid no attention to any of them, speaking as if to herself. "Yes."

"Did anyone know what you were going to do?"

"No."

"Did you tell anyone what you did afterwards?"

"No."

"How 'bout your mother or brother?"

She focused briefly on him. "I told you: No."

Her face was tense, her eyes dry. He doubted he'd get her to change her story, or even if he'd ever determine its truth or not. Julie Washburn was taking all the blame for BB's death—whether she was the sole guilty party or not.

The thought shifted his scrutiny to Sharon, to gauge her reaction. But her attention remained fastened to Julie, and nothing in her body language radiated anything beyond support and concern. If Julie was covering anyone else's involvement, Joe guessed it might've been her brother, Greg, as Willy had suspected long ago.

But the girl was giving them nothing to work with.

"Why did you do it, Julie?" Joe asked.

"He killed our father."

He waited for more, got nothing, and followed with, "How do you know that?"

"He was in love with our mother."

The authority of her tone gave it conviction and caused Sharon to squeeze Julie's hand.

"Tell me about that," Joe coaxed her, noting her use of the word "our."

Julie had resumed staring into space, but looked at him again. "*You* people told me, indirectly, when you found Dad's body at the nuke plant."

"Because you'd thought the same as everyone else? That he'd just left you?"

She kept his gaze a moment longer, before breaking off. "I never thought he left us," she almost whispered.

Joe let the pathos of that float between them—of the ignored little girl, assumed to be too young to notice what was going on around her. He imagined her suffering Hank's absence in silence, only to watch the ebullient BB Barrett trying to move in without a pause. The irony was that Julie hadn't been alone. Both Sharon and Greg had longed for Hank Mitchell's return, with Sharon never wavering in her rejection of BB's advances.

But to a brokenhearted girl, such a broader understanding had been as absent as her father, whose death by murder—confirmed so many years later—must have come as a celestial directive. As soon as Hank's body had surfaced and his cause of death made public, BB's remaining time on earth was short, probably regardless of any input from anyone else.

"You loved your father very much," Joe suggested quietly.

"My life ended when he went away," she said calmly.

"How did it feel when you killed Barrett?" he asked, genuinely curious.

"Peaceful. I've never felt so good."

"And when the news broke that you'd killed an innocent man? That we got your dad's killer?"

She stared at him again. "Innocent? He wasn't innocent of sniffing around my mom as soon as Dad was gone. If he didn't kill my father, it was only because somebody beat him to it."

Joe studied her face, her smoldering anger, and rethought his appraisal. Underneath the pitiful grieving of a longing daughter, there was the primitive rage of pure revenge. He noticed that even Sharon straightened slightly upon hearing these words, as if stung by an insight she'd never before imagined.

"My wild child," she'd once said, describing her daughter. Joe imagined that right now, the true meaning of the phrase had never been sharper-edged. Greg's possible involvement dimmed in his mind.

Joe pursed his lips, suddenly tired. He reached for the recorder, his finger hovering over the Off button. "Do you swear, Julie Washburn, under penalty of law, that everything you've told me today is the truth to the best of your knowledge?"

"I do."

Perhaps, he thought.

Truths were said to be self-evident. This one, he'd just take at face value.